The Caribbean
Prisoner

A novel

For Carolyn —

Thanks for your

support

D1617100

Scott Evans

Scott Evans

Copyright 2016, Scott Evans
Cover Design: Clayborn Press, LLC
Cover Image Credit: David B. King, Copyright David B. King, 2012
Edited by: J. S. Jones
Published by Clayborn Press, Phoenix, AZ
IBSN: 978-1549703713

Printed in the United States of America.
10 9 8 7 6 5 4 3 2 1

This Edition published in April, 2017 by Clayborn Press, LLC
Printed under authorization, all rights reserved.

CLAYBORN
PRESS

Dedicated to the men and women in the military who have been victims of sexual assault. You survive your fear and humiliation, often in silence; let this work give you voice.

-Scott Evans

No man is an island,
Entire of itself.
Each is a piece of the continent,
A part of the main.
If a clod be washed away by the sea,
Europe is the less.
As well as if a promontory were.
As well as if a manor of thine own
Or of thine friend's were.
Each man's death diminishes me,
For I am involved in mankind.
Therefore, send not to know
For whom the bell tolls,
It tolls for thee.

-John Donne

Chapter 1

After my father's sudden death, I felt so lost and alone that I took a leave of absence from San Francisco State. Just as my dad and brother and I had done ten years earlier when my mother had died after a long battle with ovarian cancer I decided to travel. I picked an island in the Caribbean, based on a poster I'd seen in a travel agent's office. But, despite its promising name, St. Thomas eventually proved more hellish than I could have imagined. I learned even more about despair. And guilt.

And the redemptive power of vengeance.

On the day of my arrival, when I stepped over the doormat of the Midtown Hotel in the center of Charlotte Amalie, I walked through a dim hall into a small courtyard and felt at peace. Lush, tall, broad-leaf plants grew in the center, surrounded by stairways and landings with black iron railings. Sunlight burned high on the pink walls, casting deep cool shadows where green ferns flourished. It seemed at first the perfect serene setting where I could try to quell the anguish I felt.

A single room on the ground floor next to the office was available, so I took it. The door was a wooden frame holding a series of frosted glass panels. The room was clean but small. Over the bed was a transom of thin metal slats that allowed little light. Above the window, an air-conditioner protruded from the wall. I turned it on, and though the air was a little stale, the room cooled quickly. The double bed was firm and neatly made, the small bathroom, smelling of bleach, was clean with white tiles on the floor and halfway up the walls.

It was late afternoon. I was hungry and anxious to explore. On the street, reggae music and the beat of steel drums - sounding so upbeat and joyful - drew my attention to the town. I strolled past a dimly lit bar filled with laughter from people whose faces I couldn't see. The smells of rum and cigarette smoke assaulted my nose. A patch of the bay's blue water was visible between the buildings, so I made my way across Main Street where cars crawled at a snail's pace. Natives and tourists alike crowded a park that gave off pleasing aroma of pork cooking on barbeques.

Politely waving off occasional invitations from people to join them, I walked under the shade of palm trees to the waterfront, checking the street map from time to time. Beyond the busy Waterfront Road was St. Thomas Harbor. To my left was a large stone building painted a deep crimson that looked like a prison. A sign in front said the grotesque blood-red castle-like structure was the St. Thomas Police Station, but the map referred to it as "The Fort". Something about it gave a chill.

I turned from the waterfront and trudged up a steep stairway. Trees with low branches created welcome shade. Halfway up the steps, I saw a tidy white building, surrounded by a low, whitewashed rock wall. A sign with carved letters over and under a portrait of a schooner read, GALLEON HOUSE - FOOD AND DRINKS - LUNCHES AND DINNERS. Through an archway, a sidewalk wound between overgrown vegetation, and disappeared behind the trunks of old palm trees. Within the walls, I smelled rich soil and the various flowers, like jasmine and wisteria, which clung to trellises. These fragrances reminded me of my mother's flower garden and took me back to moments I had spent with her when I was younger. A green lizard scurried up the cracked wall and disappeared. A small, cream-colored butterfly floated in front of my face, then fluttered into the shadows before turning back and zig-zagging through pockets of sunlight.

The stairway led to a spacious terrace opening on three sides to a view of St. Thomas Bay. The deep harbor lay below me like a sheet of pure turquoise. Yachts mirrored themselves in the water. The narrow streets of Charlotte Amalie, the steep green hillsides dappled with colorful houses, the iridescent vegetation, and the red-tiled roofs made me think of paintings by Paul Gauguin. My mother had loved art and often had me sit on her lap as she browsed through massive books filled with beautiful photos of paintings. The ones by Gauguin had been among her favorites.

"Can I help you?" A blonde man in a half-unbuttoned white shirt stood in the shadows behind the long bar.

"Fantastic view," I said.

"First time here?"

Nodding, I stepped closer, pulled a barstool out, and ordered a scotch and soda.

"Scotch? Folks come here to drink rum."

"Got sick on rum once. Doesn't have much appeal anymore."

He nodded knowingly while mixing my drink. "What's your name?"

"Randall Wake. Yours?"

He handed me the glass. "Mike."

We shook hands. Once my eyes adjusted to the dimness, I noticed the deep, rich wood of the bar top, like the deck of an expensive yacht. "Beautiful bar."

He nodded. "It's teak."

I slid my hand along the smooth surface, then scanned the room. Two dozen tables with bamboo legs were spaced evenly throughout the terrace, four sturdy bamboo chairs at each. Silverware and folded white napkins adorned each table. It looked like the kind of place my parents might have visited when they were alive.

"Where is everybody? Seems like the rest of the town is buzzing."

"Most folks come later, for dinner and dancing."

Sparkling glasses stacked behind the bartender and shelves of liquor bottles, their greens and ambers and browns added to the beauty of the island. It was as if I had begun noticing colors again after a long spell of colorblindness. I smelled the chilled scotch in my drink, the coldness rising to my nostrils, and took another sip.

"Have you lived here long?" I asked.

"Almost ten years. Came down from Houston for

a short vacation, after losing my job, and this place needed a bartender." Mike wiped glasses with a white bar towel as he spoke, stacking each one as he finished. "I'd done a little bartending to pay my way through college, so…"

"What do you do for fun? Go to a different bar and drink?"

"Not much of a drinker. Do a little scuba diving, sometimes with a few of the tourists. You dive?"

"Done a lot of free diving, mostly for abalone. But I've done some scuba diving off the coast of Santa Barbara and Catalina Island. Up around Fort Bragg and Mendocino, too, in northern California."

A few months after my mother's death, Dad had taken Richard and me to camp at Mendocino, where we went free-diving for abalone. I smiled, recalling Dad cutting the foot out of the shell, then pounding it on a tree stump to tenderize it. He sautéed it over a camp fire in a pan that sizzled with olive oil and white wine. I could almost taste the tender abalone meat melt in my mouth.

"I went diving in the Pacific one time, north of San Francisco. The water was cloudy and cold. Didn't care for it. Have you been in the water here?"

I shook my head.

"Water's warm and clear. Visibility can be a hundred feet, even on a bad day." He stepped to the cash register, pulled a brochure from a rack, and handed it to me. "There's a catamaran cruise each day that takes folks over to St. John for scuba diving and snorkeling. They supply all the equipment."

I flipped through the brochure.

"You'll notice, no one in those pictures is wearing

5

a wetsuit. Don't need one."

One of the inside photos showed a young, well-built guy swimming under water with an even younger, bountiful woman in the tightest, skimpiest bikini I'd ever seen.

"Can you guarantee I'll meet her if I go?"

He laughed. "They also provide lunch."

I glanced again at the brochure. "Looks like fun."

Two older couples dressed in slacks and bright, colorful shirts and blouses came up the steps and called "Hello" to Mike before taking a table by the railing. Mike ducked under an opening in the bar and went to their table. Once he got back, he went to work making their drinks as I watched, sipped my drink and thumbed through the brochure.

The restaurant filled with people, mostly couples in their sixties, and Mike got busy. I sat alone at the bar, but the good scotch had its effect. I felt a sense of belonging. Drink in hand, I strolled around the cheerful and chatty people to the banister and looked down. The town had become a kind of carnival, filled with music, laughter, and colorful lights.

Maybe it was just the liquor and my newfound freedom, but I felt more alive than I had in months. I'd been numb since hearing about my father's fatal heart attack, and I'd stayed numb well after his funeral.

I'd wanted to follow in my father's footsteps, which was why I had been a pre-med major at San Francisco State. But after he died, I didn't see the point. Classes were tedious, dull. On a whim, I'd decided to travel to some place I'd never seen before. St. Thomas seemed about as far away from San

6

Francisco as I could get and still be, technically, inside the U. S., since I didn't have an updated passport. So that evening I found myself at a bar in the Virgin Islands, unaware that death had tagged along.

Chapter 2

Dinner included a tender, flaky piece of white fish cooked with lemon, butter and white wine, red potatoes spiced with oregano and dill, and cool salad with slices of Mandarin oranges under a tangy raspberry vinaigrette dressing. As I enjoyed the meal, I watched the band members set up. A white-haired man put the parts of his clarinet together, a tall black man with gray hair at his temples pulled a bass fiddle out of its case and stood it up as a tall, skinny guy lit a cigarette before taking the bench at the piano. Once they started playing, I was disappointed. The music was stuff my grandparents listened to, instrumental versions of songs by Frank Sinatra and Andy Williams. But people around me laughed as they spoke, so in the fading warmth of the night, the little open dining room seemed about as pleasant as any place. Everyone seemed carefree.

I thought about my parents. Mother had been diagnosed with ovarian cancer when I was twelve. She fought hard, suffering through chemo twice, but died a couple of years later. Dad did his best to care for her in the evenings, trying not to burden me, I suppose. After Mom died, he worked even longer hours, maybe to help pay off medical bills, so I rarely saw him while I finished high school. Then I went off to college.

As I surveyed the healthy, happy couples sitting around me, I wondered how different my parents' lives might have been if Mom had not gotten ill. I couldn't recall ever seeing them as happy as the people who surrounded me.

Eventually, I went back and sat at the bar to chat with Mike when he wasn't busy. After an hour, the band took a break. The clarinetist walked over and sat down next to me.

"Whitey," Mike said, "meet Randall."

"Tom Berryman," he said, "but everyone calls me Whitey." When we shook hands, I noticed his striking blue eyes. "What brings you to St. Thomas?"

I shrugged. "Just needed to travel."

Mike handed him a drink, saying, "G & T, just the way you like it."

"Thanks, Mike." Whitey winked at me. "He knows I like it heavy on the tonic and light on the gin. At least while I'm performing." He took a sip and nodded. "Not many young people come here to the Galleon House these days. How'd you find your way?"

"Just wandered around looking for a place to hang out."

"Hope you won't be too disappointed, hanging out with us geezers." His gravelly voice reminded me of my dad's.

"Of course not." I handed my empty glass to Mike. "Can I get another?"

"How do you like her?" Whitey asked, turning around to look across the terrace.

The Caribbean Prisoner

I looked to see who Whitey meant. "Her?"

"Charlotte Amalie."

I looked into the deep-blue night sky surrounding a bright full moon. "Paradise."

"Paradise?" Whitey asked. "The island was a paradise when I first met her."

"Paradise lost then?"

He laughed. "Sometimes I don't know her anymore. It's like the storefronts and the cobblestone streets and the taxis have all become props for an amusement park."

Mike gave me another drink, and that's when I noticed the sailors climbing the stairs. They were hard to miss in their white uniforms, laughing loudly, and scanning the room. It was clear they'd been drinking and were on the prowl.

A table of attractive women who looked like stewardesses caught their attention. Since the women were with their dates, I expected the four young men to turn around and leave - they seemed so out of place. Everyone quieted as they watched the four young men amble over to a nearby table in a back corner.

A woman who looked to be about forty stood up from one table and walked over to the sailors. I couldn't hear them, but it was obvious they were ordering drinks. She stepped over to the bar, and Mike went down to speak to her.

"Does she work here?" I asked.

"That's Gillian, the owner. Doubles as a cocktail waitress when it's busy."

Gillian looked like a movie star. Her tight pink blouse and white skirt showed a good figure, and her

10

light brown hair was piled up in what I think is called a French twist. She reminded me of Tippi Hedren. I could tell she was trying to stay cool as she spoke to Mike, but she looked tense.

Mike went to work making drinks, and I glanced at the sailors. A couple of them lit cigarettes and blew out the smoke as they laughed at something one of them had said. The rest of the crowd went back to talking.

I turned toward Whitey. "You've lived here a long time?"

"Almost thirty years. Came here in 1964. Got a job on an old war sloop, re-rigged for leisure. The skipper and owner was an overweight widower, havin' the time of his life. Red, I called him. He had a bushy red beard and curly red hair. Gave me my nickname. I used to be blonder than Mike there."

"Those were the days, I bet."

"Oh, yeah. Red would get drunk and catch fish, and we just drifted in the hot sun for hours. There was a cook and two other sailors on board, and we went from island to island. Made it to the Bahamas a couple of times. Tortola, Van Dyke. There were some islands we'd sail into where the natives were still as backwards as Adam and Eve. They didn't bother with their clothes, so we didn't bother with ours."

Mike came down to our end of the bar.

"Trouble?" Whitey asked.

"Gillian says those jokers are pretty wasted." He looked at me. "If there's any trouble, will you back me up?"

"Back you up?"

"I'll need help if they start something. Until the

11

police arrive. Gillian will make the call if things go south."

"Don't count me out," Whitey said. "I can still kick a pup's butt, if I have to."

"Thanks, Whitey," Mike said. "How about it, Randall?"

"Sure. I'll do what I can."

I looked over my shoulder at the table. The owner had dropped off all the drinks and the young men were laughing and talking again, minding their own business. I was relieved. Whitey and I turned around, leaned against the bar and looked out at the hillside, sparkling with lights. It was soothing to listen to the cadence of his voice.

"The Island was a different place. Fewer cars, fewer buildings. A few shacks clustered around Magen's Bay, directly behind us, over the hill." He pointed beyond the stage to the dark hillside dotted with tiny lights. "This is Government Hill. Quite a view from up top."

"I bet." I stared across the terrace to the hillside that lifted its lights to the sky.

"Most of the islands had to import water, and cargo ships stopped en route to or from the States. Some of the islands still have water shortages." He drained his glass and set it on the bar. "Time to get back to work."

He joined the other musicians, and they warmed up. Before long they were playing "Moon River," one of my father's favorites, so I closed my eyes and let it carry me back. Right after she'd gotten so ill, Mom had danced with my dad in the living room to Andy Williams while I watched from the sofa, pretending to

12

be annoyed. But the truth was that memory had helped me through some rough times.

A cool breeze blew into the terrace and brought me out of my memories. The moon was just out of view, hidden by the awning. There had been a small birthday party at one table, but it was over and the folks had left crumpled wrapping paper on the floor. I noticed Gillian walk over to pick it up and I decided to help.

She seemed startled, but I introduced myself and grabbed handfuls of paper.

"Mike mentioned you," she said. "First night on the Island, right?"

"Yep. Glad I found your establishment here."

She grinned. She was wearing blue eye shadow and pink lipstick, and though she was almost twenty years older, I felt an attraction.

We'd picked up all the gift paper, but when the song ended, I heard one sailor yell, "Hey, bartender, can we get some more fucking drinks over here?"

Mike didn't look happy, but he nodded and went to work. I glanced at Whitey before following Gillian away from the small stage. We dumped the crumpled paper into a large garbage can at the far end of the bar, then walked back toward the stage, which took us close to the sailors' table.

One of them grabbed Gillian's wrist. "Hey, babe, fetch our drinks, okay?"

She jerked her arm away but said, "Sure thing, babe."

I shot the young guy a scowl.

"What you lookin' at, asshole?"

I ignored the question and followed Gillian to the

13

bar and waited beside her while Mike finished the drinks. He barely splashed any liquor into the glasses, and he didn't stir the drinks so the liquor would float at the top. *Smart*, I thought.

When he'd finished placing all four glasses on the tray, he pushed it over to Gillian. She picked it up expertly, as if she'd been a waitress all her life. I waited by the bar and watched, along with Mike, as she carefully placed each glass down in front of the sailors before picking up their empty glasses.

"We're closing soon," Gillian told them. "Why don't you gentlemen settle up."

The one closest to her bellowed, "Closing?" He looked at his wristwatch. "It's only fuckin' midnight."

One of the others said, "These geezers got to get to bed, Jimmy. Didn't have their Geritol tonight."

The oldest looking one of the bunch asked, "How much do we owe you, beautiful?"

"Forty bucks even," Gillian answered.

The one named Jimmy took a long pull from his drink and then pounded the glass down on the table. "This don't have no fuckin' booze in it." He swiveled his head from Gillian to us. "Hey, bartender. Put more fuckin' bourbon in my damn drink."

Mike frowned but waved for the glass. Gillian grabbed it and handed it over.

Mike made a big display of pouring bourbon into the glass until it was full to the rim. "There you go, sir. No extra charge."

Gillian took the glass back to the table and handed it to Jimmy. "Is that more to your taste?"

He grabbed the glass, spilling some of the drink

14

on his lap. "You'd be more to my taste, if you was twenty years younger, bitch."

"Hey," Mike yelled. "Watch your language."

"Punks," I said, thinking I wouldn't be heard.

Jimmy looked at me over his glass as he took a long drink. When he'd finished, he placed the half-empty glass down on the table and said, "Who the fuck are you?"

That's when I noticed Whitey and the other two musicians walking up behind him. Customers sitting close by had fallen quiet and were watching.

Whitey put his hand on the sailor's shoulder, so I stepped to the table and stood between Gillian and the sailor who'd spoken to me.

"Why don't you guys drink up and shove off?" Whitey demanded.

Jimmy's head swiveled around to look up at him. "Why don't you take your fuckin' hand off my fuckin' shoulder, grandpa, before I break it off and shove it up your ass."

The three other young sailors smiled and stood up, as if looking forward to a fight. Then I sensed someone behind me. When I turned, I noticed Mike standing beside me holding a baseball bat.

"You boys drink up and leave right now, and we'll say the drinks are on the house. Otherwise, you're gonna find yourselves in jail."

Jimmy squirmed from Whitey's grip and stood, swaying as he looked from me to Mike and back again. The older sailor stood, too, and grabbed Jimmy before he could take another step.

"Time to ship out, Collins, before you wind up in the brig."

I didn't think Jimmy Collins was going to go along with his pal's request, but the young sailor's expression softened and he nodded, his eyelids drooping. The change was so dramatic, I wondered if Mike had slipped something into his drink.

The four men in their white uniforms staggered to the staircase, grabbed the railing and started down. We stood there—Mike, Gillian, me, Whitey and the other musicians—watching as they disappeared into the darkness. Once they'd been gone for several minutes, Gillian turned to Whitey.

"Play something up tempo, Whitey. I want to get folks out on the dance floor."

The other two musicians had already started back to the stage. "Sure thing, boss," Whitey said. "But, Mike, make me another G and T, please."

"Want a double?" he asked.

Whitey smiled. "You read my mind." He walked over to the stage and picked up his clarinet. In a few minutes, they were playing "The Girl from Ipanema."

"How 'bout you?" she asked me. "Want another drink? It's on the house."

"Yes, ma'am," I said. "Make it a double, too."

"By the way," she said, "who in the world drinks scotch when they're in the Caribbean?"

I smiled at the gentle jab. "Make mine a G and T, too, then."

Gillian flashed me a toothy grin and walked to the bar with Mike. The crowd behind me started chatting and laughing again. I looked at the stairs that descended into darkness, to see if the four sailors had really gone. I wondered if they were waiting in the garden below. I'd have to leave at some point and go down the street to my hotel, and I had a feeling I'd see them again.

Chapter 3

The next morning, I woke up groggy and disoriented in my small, dark room. After a shower, I climbed the long steps to the Galleon House, where the pleasing scents of bacon and toast drifted from the terrace. A smiling waitress handed me a cup of coffee, and I sat at a small table near the edge. Charlotte Amalie in the morning came into view—the clear, azure sky, the brightly painted houses shimmering in the sunlight, the deep green palm fronds rustling in the breeze.

I sipped coffee and thought about what had happened the night before. After the sailors had left, I'd waited until the band was done so I could leave the terrace in the company of Whitey and the other two musicians. When the four of us reached the street, the sidewalks looked empty, and I could see the entrance to the Midtown Hotel just down the hill.

Whitey and fellow musicians, whose names I never got, loaded their instruments into an old station wagon. I shook Whitey's hand before he climbed into the back seat. "Thanks for the music," I said. "Glad we didn't get into World War Three with those sailors."

"Oh, I wouldn't worry about those runts. If push

had come to shove, I'd have shown 'em Betsy here." He'd reached into his trousers pocket and pulled out a little silver pistol.

"Is that real?"

He nodded before sliding it back into his pocket. Then he'd folded himself into the back seat and closed the door with a thud that startled me. As their car drove away, I stumbled down to the hotel and somehow felt my way through the darkness to my room.

*   *   *

After breakfast, I killed a few hours exploring the little shops in town. Then I strolled along the Waterfront, breathing in the salty sea air and enjoying the turquoise water and the painted boats. Among their sagging fishing nets stood fishermen wearing straw hats with hooks and ribbons in them. St. Thomas Harbor came into view. Two enormous white ocean liners, looking like floating hotels, must have docked quietly before dawn. The way they towered out of the water seemed to defy the laws of physics. The closer I got to the park and beach, the more crowded the town became. An attractive woman in her twenties walked by, wearing a tight tee-shirt, with the words I'M A VIRGIN (ISLANDER) printed across her bust.

I found a little café with outdoor seating near the waterfront between Orchid Lane and Hibiscus Alley. A canvas awning shaded most of the tables, which were filling up. I could see the entire bay, and, to the east, the yacht harbor. After ordering a beer, I watched the flow of tourists and cars against the backdrop of painted buildings.

Two more beauties in their mid-twenties strolled down one of the pathways. They stood at the entrance to the patio, ostensibly scanning for seats, but really striking a pose so everyone would notice them. I certainly did. Both were wearing sheer white sundresses over dark print bikinis, floppy hats and high-heeled sandals. Both carried similar large, square beach bags on their arms like *Vogue* models. One was slightly taller and lighter-skinned than the other; the shorter woman had larger breasts and a deeper tan.

The two beauties glanced in my direction when the waitress brought my green bottle, so I lifted the Heineken to my lips and smiled at them before taking a sip. The shorter one smiled back and whispered something in the other woman's ear. She seemed distracted but glanced in my direction before they both walked over and sat at a table next to mine.

I leaned toward them. "Is *Vogue* doing a fashion shoot on the island today?"

"We're not with *Vogue*," the slenderer one said. "We're with *Cosmo*."

"What a coincidence. I'm doing a shoot for *Playgirl*."

"Oh?" she replied. "But the February issue has already come out."

It was mid-March, so I was confused. "Why do you assume I'd be in the February issue?" I asked.

"It's the shortest month."

They had a good laugh. I felt myself blush, but I grinned and tried to hide it. Fortunately, the waitress
20

came and took their orders, giving me time to recover.

"Where are you ladies from?"

The slender, lighter-haired woman ignored me, but the dark-haired woman said, "Boston. How 'bout you?"

"Boston? But you don't have that famous Boston accent."

"You expect all Bostonians to sound alike?" the fairer one asked. "Drove my cah to the bah at Hah-vahd?"

"Does Harvard even have a bar?"

"Yes. Several."

"We're both from Albany, New York, originally," the darker-haired woman explained. "But we met at the company we work for and got transferred to Boston. How 'bout you? Where are you from?"

"California," I said.

The slender one looked at me. "You left California to come here? Why?"

"I live in northern California, just north of San Francisco. Trust me, the beaches there aren't as nice as the beaches here, and the water's a lot colder."

"Why not just go to San Diego?" she asked.

I shrugged. "Wanted to go somewhere I've never been before."

"My name's Margaret," the tanned one said, "but everyone calls me Maggie."

I extended my hand. "I'm Randall."

She reached over and we shook. Then I reached for the other woman's hand, but she pretended to look for something in her bag.

"I'll bet they call you Randy for short," she said.

"Nope. I'm not randy, just interested."

That got a smile from the slender one. "I'm Sherry, not Cherry."

"Don't ever call her Cherry," Maggie said. "She thinks that's a hooker's name."

"Cross my heart," I said.

Their salads came. Sherry had a shrimp Louie and Maggie, a Cobb. They'd also ordered white wine, and the waitress took great care in placing the glasses down because both were full.

"Now that's what I call a glass of wine," Maggie said happily.

I raised my bottle. "Here's to the Virgin Islands."

Sherry picked her glass up without spilling a drop, but Maggie leaned forward and sucked some of the wine before lifting hers. We toasted and sipped our drinks.

"That shrimp salad looks good," I said. "How's it taste?"

Sherry took a bite with a good portion of dressing on the fork and nodded.

"Not bad. How's yours, Maggie?"

I watched Maggie dig around to get as much on her fork as possible before shoveling it into her mouth. She chewed for a few seconds, then mumbled, "Good."

"So, Randall, not Randy," Sherry said, "entertain us while we eat. What's your story?"

"And I hope it's not a short story," Maggie said, laughing.

"I'm just taking a break from medical school," I fibbed. I could tell they were at least twenty-five, and I was barely twenty-one, but I knew I looked older.

22

"You're in medical school?" Sherry asked. "What year?"

"Halfway through my second."

"What kind of medicine are you going to practice?" Maggie asked.

"Not sure yet. Maybe a general practitioner."

"You should specialize," Sherry said between bites. "That's where the money is."

"My father was a general practitioner. He did pretty well for himself."

"Was?" Sherry asked. "Is he retired or something?"

I took a long pull from my beer.

"Or something."

"What's that supposed to mean?" she asked.

"Let's just say, he doesn't have to practice anymore."

Sherry ate in silence. Maggie had a quizzical expression but followed Sherry's lead and ate quietly. I flagged over the waitress and asked for another beer.

"Would you ladies like another glass of wine? It's on me."

"No," said Sherry. "We're headed to the beach."

"Yeah," Maggie added. "The one on the other side of the point is spectacular."

"What a coincidence," I said. "That's where I'm going."

"Maybe we can share a cab?" Maggie suggested.

Sherry shot her a dirty look, which Maggie ignored as she smiled in my direction.

"I'd love to," I answered.

"Then you'd better cancel that order," Sherry said, scowling. "You won't have time to drink a beer

23

before we go. We're leaving as soon as we're done."

"Don't worry. I've had a lot of experience drinking beer."

Maggie smiled again and picked up her glass. There was only a little wine left, but a black fly was floating on the surface, and she swallowed the last gulp before I could stop her.

"Ooo," she said, "I think there was piece of cork in my glass."

Sherry had noticed, too, and glanced at me.

"Yeah," I said. "It must have been a bit of cork."

Sherry flashed me a satisfied smile and then picked up her own glass. She inspected it closely. "I don't think there's any in mine." She swirled the remaining wine around the bottom of her glass and then poured it into her mouth, pursing her lips and sucking in some air before swallowing.

"That's the proper way to taste wine," Maggie said. "We took a gourmet cooking class. That's one of the things we learned."

That must have struck Sherry as funny, for she burst into laughter. There was something about swallowing a fly and claiming to have a gourmet's palate that struck a chord with me, and before I could help myself, I was laughing, too.

Maggie looked confused. "What so funny about that?"

Sherry shook her head. "Nothing, nothing." Then she laughed again.

Maggie looked indignant. She folded her napkin, saying, "Well, I don't know what's so funny about us taking a gourmet cooking class, Sherry."

Sherry and I laughed again so loudly that the

24

waitress who had my beer just stood for a moment, as if wondering what to do. The more indignant Maggie got, the funnier it seemed, but eventually we regained our composures.

After paying our bills, we hailed a cab.

"Can you take us to Morningstar Beach, please," Maggie asked.

"You know where that is, right?" Sherry asked the cabbie

"Of course," he said. "Dat's our most popular beach." He was a small, skinny man with a gold tooth in the front of his perpetual grin.

Holding the door open, I asked, "How'd you hear about it?"

Sherry climbed into the back seat next to Maggie. "We've been here before, Randall."

"Oh?" I closed the door and sat in the front passenger seat.

Maggie, still fuming, glared at Sherry. "I wish you two would let me in on the big joke."

Sherry touched her shoulder. "There's no joke, Honey. There was just something about the way you said gourmet cooking class that seemed funny. I don't know why."

Maggie glared at me. "What about you? What did you find so funny?"

"I laughed because she was laughing," I said. "Her laugher is infectious."

"Infectious, or contagious?" Sherry asked.

"I don't know," I answered. "I'm not a doctor yet."

"Ha, ha, ha," Maggie said.

The cab swung up a hill, and we looked back at

the town and the bay receding in the background. With its white houses stacked against the steep green hillside and the white yachts floating on the azure water, the scene reminded me of Sausalito in north San Francisco Bay.

The steep road had several narrow curves, but it afforded a spectacular view of the bay. Sometimes the drivers of small trucks honked at our cab as if we were crowding the road. Or maybe they recognized our driver.

"How much farther?" I asked.

In his thick Caribbean accent, the cabbie replied, "We be there in fifteen minutes, mon. No problem."

We turned away from the bay and headed east. Several large resort hotels came into view, and I saw where the wealthier folks stayed.

"Did you even bring a bathing suit?" Sherry asked. "Obviously, you didn't bring a towel."

"My shorts double as trunks." I had on a regular pair of khaki shorts, along with a white cotton polo shirt, but what the hell. I was going to be with two bikini-clad women.

"What about a beach towel?" Maggie asked. "We only brought our own, and I don't think mine's wide enough to share."

Without taking his eyes off the road, the driver said, "You can buy a nice towel at the beach. Fine souvenir. They got a good concession stand, mon."

I grinned at the girls.

Finally, we pulled into a narrow parking lot on a small bluff overlooking the beach. I paid the driver and climbed out to admire the view. The calm turquoise sea spread before us like some magical

26

eternity, a steady breeze causing the fronds of the palm trees to wave in our direction, as if welcoming us, and below was a strip of sugar-white sand. A well-worn path led from the blacktop of the parking lot to the shimmering sand below.

"Randall," Maggie said, sweeping her arm along the horizon like a game-show beauty, "I give you Morningstar Beach."

I nodded and smiled at her. "Thanks. I'll take it."

Chapter 4

The beach was narrower than I'd expected, but the sand much whiter than on California beaches. Palm trees shaded various spots like umbrellas. A few dozen people were scattered about in clusters - some couples, some foursomes, some old, some young.

"Lead the way, ladies." I waved them ahead, not wanting to be pushy.

Maggie and I followed Sherry down the path and onto the beach. Low waves rolled in lazily. The water looked clear enough close to shore, but twenty yards out, it turned turquoise and looked pristine. In the distance, a small island rose out of the sea like the back of a gray whale.

Sherry chose a spot under a palm tree where we could be in shade if we wanted it. The white sand was inviting, though I tossed a few cigarette butts away. The girls pulled towels out of their bags and spread them out next to each other, with about six inches of sand between.

"You know," Maggie said, "if we put our towels right next to each other, there might be room for Randall."

Sherry shot her an evil look. "I need my space,"

she said. "No offense, Randall, but I don't want to rub up against a sweaty body all day."

I smiled. "Yeah, I'd rather rub against a sweaty body all night."

Sherry pulled her sundress over her head, saying, "Ha, ha." Lean and toned, she could have been a model and she already had a good start on her tan, though a tantalizing bit of white flesh appeared when she adjusted her top.

"Look," said Maggie, pointing to something behind me. "That must be the concession stand."

A small shack stood at the far end of the beach, a large red Coca-Cola sign hanging over the opened window.

"You ladies want anything? A cold drink? Potato chips?"

"No, we're good," Sherry said.

"Actually, if they have some Lays, I'll take a bag."

"Okay," I said, grinning. "The lady wants to get Lays. I'm your man!"

She swatted my arm and laughed. "Don't make it sound dirty!"

Sherry rolled her eyes and lay on her back without comment.

The concession stand was a wooden hut with odd pieces of bamboo, netting, and broken shells nailed to the walls. On a shelf inside were several stacks of beach towels. I found a blue one with an orange sunset behind silhouettes of palm trees.

With my new towel in hand, along with two bags of chips and a cold bottle of Coke, I returned to the girls. Both were on their backs, their faces in the shade, but their bodies glistened in the sunlight.

Sherry's body was long, lean and athletic. Maggie was voluptuous. Her top barely contained her breasts and her hips were wide. She was tanned, but several moles stood out on her stomach. If I used a pen to connect the dots, I'd be able to draw an irregular star on her stomach. Or maybe the Big Dipper.

"Like what you see?" Maggie asked.

"Just trying to decide where to spread my towel."

The trunk of the palm tree was next to Sherry's head—by design, I suspected. Maggie patted the shaded sand next to her and said, "Feel free." She lifted her sunglasses and smiled. Sherry stayed as stiff as a cadaver. I spread the towel on the sand next to Maggie, pulled off my shirt, which brought another grin to Maggie's full lips, and plopped down on my side, facing her.

"So, Maggie, tell me the story of your life."

"Okay, but don't you have something for me?"

"Ah, yes."

She took the bag, opened it and ate the chips one at a time as she told me her story.

"After college, I interned at Met Life in Manhattan, where I met Sherry, and then we both got jobs in Boston. We've been best friends for three years. Isn't that right, Sherry?"

Sherry nodded, but it was clear she wanted to doze. Maggie ate another chip.

"What about boyfriends?" I asked. "You're not engaged or anything, are you?"

She laughed. "Do you see a ring on my finger?"

I shook my head as I grabbed a potato chip.

"In high school, I went steady with a boy for two

years before breaking it off when it was clear we were going to different colleges. He was the first."

"The first what?"

She gave me a look. "The first boy I went all the way with. He'll always have a special corner of my heart. Then I went steady with an older boy during freshman year in college, but I caught him cheating, so I dumped him. I dated a lot after him. Sherry says it was revenge sex."

I pretended to be enthralled as I imagined taking off her top. She rattled on as if her life were a romance novel. She'd been engaged to a young divorce lawyer for six months while living in Manhattan, but he'd left her for a client.

"I'm focusing on my career now," she explained, "so I'm not dating much anymore. And I don't want to get serious until I'm ready to settle down. Sherry and I hope we'll find guys at about the same time, in a couple of years. Isn't that right?" She turned and saw that Sherry was asleep, her mouth sagging open, producing the cutest little snore.

"Anyway, I want to keep working, at least part time, after I get married. Even when I have kids."

I nodded and smiled, wishing I had another beer.

"So tell me more about you, Randall. You know almost everything there is to know about me, but I know almost nothing about you."

I wiped the sweat off my forehead. "How about we take a swim first? I'm getting hot."

She nodded and stood up, leaving her sunglasses on the towel. I left my wallet and room key inside my shoes, where only the cleverest of thieves would think to look, and, hand in hand, we ran into the water together. I'd expected it to be cold, but it felt as lukewarm as bath water. We walked through the low surf and then swam together into the clear water. Small waves lifted us gently, and I was surprised by how buoyant I felt. We could float on our backs with little effort, and I stared up the clear blue sky, expecting to spend the rest of the afternoon and evening in the company of these two women, hoping that one of them would come to my room that night.

"This is paradise," I said.

"Yeah." She scanned the depths. "The water feels great. I hope there aren't any sharks around."

"You want to go back?"

She smiled and wet her lips with her tongue "In a little while. I'm enjoying your company."

Her hand brushed against mine, so I reached over. We were in shallow enough water that we could stand face to face, and a minute later, we were in each other's arms kissing.

We kissed long and hard several times until the water level rose. Then she put her arms around my neck and I put my hands under her butt to hold her up so we could kiss again. She wrapped her legs around my waist. It was nice. I hadn't been with anyone in months. My girlfriend had broken up with me before Thanksgiving, saying she didn't see us going anywhere—whatever that meant.

"The tide's coming," she said, grinning.

I smiled at her innuendo, but the water was lapping at our chins, so I carried her to shallow water and then let her down. We walked back up to the beach holding hands. Sherry had rolled over onto her stomach and was fast asleep.

"Did she sleep at all last night?" I asked.

"No, not much. We stayed out at a bar until almost two, and she's not used to drinking so much."

"A lightweight?"

I was drying off when I noticed three of the young sailors from the night before walking down the beach in our direction wearing matching dark-blue swimsuits and white tee-shirts. They were laughing and talking loudly. Each carried a six pack of beer in one hand and a towel rolled up in the other.

The one named Jimmy looked at Maggie as he walked by. She was drying herself off and stopped long enough to cover herself with the towel. One of the others whistled, and Jimmy laughed, saying, "Hey, sexy! Why don't you come with a real man?"

I laughed. The one named Jimmy stopped, the obnoxious smile leaving his face, and his two pals stopped as well.

"What're you laughing at?"

"Just a couple of punks who don't know when to shut up," I answered. I was taller and better built, so I felt confident I could take them, as long as it was one at a time.

Sherry sat up. "What's going on?"

"It's those same guys who hassled us last night," Maggie told her.

I looked at Maggie. "These guys bothered you last night?"

"Yeah," she answered, "but there were four of them and they were wearing uniforms."

Sherry stood up, and it looked like she was ready to fight, which made me feel braver. I turned back to the one named Jimmy. "Jesus, you guys make friends everywhere you go, don't you. They got asked to leave the bar I was at last night, too."

Jimmy looked me up and down. "You the guy with the bat?"

"That was Mike. He'll be back in a minute. Went to his car to get something. A tire iron, I think."

The kid in the middle transferred his towel to his beer-holding hand and grabbed Jimmy. "C'mon, man. We came here to have fun in the sun, not brawl."

Jimmy stared at me with hatred in his eyes for a second or two, but then let himself get dragged away. Soon they were back to laughing and talking too loud, with the occasional swear word accentuating their banter.

"Those guys are assholes," Maggie said.

"Especially that one guy with the dark eyes," Sherry added.

"His name's Jimmy," I told them. "Jimmy Collins."

"I don't care what his name is," Sherry said. "He scares me."

We watched them grow smaller and smaller as they walked to the far end of the beach and then turned to find their own place under the palm trees. I couldn't see them after that, but I kept looking out for them, worried that, once they'd finished their beer, they'd look for some other form of entertainment.

Maggie asked me to rub lotion on her back, and I did, as she lay on her stomach. I massaged the lotion into her skin and on the backs of her legs while she smiled with her head turned toward me. If we had been alone, I would have kissed the back of her neck and between her shoulder blades, but Sherry had sat down and was watching from behind her sunglasses, even though she pretended to be reading a book.

I could tell Sherry was troubled about something, but I wasn't sure if it was jealousy because I was giving all my attention to Maggie now, or if she were still worried about the three sailors.

Eventually, Maggie fell asleep. Her snoring was deep and phlegmy as if she were an occasional smoker. Sherry put her book down, hugged her knees and stared at the horizon.

"You okay?"

She nodded half-heartedly, and then whispered, "I wish Maggie and I could go somewhere without being bothered by men all the time. No offense."

"I hope you don't put me in the same category as those assholes."

She lowered her cheek to her knees and looked at me. "You're much smoother, Randall, it's true. But you want what those guys want."

"And what's that?"

"To get into our pants, of course."

"But you aren't wearing pants, Sherry."

She neither laughed nor smiled, just turned her face back to the water.

I wanted to hold her, to make her feel better, and I knew then, that even if I slept with Maggie, it was Sherry I had a crush on.

Chapter 5

L ike the ladies, I dozed for almost an hour. When I awoke, the scene had changed. Clouds had built up along the horizon, and the air had grown thick with humidity. After the women stirred, we decided to call it a day, packed up, and headed back to the bluff. Taxis on the edge of the road held drivers smoking cigarettes and reading newspapers. We climbed into the one in front, manned by a different driver, but he could have been the other driver's brother.

"Where to?"

"I'm staying at the Midtown," I told him, "but you can take the ladies to their hotel first."

Maggie laughed. "Are you kidding? That's where we're staying, too."

I glanced back. Maggie was beaming, but Sherry just stared out her window.

The taxi lurched forward and made a U-turn when there was an opening in the traffic. Maggie put her hand on my shoulder and rubbed my neck, saying, "That was fun, being in the water together."

I nodded, craning my neck to look at her. "Want to meet for dinner?"

Sherry looked at Maggie and shrugged. "I need a nap, and a cold shower."

Maggie squeezed my shoulder. "Why don't we

meet around seven at the same place we had lunch?"

It was a little after four, so a couple hours of rest sounded good to me, too.

"Sure," I agreed. "That place has a nice view."

*   *   *

When I woke up, it was almost seven. I jumped in the shower, dressed in record time, and raced to the little café with its charming patio. Maggie and Sherry, wearing colorful tight sundresses, were at a table with two young guys. They seemed to be having such a good time, I wasn't sure if I should join them. Fortunately, Maggie noticed me and waved me over.

Grabbing a chair, I squeezed between the two women. "Sorry I'm late."

"Randall," Maggie said, "meet Jerry and Stewart."

I reached across the table and shook hands with each of them. They appeared to be in their late-twenties and fairly well off, by the look of their wristwatches and clothes.

"Stewart just got his broker's license," Maggie said, "and Jerry's interning at the same real estate agency in Manhattan."

"How 'bout you?" Stewart asked, looking at me.

"I'm in medical school in California," I fibbed again.

"Wow," Jerry said. "Med school. That must be challenging."

Maggie leaned over, kissed my earlobe, and whispered, "I'm really glad to see you. I was

37

beginning to think you'd changed your mind."

I glanced at her and smiled. Her expectant eyes glistened in the evening light.

The girls already had Mai Tais, Jerry and Stewart had what looked like rum and cokes, so I ordered a gin and tonic. When the waitress came back with our glasses, we ordered dinner and settled into polite, vapid conversation, sipping our drinks. The sun had disappeared behind Government Hill, and a light breeze brought with it the salty smell of the ocean. At the tables surrounding us sat other groups of vacationers in their colorful clothing, talking and laughing. Most of the men wore Hawaiian shirts that made them look like peacocks, so I felt a bit out of place in my simple white polo shirt and khaki shorts.

When the food arrived, I realized how hungry I was. I'd ordered a shark steak, Jerry and Stewart, the sea bass, Sherry had crab cakes, and Maggie, the seafood linguini. We asked for another round of drinks before we dug into our meals.

"The shark's delicious," I said. "How's everyone else's?"

The guys nodded, Sherry said, "Tasty," and Maggie added, "Mine's tender and tasty, too." She held a forkful up to my mouth, asking, "Would you like to try some?"

Her impish grin told me the innuendo was intended, so I wrapped my mouth around her rolled up pasta and pulled it off the fork slowly.

Sherry gave us a disapproving "Hmm," and said, "Will someone please pour a glass of cold water on those two?"

Jerry picked up his water glass and threatened to

douse us, but then laughed and took a sip.

I could tell Sherry was sizing up Stewart. She listened to him answer questions as if interviewing him for a job, nodding approval at some answers, scowling at others.

Stewart was good looking and knew it.

Jerry, on the other hand, seemed lost, destined to play Stewart's sidekick for the rest of their stay, if not for the rest of their lives.

Once dinner was over, we ordered more drinks. Under the table, Maggie rested her hand on the inside of my thigh, sliding it up and down my leg slowly. I followed the banter, but I was distracted.

Sherry had a way of smiling that was too sexy to ignore. Her upper lip drew up, revealing her teeth, but she bit her lower lip almost every time she grinned. And her eyes sparkled. Little crinkles at the corners of her eyes made her seem wiser than her years. She wore her hair up, and little strands made me notice her long neck.

She'd gotten just enough sun, her skin the shade of honey. Her blouse was loose, and she wasn't wearing a bra, so whenever she moved or laughed, I could see her breasts sway inside the light fabric.

Maggie squeezed my thigh and slid her hand toward my crotch. Her eyelids were drooping. I wasn't sure if she was trying to look sexy, or if she was just tired—or maybe even drunk.

"How you feeling?" I asked.

"With my hand," she said. Then she burst into laughter, startling the others.

"You okay, Maggie?" Sherry asked.

"Let's go dancing!" she blurted. "I want to dance

with these guys."

"There's a bar just down the street," Stewart offered. "We were there last night. It has a dance floor and a little Reggae band."

"Let's go!" Maggie said. She pushed her chair back and tried to stand, but needed help. "Wow. I've been sittin' too long. I need to move."

I glanced at Sherry. She nodded. "Might do us all good to walk around."

While the ladies made a trip to the bathroom, we three guys split the bill.

"How long have you known Maggie?" Stewart asked.

"Just met this morning."

"Oh? Seems like you two have been dating for awhile."

"They're what you call 'fast friends,'" Jerry offered.

The girls came back, and Maggie looked better. We strolled down the street. It wasn't hard to find the bar—we could hear the steel drums blocks away.

The place was dark and smoky, packed with natives and tourists, dancing, drinking, and laughing. Stewart had led the way but seemed stymied when he couldn't find a table.

Being taller, I scanned the room and noticed an empty table in the back corner. "C'mon," I said, grabbing Maggie by the hand. I weaved through the crowd, brushing against hot, sweaty bodies. A mixture of perfumes, cigarette smoke and the scent of rum assaulted my nostrils, but I found the corner table. It had only two chairs, so we let the ladies sit while we stood behind them.

Scott Evans

The band played reggae on a small stage under a few colorful lights, but the steel drums were so loud I couldn't understand the singer's tonal, rhythmic moaning. The lyrics didn't matter to the dancers close to the stage. They rocked and swayed, with arms in the air and wide smiles on their faces. It looked like an orgy. I wasn't much of a dancer, but even I wanted to get into the action.

I yelled in Maggie's ear, "Want to dance?"

She looked up with drooping eyes and shook her head. "Feeling a little queasy."

"I'll dance with you," Sherry yelled.

I led her to the dance floor where we squeezed into the crowd. At first, with our arms in the air, we tried to stay a polite distance from each other, but the sweaty bodies around us pressed us together. The top of her head was just below my nose. The musky fragrance of her perfume and the flowery scent of her shampoo filled my nostrils. She turned and pressed her back against me, maybe aware of my excitement, and I simply danced and enjoyed being close to her. We danced close to each other through several songs. My shirt was drenched, and whenever I tried to spin Sherry, I could see that her blouse was clinging to her wet skin, revealing the contours of her breasts and the tips of her nipples.

Then the music stopped, and the singer said something about taking a break, producing a collective groan from the crowd. I glanced at Sherry. She smiled in a knowing way, and I knew she felt an attraction.

As we headed to the table, I was stunned to see the three Navy boys from the beach standing at our table, talking to Jerry and Stewart. Maggie's head hung down. I couldn't tell if she was asleep or terrified.

When she noticed them, Sherry stopped me, saying, "Oh, no."

"Be cool," I said.

When we got back to the table, the one named Jimmy Collins grinned, cigarette smoke rolling out from between his teeth.

"Hey," he said, "fancy meeting you here."

"Yeah," Sherry replied, "fancy."

He was undeterred. "Isn't this place great?"

Maggie looked up and clutched Sherry's hand. "I'm going to be sick."

Sherry helped her stand, and they pushed through the crowd to the restroom.

"Mind if I sit down?" Jimmy asked.

Before anyone answered, he took Maggie's seat and set his glass on the table. Stewart sat down next to him in the chair he'd been saving for Sherry. The other two Navy guys shot me indifferent stares, then returned to scanning the crowd—probably for available women.

Jerry stepped closer to me. "Do you guys know each other?"

I nodded. "We've run into each other a couple of times."

"Yeah? Us, too," Jerry answered. "We partied with these guys last night. They can get pretty crazy. I guess this is their first furlough, or something, since they finished boot camp."

"Did someone mention boot camp?" Jimmy yelled. "Don't nobody talk about boot camp. Fuck boot camp!"

The three of them raised their glasses and toasted, slamming back their drinks. I tapped Jimmy's shoulder. "Where were you in boot camp?"

He glared at me. "Didn't you hear me? I don't want to talk about no fuckin' boot camp?"

One of the other sailors leaned across the table. "Orlando, Florida. It was a bitch, a friggin' bitch."

Jerry leaned in. "Did you guys go to Disney World? I went a few years ago, and it was amazing."

"We had this conversation last night," Jimmy said. "Don't you remember, Jerry. You told us all about going there on your senior trip in high school. Told us you got a blow job on some scary ride from some slut, remember?"

"Oh, yeah," Jerry said. "Guess I was pretty wasted last night."

Jimmy took another drag of his cigarette and then blew the smoke out, saying, "Your boyfriend Stewie had to walk you home, you were so plastered."

The other Navy guy leaned across the table again and said, "We got kicked out of this place shortly after those guys left."

"That must have been when you came to the Galleon House," I said.

"The Galleon House?" Jimmy asked. "You mean that geezer bar?"

"Definitely for an older crowd," I admitted, "but the food's good."

The other Navy boy reached out to shake hands and said, "I'm Frank. I'm an E-3. I have a couple of years of college."

I shook his hand. "What's an E-3?"

"It's just my rank, but I get a little more pay than these two clowns."

"Yeah, Frank," Jimmy said. "You're such a kiss-ass."

Ignoring Jimmy's comment, I leaned over his back and asked the third Navy guy his name.

"Tony," he answered. He reached for my hand, so I extended mine.

"Get off me, man," Jimmy grumbled, pushing his shoulder into my stomach. "You some kind of fag?"

I stepped aside and looked down at his scowling face.

"No," I said. "Are you?"

He jumped to his feet, knocking his chair over, and took a swing at me. I stepped aside before his right could connect. He threw another wild punch that missed. The other sailor, Tony, grabbed for him, but Jimmy shrugged him off and fell into me as his right fist grazed my chin. As he straightened up, I saw the rage in his eyes and knew he wouldn't quit unless I stopped him.

I was a good head taller, my reach longer, so my right fist caught him squarely on the jaw. I followed with a left uppercut that straightened him up. He took another wobbly swing, but I jumped back, then stepped in and slammed my right fist into his nose. It exploded with blood, and Jimmy clutched it as he fell on his ass.

Even in the darkness, I could see blood gushing from his nose when he pulled his hand away and looked at it. He glared at me, rage in his eyes, but stayed on the floor.

The crowd around us quieted. Jimmy's friends

stepped around the table and helped him up. Stewart handed him a handkerchief which Jimmy pressed against his blood-smeared face. With Frank on one side and Tony on the other, they started for the door.

As he brushed by me, Frank said, "That wasn't necessary."

"No?" I said. "What would you have done?"

Once they were gone, I picked up the chair Jimmy had occupied. His half-empty glass was on the table, next to his smoldering cigarette in the ashtray.

"Jeez," Jerry said, "you're pretty good. Did you box in college?"

"A few times," I said, smiling. "But not on the team."

"That guy was right, though," Stewart said. "That wasn't necessary."

I crushed out the cigarette. "He took a swing at me."

Stewart drained his glass and waved for a waitress. People around us went back to talking and laughing.

"At least the ladies didn't see it," Jerry said. "They'd be upset. Hey, what do you think of Mike Tyson getting convicted of rape?"

"What the hell made you think of that?" Stewart asked.

"I was thinking about boxing," Jerry said.

I didn't respond. A month earlier, Tyson had been convicted earlier of raping an eighteen-year-old woman named Desiree Washington—a beauty contestant winner. To be compared to him in anyway was insulting.

When the waitress came, she cleared the empty

glasses and took our orders. I handed her the ashtray before she left. The fight had happened so quickly, no one who worked in the bar seemed to have noticed.

Sherry made her way back to the table alone.

"Where's Maggie?" I asked.

"Bent over a toilet. I'm not sure if it's food poisoning or just too much to drink, but she's losing everything."

"Poor thing," Jerry said.

"Can one of you help me get her back to the hotel?"

I said, "Of course," and stood.

Stewart touched Sherry's shoulder. "Want me to help?"

"Randall's staying at the same hotel we are, so the two of us can take her."

He drew his hand away. "Well, let's find each other tomorrow, okay?"

"Okay. Let's meet around noon at the same place where we had dinner, only—"

"Only we won't eat."

"Agreed."

I followed Sherry to the Ladies room and waited while she went in. A few minutes later, she staggered out, propping up Maggie as well as she could. I got on Maggie's left side.

She threw her arm over my shoulder, mumbling, "I'm sorry, I'm sorry."

"It's not your fault," I whispered.

On the street outside, I looked for a taxi but didn't see one, so we staggered together like we were in a three-legged race. Fortunately, we were only a few blocks from the hotel. Maggie seemed to grow stronger as we walked. She glanced at me and tried to smile, but then noticed my shirt.

"What's all over you?"

Sherry peered around her. "Is that blood?"

"Yeah," I admitted. "One of the sailors had a nose bleed."

"And you tried to help?" Sherry asked.

"Sort of."

Maggie shook her head disapprovingly. "You'll never get that out of your shirt. It's ruined."

Their room was on the third floor and the hotel had no elevator. Sherry and I helped her climb the stairs, and once we got to the door, Sherry took out her key. "I can manage from here."

"Are you sure?" I asked. "I'd be happy to help get her into bed."

"I bet you would."

"I didn't mean it like that."

"Don't scold him," Maggie said. "He's just tryin' to be nice."

Sherry swung the door open. Cold air billowed out—the air-conditioner was running at full blast. Their room was twice the size of mine and had two double beds.

"Nice room," I said.

"That's as far as you go," Sherry warned.

Maggie, still hanging on Sherry's shoulder, looked at me with sad, bloodshot eyes. "Night, Randall. Except for barfing, I had a really great day."

Sherry kicked the door closed in my face.

As I descended the stairs, I noticed my hands. Dried blood coated my knuckles. I went to my room, washed my hands and then tried to rinse out my shirt.

The dried brown blood turned orange in the water and swirled down the drain, reminding me of the bathtub scene in *Psycho*. I tried to rinse the blood out of my shirt, though it still appeared splattered with orange mud, and hung it up on the shower rod knowing it was probably a lost cause. Then I turned and looked at myself in the mirror.

People had always said I looked like my father. We both had dark hair and thick eyebrows, but my nose was narrower than his and he had a slight cleft in his chin. He told me I'd gotten my dimples from my mother. Dad had trained me to box in a little gym he'd carved out in our basement, but he'd always said, "You should turn to violence only as a last resort." I knew he would've been disappointed with me, but I had to admit, there was something very satisfying about breaking the nose of that obnoxious sailor.

Then I heard a light tapping on my door. I opened it carefully, half expecting the sailor's friends, but the light from my room illuminated Sherry's lovely face. She was smiling though her brow was knitted with concern.

"Everything okay?"

"Yeah. I got Maggie into bed. She's sleeping on her side, in case she gets sick again."

I thought of something and smiled. "I wonder if it was that fly she swallowed."

Sherry frowned. "It's not funny. She's very embarrassed. That's why I came down. She begged me to apologize for being rude to you at the door. She really likes you, you know."

"You weren't rude," I said, touching her shoulder.

48

She didn't squirm away as I'd expected. "Want to come in?"

"That wouldn't be a good idea." She peered into my eyes. "I just wanted to thank you for helping me and to say I'm sorry."

I held out my hand as if to shake. "Apology accepted."

She took my hand and then stood on her tip-toes, kissing me lightly on the cheek before turning away. I watched her as she padded barefoot up the stairs until she disappeared in the darkness. Then I slowly closed my door, grinning stupidly as I touched my cheek where her lips had landed like a butterfly on my skin.

Chapter 6

I awoke early, still feeling the brush-stroke of Sherry's lips on my cheek. I climbed the stairs and tapped on Sherry and Maggie's door. Nothing. I tapped again. Sherry opened the door a crack, squinted at me and rubbed her eyes.

"What time is it?"

"About seven. Were you still asleep?"

"God, yes. Why aren't you?"

"I don't know. Just woke up feeling pretty good." I wanted to tell her that she'd given me a new sense of hope, a feeling like I could go on. I wanted to tell her everything—all the deep feelings I'd had since my father's death, all the doubts I'd felt. But all I could think to say was, "You want to go for coffee?"

"Come back in a few hours, Randall, when normal folks on vacation get up."

With that, she closed the door.

I was disappointed but not discouraged. After all, she'd told me to come back. I went to the Galleon House for breakfast.

Over bacon and eggs, I read a well-worn, two-day-old *New York Times*. Killings in the Middle East, a slumping economy, protestors clashing over abortion—each story more depressing than the last. I

50

tried to find at least one story that had something positive and uplifting, but the best I could find was my Horoscope, which said, "Embrace new adventures and your life will find new purpose." *Wow,* I thought. *How appropriate!*

I'd killed enough time to go back to Sherry's room, but when I knocked, there was no answer. I put my ear to the door, but heard nothing. I knocked one more time and waited. The hallway on that floor led to a little terrace, so I walked out and sat down on one of the four worn lounge chairs. The terrace afforded the opposite view as the one from the Galleon House. From that higher perspective, I'd had a view of the red roofs of buildings, the town, and the bay, but from this terrace, all I could see was the hill and the wall around the gardens of the Galleon House.

Something about the odd combination of scents in the air—of bacon and flowers—made me remember the morning of my mother's funeral. One of the nurses in dad's office, a heavy woman who wore too much make up, had come to the house to cook for us. We'd eaten in the dining room, which was filled with bouquets of flowers. I followed Dad's example and ate politely, commenting on how good everything tasted, which only made me miss my mother's cooking.

I must have sat there for an hour, thinking about my parents. Finally, someone honked a car horn on the street below. The noise startled me, so I looked over the railing. A taxicab was parked across the street, and two women in their late thirties climbed out of the back seat. They laughed at themselves as they fumbled with their bags, nearly tripping over one another. Their high-pitched banter rang with excitement as they disappeared below to check into the hotel. The laughter reminded me that I, too, was a tourist, so I should stop moping and act like one.

I walked around town searching for Sherry and Maggie, but they weren't at the café we'd eaten at the day before, nor anywhere else. After an hour or so, I went back to my room, killed a cockroach on the bathroom floor, pulled off my damp shirt, then collapsed on the bed and fell asleep.

I dreamed that someone was slapping the walls, trying to kill cockroaches as they scurried in circles, and then I awoke to the sound of knocking on my door. I opened it, hoping to see Sherry, but it was Maggie who stood in front of me, smiling.

"We missed you this morning," she said. "Knocked on your door about nine, but there was no answer."

"I must have been across the street eating breakfast."

She put her hand on my bare chest. "I really wanted to see you."

I grabbed her and kissed her, pulling her into my room and closing the door. She returned my kiss fiercely, and we tore each other's clothes off. Once we were naked, she pulled me onto the bed on top of her, kissing me passionately and moaning—almost whimpering. She smelled like roses. I was fully aroused, but before I entered her, I looked into her eyes and whispered, "Are you sure?"

She nodded and pulled my head down to kiss me. Her legs opened, so I entered her, feeling how wet she was. "Oh, God," she murmured, and we made love, rocking and undulating in rhythm.

When I couldn't hold it any longer, I released and moaned, and she smiled and moaned with me. Whether she was faking or not, I didn't care, because the sounds she made intensified my ecstasy. I finally rolled off and collapsed beside her, panting.

"God, I needed that," I said.

She rested the back of her hand on my shoulder and said, "So did I." Then a few minutes later, she said, "You were just how I imagined you'd be."

"Oh? How do you mean?"

She rolled onto her side and looked at me, stroking hair away from my sweaty forehead.

"Passionate, intense, powerful."

"And you liked that?"

"Of course, I did." She kissed my eyebrow. "Every woman wants to be taken like that sometimes." She ran her fingers over my chest. "I know I shouldn't tell you this, but I wanted you the moment I saw you."

I smiled. "Wow. That's really... honest." I glanced at her breasts. Her aureoles were deep brown, as large as saucers, her thick nipples, still hard. "Why?"

"Why did I want you?" She laughed. "Because you're handsome and sexy, and you have a great body, and you're nice. And when I found out you're going to be a doctor, well, that was just icing on a great-looking cake."

I kissed her lightly on the lips.

"How 'bout me?" she asked. "Did you find me attractive when you first saw me?"

"Of course."

"Really?" Her fingers made circles on my abdomen. "What did you like about me?"

"You're pretty and sexy, and you have a great body, and you're nice. And when I found out you were in the insurance business, well—"

She slapped my stomach and laughed.

"Where were you this morning?" I asked. "I went to your room about an hour ago, and no one was there."

"Out to brunch. We met up with Jerry and Stewart."

"Oh? How was that?"

"Oh, my God," she said, suddenly changing positions. She sat cross-legged, looking down at me, grinning. "They told us all about the fight last night, how you broke that annoying asshole's nose."

"It wasn't much of a fight."

"That's what Jerry said. He went on and on about how fast you were, throwing punches left and right, and then smashing that guy's nose."

"Yeah, well, that guy's shorter than I am, and he'd had more to drink, so…"

"Stewart said it was a little unfair."

"He did swing at me first."

She spun around and lay back down, nuzzling into my armpit. "I wished I'd seen it. I mean, that guy's a jerk." She laughed. "And you told us he'd had a nose bleed, and that's how the blood got on your shirt."

"I was telling the truth. He did have a nose bleed. I just left out the reason why."

"In the insurance field, we'd call that a lie by omission." She fell silent then, but I could see her satisfied smile.

I stroked her hair. "Where's Sherry? In your room?"

"No. She went to see the house Stewart and Jerry are renting. They call it their 'villa,' but it's just a two-bedroom house. Jerry says it has a big veranda and a good view of the bay. They're talking about throwing a party tonight."

"Sounds like fun," I said. But a pang of jealousy stabbed my heart as I imagined Sherry and Stewart preparing decorations together as if they were organizing a high school prom.

"We're invited, of course." She looked into my eyes. "Want to go?"

"Sure. As long as you won't flirt with any other guys."

"I won't flirt with anyone but you," she whispered. And then she brought her mouth to mine, and we kissed deeply again, as if we really loved each other.

I nudged Maggie onto her back and kissed her mouth, her ears, nibbled her lobes, kissed her neck and both breasts, sucking each nipple until it was harder still. I looked into her eyes and smiled. "I want you again," I whispered.

She said nothing but opened her legs, closed her eyes and turned her face, biting her finger.

It wasn't the frenzied sex we'd had earlier, but soon her body was working in rhythm with mine, and when she moaned, her body shuddered and trembled. She wasn't faking this time.

"Don't stop, don't stop," she cried.

Her hands pulled at my buttocks, and she cried

loudly as she made me work faster, until finally she screamed so loud, I worried someone would call the police. But then I reached a blinding ecstasy as if I'd fallen backward into a warm dark pool. Helpless, I collapsed on top of her and rested there in sweet exhaustion.

When I rolled off, we were both dripping with perspiration.

"Wow," she said, "that was better than before. I didn't think it would be at first, but then…"

Breathing hard, I managed to say, "It's been a while for me. My girlfriend and I broke up over a few months ago."

She stared at the ceiling while her breathing grew calmer. "How often did you two make love?"

Still catching my breath, I said, "All the time, at first. Then we sort of settled into a routine of a couple of times a week."

She nodded and closed her eyes. "Then it got stale, right? That's what guys have told me."

I chuckled. "Guys have told you, you got stale?"

"No, not me in particular. Just having sex with the same person over and over again. For guys, it gets boring. Anyway, that's what a few guys have told me."

"No chance of that happening with us," I said.

"Why? Cuz we're so good together?"

"No, because we'll be going our separate ways when our vacations end."

Her face fell. I'd hurt her, but she tried not to show it. "Yeah, that's true," she said, "but maybe we can stay in touch."

"Sure. Of course," I said, trying to heal the

wound. "Maybe you could come to California. I'd love to show you the sights."

"That'd be nice," she said, looking away. "I've got to shower." She rolled off the far side of the bed and walked around the foot, picking up her clothes as she made her way into the bathroom.

I checked the clock. It was mid-afternoon, and I was famished. I got off the bed, turned the air-conditioner up high, and picked up my clothes, laying them out on the bed. I needed a shower, too, and thought it would be nice to join Maggie and wash her back.

When I pulled the shower curtain aside, she looked at me, crying.

"Hey, hey," I said, pushing hair away from her face. "What's this for?"

"I'm being stupid, I know. I thought we connected, you know?"

I stepped into the shower and wrapped my arms around her, whispering in her ear, "We have connected, Maggie. We are connecting." I kissed her neck and then her lips. "It's a little too soon to say we're going to last forever, but I really like you. Let's see where it goes, okay?"

She nodded.

I washed her hair and used a soapy washcloth on her back, and she scrubbed mine. Soon she seemed to be back to normal. We dried off, and I gave her privacy while I got dressed. I perched myself against the pillows and enjoyed the cold air blowing down from the air-conditioner.

Finally, the bathroom door opened, and she stood in the steamy light, smiling. "How do I look?"

"Lovely."

"You messed me up pretty good," she said. "My hair's a wreck, and I don't have my make-up, so you're seeing the real me."

Sensing she needed to be re-assured, I stood and gave her a hug, saying, "The real you is beautiful."

We went upstairs to her room where we found Sherry sitting on the bed. Stewart and Jerry were seated in different chairs. All three of them had green bottles of Heineken in their hands and smiles on their faces.

"Where have you guys been?" Jerry asked.

Sherry looked at Stewart, and they laughed.

"A gentleman doesn't tell," I said. But I noted a glimmer of disapproval in Sherry's eyes, even though she tried to laugh it away.

Jerry turned bright red. "Oh, I'm sorry."

Maggie stepped over and patted him on the shoulder. "It's okay, Jerry. How could you know we were having the most amazing sex of our lives?"

He turned a deeper shade of red and took a long drink from his bottle.

"So what's the plan?" Maggie asked. "Are you guys throwing your party?"

"Tomorrow night," Stewart said. "We found a really cool thing to do tomorrow and thought a party afterward would be perfect."

Sherry slid off the bed and grabbed a brochure from the nightstand, handing it to Maggie. "There's a catamaran cruise every day from St. Thomas to St. John. It takes an hour to get there, and then they serve you lunch and you can swim or scuba dive or just lie on the beach all afternoon."

"We bought four tickets," Stewart said. "Of course, Randall, if you want to join us, you can probably get a ticket in the morning. The boat leaves at ten."

"I heard about that," I said. "Sounds fun."

"The boat holds about twenty people," Sherry added, "so we thought we'd invite some of them to the party afterward."

Maggie looked up from the brochure and grinned. "That sounds exciting, doesn't it?"

I nodded. "Count me in."

"Assuming they haven't sold out," Stewart added.

"Hopefully, we can squeeze you in," Sherry said.

The way she said it was intended to make me feel like the fifth wheel, but I let it roll off my back. I knew Maggie wanted me.

"I'm famished," I said. "Have you guys made dinner plans?"

"We were just talking about that when you came in," Sherry said. "We don't want to go back to that same café, in case Maggie did get food poisoning. How about taking a cab up to one of the resort hotels and splurging."

"Ooo, that sounds fun," Maggie said. She turned to me, asking "Are you in?"

"Sure, if you guys want to do that, I'm game."

"You have a better suggestion?" Stewart asked.

I shrugged. "I like the Galleon House. It's right across the street, up the hill, and it has a great view of the bay. An older place, but it's got history."

"How's the food?" Sherry asked.

"The dinner I had was delicious. I've gone back for breakfast both mornings." Sherry looked at

Stewart He shrugged.

"Sounds okay to me," Jerry said. "I'd rather save the resort hotel for our last night, anyway. Gotta stretch my dime."

"Do we need reservations?" Stewart asked.

"Nah. I know the bartender, Mike. He'll take care of us."

"Well, I'm not going anywhere," Maggie said, "until I've done my hair over and put on my face. Randall mussed me up something awful." She kissed my cheek before stepping into the bathroom.

I sat on the edge of the bed across from Sherry and smiled. She drained her beer and opened another, which I took as a sign she was a little jealous. I could have sworn she even looked a little hurt, which confused me.

"Would you like a beer, Randall?" she asked.

There was only one bottle left on the dresser. "I don't want to take your last one."

"Take it, if you want it," Stewart said.

"That's okay. Someone else can have it."

"Oh, for God's sake, take the beer already, Randall," Sherry demanded. "You probably need it more than we do, after—" She stopped herself abruptly and looked out the window, taking another swig of beer.

I sheepishly opened the beer and took a sip. "That does hit the spot." It sounded lame, but it was all I could think of.

Jerry leaned over a clinked his bottle against mine. "Here's to a pleasant evening."

Stewart touched his bottle to mine before tapping Sherry's with his. "To a pleasant night, without any

60

rowdy sailors, hopefully."

"I'll drink to that," Sherry replied.

We all took a long pull from our beers, hearing Maggie hum some unrecognizable love song from behind the bathroom door.

Chapter 7

The terrace dining room was half full when we got there, but only a few single men sat at the bar. It must have looked a bit dated to the others, maybe even a little shabby, but it had its charm—the kind of place where you would have seen Frank Sinatra, Dean Martin and Sammy Davis, Jr.

"Hey, Mike," I called.

"Hi, Randall," he said, smiling. "Good to see you again."

Just the response I was hoping for. I led the way to a table by the edge of the terrace so we'd have a good view, and dragged an extra chair over, since there were five of us. We were close to the little stage where Whitey and his friends had performed.

"What a beautiful bar," Sherry said. She was stunning in a loose-fitting Royal blue blouse and tight white slacks.

"The bartender isn't bad, either," Maggie noted. She grinned at me, adding, "For an older guy." She was wearing a low-cut yellow print dress that made her tanned skin glow. With her long, dark hair hanging in curls, she looked like a Spanish flamenco dancer, especially with her gold hooped earring and bright red lips.

"Mike's cool," I said. "Left the corporate world and carved out a pretty nice life here on the island."

"Wow." Jerry said. "Sounds heavenly."

"Heavenly?" Stewart balked. "Sounds like he couldn't cut it in the real world."

I ignored the dig. "Can I get you a drink, Maggie?"

"What are you having?"

"Gin and tonic," I said.

She smiled. "A gin-tonic sounds refreshing."

Sherry leaned over. "You think you should drink tonight?"

Maggie beamed at me. "I feel like a new woman."

I should have kissed her then and there, but instead, I turned to Sherry. "You want something?"

Sherry sat back as if contemplating her options. "I'll have a dry white wine as long as it's chilled."

"Any particular brand?" I asked.

"You're from California," she replied. "You choose."

I nodded, smiling at the frustrated look on Stewart's face. "You guys want me to get your drinks, too," I asked, "or are you coming to the bar?"

"I'll go with you," Jerry said, standing. "What'll you have, Stew?"

"The usual," he answered.

"Long Island iced tea, just like me," Jerry said.

I couldn't help but laugh. They were like an old couple who knew each too well.

We went to the bar and ordered. Mike chatted with Jerry as he mixed the drinks, asking the same questions he'd asked me when we'd first met. I watched Stewart flirt with Sherry. They looked good together. I could imagine them married with kids. Maggie waved, so I waved back and then turned to Mike.

"Make mine a double."

"Yours is on the house, for helping me out the other night."

Jerry turned to me. "How'd you help the other night? Doing dishes or something?"

I was angry at first but saw his innocent face. He'd meant no disrespect and seemed incapable of guile.

"Are you kidding?" Mike said, placing the drinks in front of us. "Randall helped me kick some troublemakers out when they started bothering they owner."

Jerry looked at me in awe. "Was it the same guys?"

"Yeah. The one guy grabbed the owner's arm and was saying some nasty things."

He told Mike about the fight the previous night, and Mike laughed.

"You broke his nose?"

"I think so. It bled pretty badly."

"Well, he needed to be knocked down a rung or two."

We paid for the drinks and carried them back to the table where Jerry shared what he'd learned from Mike. I sipped my drink, which was good and strong and cold, and soaked up the admiration, until Stewart interrupted.

"Jesus, Wake. Do you get into fights everywhere you go?"

My first instinct was to hit him. "No, just when some asshole deserves it."

He shook his head but said nothing. He and Sherry exchanged looks, and I knew she was his now.

"Well, I think Randall's a hero," Maggie said. Then she leaned over and kissed my face.

I sipped my drink, remembering Sherry's lips on my cheek the night before. A pang of sadness stung me, but I grinned and listened to the chatter. They were discussing the view from the terrace, and I was glad the topic of conversation had changed. I'd sat with my back to the view, Maggie on my left and Jerry on my right, so the others could see the red Spanish tile of the rooftops and the lush, green vegetation, and the blue-green water of the bay.

I'd come to St. Thomas to escape the pain and sadness I'd been feeling, but there it was again, like a stowaway, a parasite that had burrowed into my heart. I wanted not to feed it anymore, but every breath I took seemed to breathe more life into it.

After another round of drinks, we went upstairs to the buffet and filled our plates. The food—a white fish, crab cakes, shrimp cocktails, green beans, and fruit salad—all smelled as good as I remembered. Then downstairs on the terrace, we settled into eating together like one happy family. I tried not to let the nagging aloneness bother me. The night sky was turning a deep blue and the town's lights were coming on, as a breeze blew in off the water. Everyone seemed pleased with my choice of the Galleon House. Even Stewart.

Looking like a movie star in a tight green and white Hawaiian-print dress, Gillian came to the table and introduced herself, telling the others how lucky she'd been to have me there two nights ago. I was afraid that would ignite another volley of insults from Stew.

Instead, he raised his nearly empty glass and toasted me. "To Randall, the knight in shining armor, who rescues fair damsels in distress."

I ignored his sarcasm and raised my glass.

"To Randall," Jerry said.

Gillian began picking up our plates. "You folks want another round?"

Maggie looked at Sherry, who shrugged. "It's really pleasant here," Maggie said. "I wouldn't mind staying."

Jerry nodded as he drained his glass and balanced it on the stack of dishes in Gillian's arms. "This is a great place."

"Two G and T's," Gillian said, "two Long Islands, and one glass of chardonnay, right?"

Pleasantly surprised, I asked, "How'd you know?"

She smiled. "A good hostess knows what her guests are drinking."

After she left, Maggie leaned over. "She's got the hots for you, Randall. You'd better watch out."

"Don't be silly," I said. "She's old enough to be my mother."

Jerry scratched his scalp. "Not really. What is she, about thirty?"

"I'd say she's a little older," Sherry said. "Early forties, maybe."

Jerry craned to watch Gillian walk across the room. She moved gracefully, like a ballerina in her tight dress.

66

"Well," Jerry added, "I think she's sexy."

Stewart laughed. "We've found you a girlfriend, Jerry. Is she single?"

"I think so," I answered. "What about it, Jerry? Want me to fix you up?"

He turned bright red and chuckled nervously. "Stop it, you guys. I don't need to be fixed up."

As Gillian brought our drinks over, Whitey and the other musicians came up the stairs and walked to the stage.

"Well, hello there, Randall Wake," Whitey said, noticing me just as he stepped up on the stage. "You brought friends."

"Hi, Whitey." I stepped over and shook hands with all three men. "Can you play something we can dance to?"

Whitey leaned toward me. "The truth is, we only have about twelve songs in our repertoire. But we'll start with 'I Left My Heart in San Francisco' in your honor. How 'bout that?"

They warmed up as several older couples arrived, and soon the terrace was three-quarters filled. I think Whitey's trio had a small but loyal following.

"Jesus," Stewart said, "it looks like our parents are here, or maybe our even grandparents."

Jerry raised his glass, grinning. "Least the drinks are good." He seemed very cheerful. I was growing fond of him.

"You're a nice guy, Jerry," I told him. I lifted my glass for a toast. "Here's to nice guys like you."

He beamed and raised his glass. "Thanks, Randy. You're nice guy too."

"Yeah, just remember," Stewart said, "nice guys

finish last."

Maggie laughed. "Well, I think that's only polite."

Stewart looked confused. "What do you mean?"

She giggled. "No woman wants a lover who finishes first."

Sherry spit out a mouthful of wine. "You're awful, Maggie."

I leaned over to kiss Maggie lightly on the lips, but she pulled me in for a deeper one.

"Oh, get a room," Stewart said.

Then the microphone crackled, and the crowd quieted. Whitey was at the mic, holding the stand in one hand and his clarinet in the other.

"Good evening, ladies and gentlemen. We're going to start with one of our favorites, which we're dedicating to our new friend Randall there—"he nodded in my direction "for helping to keep the peace the other night. Randall's from California, so we thought he'd enjoy this little Tony Bennett tune."

Before they could begin playing, several couples stood and walked to the dance floor.

I reached for Maggie's hand. "Want to dance?"

"You know I do," she said, smiling.

I held her in my arms and moved her in wide circles around the floor, expecting Stewart and Sherry to join us, but whenever I glanced in their direction, Stewart was scowling and Sherry looked annoyed. I didn't care. I closed my eyes and enjoyed feeling Maggie's soft, warm body against mine. Her hair smelled like jasmine and made me remember the afternoon.

When the first song ended, the band transitioned to "Moon River," and Maggie said, "Ooo, I love this song." We stayed on the dance floor with the other couples.

Soon Jerry and Sherry were dancing next to us. Stewart waved to Gillian for another round.

After the song, the four of us sat down.

Stewart leaned over to Sherry. "I don't see anyone under forty."

"Oh, relax," Sherry said. "It's nice."

Maggie nodded. "Better than the place we went to last night. I don't have fond memories of that place."

"Whatever," Stewart said. "Look, I ordered another round, but when we finish, let's go up the street to our place. It has a patio in the back, with a view as good as this."

"Well, not quite as good," Jerry corrected, "but still very scenic. A terrific place for a cocktail party."

"Cocktail party?" Stewart said. "No wonder you like it here, Jerry. You fit right in."

Jerry shrugged.

"You guys have anything to drink?" Maggie asked.

"We've got everything," Jerry said. "Bourbon, rum, scotch, gin, vodka, wine, beer. We stocked up as soon as we got here."

Gillian came with our drinks.

"Can we get the check, please?" Stewart asked.

She pouted. "Leaving so soon? You guys are the life of the party."

"We've got to get young Jerry here to bed," Stewart said. "Got a big day of sailing tomorrow."

Jerry giggled, staring up at Gillian with a schoolboy's crush. "Maybe you'd like to tuck me in?"

Gillian patted Jerry's head. "You're cute. I'll get

69

your check." Then she turned and walked back to the bar.

Jerry almost fell off his chair watching. "Her parts move together really well."

Sherry grabbed his Long Island. "You've had enough."

Jerry looked indignant. "Are you going to drink my Long Island and your glass of wine? At least give me your glass."

She took a long pull from her wine glass and handed it to Jerry.

He stared at it scowling. "This glass is half empty."

"Don't look at it that way, Jerry," I said. "Think of it as—"

"Yeah, yeah, as half full," he answered. "Either way, there's room for more."

I patted Jerry on the back. "Good one."

By the time the band was ready to take a break, we'd finished our drinks. I said goodbye to Whitey, then followed Stewart and Sherry out of the courtyard of the Galleon House, up the hill for several blocks.

The houses along the way were large at first, but the higher we climbed, the smaller they got. Lights glowed from their windows, and music and laughter erupted from within some of the houses. It was obvious which were rentals—the tiny front lawns and porches were neat and sparsely furnished. The other houses had piles of wrecked furniture and broken toys cluttering their front porches. A small dog—maybe a terrier—tied to a railing barked incessantly as we walked by one place. I felt sorry for it.

Finally, we reached "The Villa," a two-bedroom

house, with the kitchen and breakfast nook in front facing the street, and the living room and bedrooms in back, with sliding glass doors opening onto a long stone patio. Four bamboo chairs and a glass-topped table took up most of the kitchen. The living room was sparsely furnished—only a red davenport, a worn brown loveseat, and one green vinyl easy chair, with a couple of floor lamps for light. Some local artwork adorned the white walls.

Jerry gave us a tour of the bedrooms while Stewart made drinks. Each room had a double bed, nightstand, lamp and dresser. Despite the walls having been painted bright colors, the rooms seemed drab, the tile floors bare.

After inspecting both rooms, we rendezvoused with Stewart in the living room and grabbed our drinks.

"To the villa," I said, trying to mask my sarcasm.

Stewart waved us to the patio. "Let me show you the view." He slid the heavy glass door open, and we followed him outside.

Sounds of buzzing insects filled the night air. Through the trees, we could see some of the lights of the town below. The bay was black as marble. The view wasn't nearly as impressive as the one from the Galleon House.

Stewart had put some music on—much more contemporary stuff than we'd been listening to—and Sherry lit a dozen or so candles around the patio. We settled at a table, talking and laughing. I felt Maggie's hand on my thigh. When we finished the drinks, Stewart asked if we wanted another round.

It was after midnight, and I was ready to call it a

night.

"I don't think so," I said. "Not if we're getting up early to go on the catamaran by nine-thirty."

Maggie and I stood together, and I shook hands with Jerry, who was practically asleep in his chair. I overheard Stewart whisper to Sherry, "You want to stay here tonight?'

She glanced at me, knowing I'd heard. "Maggie and I better get a good night's sleep."

Jerry stood up, said good night, and staggered out of sight. Maggie and I went out the front door and waited on the street while Sherry let Stewart kiss her as we watched.

"Are you sure you won't stay?" he asked again.

She shook her head and pushed away, saying, "See you tomorrow at the dock."

With that, the three of us walked arm-in-arm down the hill, Sherry on my right and Maggie on my left.

"That was an enjoyable evening," Sherry said.

Maggie smiled at me. "The whole day was enjoyable."

Once we'd reached the hotel, Maggie waved Sherry on. "I'll be up in a minute."

Sherry climbed the steps slowly. When she was out of sight, Maggie leaned into me and we kissed again, deeply, softly, sensually.

"You want to stay?" I asked.

She smiled but shook her head. "I'd better keep Sherry company. We've got girl talk to take care of."

"That's fine," I told her. "See you bright and early."

We kissed again, and then I released her and

72

watched as she ascended the stairs. Before she went out of sight, she looked back and blew me a kiss which made me smile.

Inside my room, I examined my face in the bathroom mirror again, as I had the previous night. Despite a sense of nagging loneliness, I was feeling quite pleased with myself. I'd become something of a minor celebrity at the Galleon House, and my new friends seemed adequately impressed. Tomorrow would bring a new adventure, and, for a few hours, I'd forgotten all about my dad's passing.

Suddenly, I was exhausted.

Chapter 8

I awoke to someone pounding on my door. I'd overslept. It was a little after nine. Wearing nothing but my boxers, I opened the door to find Maggie and Sherry standing in front of me decked out in beachwear, clutching their large bags.

"Geez, Randall," Maggie said, "aren't you coming?"

I rubbed my eyes, trying to remember what she meant.

"I'll call for a cab," Sherry said. "We'll never make it now, if we walk."

"Oh, the boat trip!" I tapped my forehead. "Give me two minutes."

Hopping around the bed, I swapped my boxers for swim trunks, threw on a clean shirt, rubbed deodorant under each arm and squeezed a dollop of toothpaste into my mouth, working it around my teeth with my tongue as I tried to do something with my deranged hair. *No use.* The stubble on my face looked like I'd fallen chin first into a pile of splintered pencil lead.

"Ready," I called as I relieved myself at the toilet.

When I turned around, Maggie was standing in the bathroom doorway, grinning and holding my sandals.

"Geez, how much did you drink last night anyway?"

"Too much," I said, snatching the sandals and slapping them on as I followed her out. I pulled the door closed before realizing that I hadn't grabbed my wallet or room key. "Oh, shit. I don't have my wallet."

Maggie patted my shoulder. "I've got you covered. You can pay me back tonight."

I kissed her lightly on the cheek. "Does that make me your gigolo?"

She laughed. "Yes, you're my slave for the day. Now carry my bag."

A taxi arrived a few minutes later, and we climbed in, all three of us squeezing into the backseat. The ride to the dock took us around the east side of the bay where Jerry and Stewart were waiting. Stewart, holding a small backpack on one shoulder, checked his wristwatch, looking annoyed.

"You guys are late."

"My fault," I admitted. "Overslept."

We walked together down the dock to a sign that read, HO-TEI CATAMARAN CRUISES. Maggie bought a ticket for me from an elderly woman sitting inside a little white and red booth, and then we followed Stewart down the dock.

It was a gorgeous morning. The sky was cloudless and the blue water was calm as glass. Several boats were tied to the dock, but once we'd walked by them, we saw a large, white, two-hulled catamaran glimmering in the sunlight, with a main mast taller than a telephone pole.

A dozen or so people of various ages were already on board, dressed in an array of colorful outfits. The crew all wore the same khaki shorts and dark-blue polo shirts with some sort of sailboat as a logo over their hearts. A tall, good-looking guy in his mid-thirties, I guessed, manned the wheel. He donned a Captain's hat, which reminded me of Thurston Howle from *Gilligan's Island*, and then commanded his crew—two guys in their twenties and one gal in her early thirties—to cast off.

The Captain throttled up, and we backed away from the dock before making a wide turn toward the mouth of the harbor and the open sea. Most of the people had crowded onto the stern, so I waved for Maggie and the others to follow me to the front of the boat. Only two other couples, about our age, were sitting on the front deck, leaning against the slanted cabin windows, smiles plastered on their faces. The women had already removed their sundresses and were tanning themselves in their skimpy bikinis. The five of use sat in the center of the forward dock, a few feet in front of the other couples.

"Have you ever done this before?" Maggie asked them. "Taken this boat, I mean?"

One of the guys nodded. "I was here last year. This trip to St. John is one of my best memories."

We motored out to the mouth of the bay, going slowly by one of the ocean liners, and it still awed me that an object that massive could sit upright in the water. The other ship must have pulled out earlier that morning. I wondered if we'd catch a glimpse of her once we got out on the open sea.

I'd been sailing a few times on the San Francisco

Bay with my father and a few of his friends who owned yachts. Only once had we gone out of the bay into the Pacific where we'd stayed fairly close to the shore south to Half Moon Bay. I'd never been on a catamaran, so I was looking forward to the ride. On a yacht, when you catch the wind, the boat leans at a steep angle, but I'd seen good-sized catamarans on the Bay and they stayed much more level in the same breeze.

Once we were on the open water, the Captain cut the engine and the crew hoisted the main sail, which was huge—mainly white, with three deep-blue stripes slanting at a ninety-degree angle and a bright orange sun symbol at the top. As soon as the wind caught the sail, we picked up speed and Maggie clutched my arm.

"Geez, we're going fast."

"Yeah, but the water's calm," I said. "It'll be smooth sailing."

We turned into the sun, and the glare was so bright, I had to shade my eyes—I'd also forgotten my sunglasses.

Sherry pulled her sundress off and rolled it up, placing it under her head for a pillow when she stretched out. Stewart pulled off his shirt and rolled it up, too, stretching out beside Sherry. Jerry, who was sitting cross-legged in the middle between Maggie and Sherry, stretched out as well, leaving his shirt on.

Maggie tugged her dress over her head and rolled it up, pushing it into her bag before taking out a plastic bottle of suntan oil, which she handed to me.

"Will you do my back?"

"Sure," I said, scooting behind her. She sat

77

between my legs and I rubbed oil over her back, massaging her as I worked.

"Ooo, that feels so good."

When I'd finished, she took the bottle and coated her arms and legs, and saved her stomach and breasts for last, smiling back at me as she rubbed the tops of her breasts.

"No fair," I told her. "I can't do anything to you here."

"I've got to tease you a little, don't I?"

"Yeah, as long as you give—"

"Shh!" she hissed, glancing around.

Jerry was watching us, grinning. "I think Randall was going to say, as long as you give to charity."

"Yeah, Jerry, that's exactly what I was going to say." I laughed. "You must be a mind reader."

"Yes. I have ESP."

Stewart glanced over. "Did you say you have to pee?"

Sherry started laughing—it was noisy, after all, with the air sweeping over the boat as we cut through the water. "No, no. He said he has ESP."

"Oh," Stewart said. "Well, what am I thinking right now, Jerry?"

Jerry held his hand to his forehead. "You'd like me to shut up so you can sleep off your hangover."

"You're good," Stewart said.

"What am I thinking?" Sherry asked.

"Difficult to say. Your mind is much more complex than Stu's, but I'm getting the impression that you wished you'd chosen Stu's funny, baby-faced sidekick, Jerry."

Without opening her eyes, Sherry smiled and

78

touched Jerry's shoulder with the back of her hand. "I'm going to have to watch what I think from now on."

Maggie stretched out beside Jerry. "Can you read my mind?"

"Let's see. You're thinking about Randy—I'm sorry, Randall—hoping he finishes medical school, marries you, and makes lots of babies with you."

Maggie grinned but said nothing, looking a little sad, as if Jerry's "reading" had hit too close to home.

After pulling off my shirt and balling it up, I stretched out on my side, looking across Maggie's ample chest at Jerry. "You must have read my mind by mistake."

"It's possible," he replied. "All these random desires are messing up my powers."

"Random desires," Maggie repeated. "I like that, Jerry. It's poetic."

I rolled onto my back and lay under the warm sun, my balled shirt for a pillow. The boat's motion was soothing, and I fell asleep, feeling very content.

* * *

Something—a change in direction or the boat's speed—jarred me awake. I glanced at Maggie, who was snoring away, a glistening stream of drool hanging from the corner of her mouth. Stewart and Sherry were sitting up, Sherry holding her knees.

Jerry struggled to sit up while rubbing his eyes. "Are we there yet?"

"Looks like it," Sherry answered.

Green filled the horizon. We were headed toward

a crescent-shaped beach whose sand was white as sugar. The vivid blue of the water, the white of the sand, the deep green of the vegetation, and the clear, azure blue of the sky, where a few cotton ball clouds hung lazily above, as if admiring the scene below—all of it postcard perfect. "Man, I wish I had a camera," I said.

"Stu," Jerry called, "give me the bag."

Stewart handed him the little backpack and Jerry dug out an expensive-looking camera with a telephoto lens. He snapped a few pictures of the island, and then turned the camera on Sherry and Stewart, taking a few of them as well. Sherry titled her head, resting her cheek on her knee, and smiled for the camera.

"See?" I said loud enough for Sherry to hear. "You are a *Vogue* model."

"The hell with *Vogue*," Jerry said. "I'm sending these to *Playboy*!"

Sherry slapped Jerry's shoulder, grinning broadly.

The Captain shouted an order, which woke up Maggie, and then the crew lowered the sail and our speed dropped dramatically. He started the engine and motored us right up to the beach, landing the front of the pontoons on the sand. The water was so calm that we had made the larger waves. The Captain cut the engine, and the crew came forward, walking by us, and lowered a metal staircase onto the sand.

"Okay, folks," the girl shouted. "Grab your gear and disembark. We'll serve lunch in about an hour, and then we'll be here for a few hours afterward, depending on weather."

We were the first to climb down the narrow stairs, assisted by the crew members, and the two couples who'd been behind us followed us onto the beach.

Sherry looked at the guy who'd said he'd made the trip before and said, "I can see why you liked coming here. It's beautiful."

"Yeah," he answered. "This is a preserve, so it's protected, which means it remains pretty close to pristine."

Stewart reached back to shake hands and introduced himself, so we all stopped walking and made introductions. Matt and Tina made one couple, and Ted and Gloria were the other. They seemed friendly enough, but I didn't want to make small talk. I took Maggie's hand, and we walked down the beach to a place where the waves were small and a palm tree hung over the sand.

We spread Maggie's beach towel under the shade of the palm and sat down, side by side, grinning at each other and the beauty of the water.

"Do you want to SCUBA dive after lunch?" I asked.

She shrugged. "It's sixty bucks more, per person."

"I'll pay you back." I wouldn't have to worry about money because of Dad's insurance policy, and Rich and I had agreed to sell the house and split the equity.

"We can just snorkel for free, you know."

"We can do that, too, but don't you want to go diving?"

She frowned. "I've never been SCUBA diving, so I'd be too scared. I'm not a strong swimmer."

"I'll be right beside you, Maggie. I won't let anything happen to you."

"I'll think about it," she said. But I could tell she

didn't want to do it.

The others—including the two new couples—joined us, and soon we were our own little party, chatting, laughing, commenting on the scenery. I stayed quiet, pretending to doze, and listened to the others share biographies.

One of the guys—Matt, I think—had just passed the bar exam and was working in his uncle's law firm in Connecticut. The other was a civil engineer who worked in the New Haven city planning office. They'd been friends since college. The way Stewart soaked up their trivia made me realize he was working them, not just to invite them to the party, but to make some business connections.

Soon, the crew had put up tables and spread food out, so we strolled back down toward the boat and grabbed something to eat. An array of cold cuts, sliced cheese, lettuce, tomato slices, pickles, different kinds of bread and all the condiments awaited us. I made myself a ham and Swiss on rye and waited as the female crew member removed saran wrap from large bowls of fruit salad and potato salad.

"Hungry?" she asked, grinning as I loaded heaps of fruit salad on my plate.

"Starving. I missed breakfast."

"That's too bad. I've always said, breakfast is the most important meal of the day."

"Well," I said, "it's certainly the most important meal of the morning!"

That got a good laugh out of her, and I moved on to the ice chest, where I grabbed a cold bottle of Coke.

We took our plates back to our towels and ate. It

was pleasant, the heat tempered by a light breeze blowing in from the water, the rustle of the palm fronds above us, and the little waves lapping against the clean sand.

Stewart brought up the house party and invited his new potential clients.

Matt looked at Tina and said, "We've got no plans, so, yeah, that'd be great."

"What should we bring?" Tina asked.

Jerry chimed in. "Maybe some potato chips and onion dip?"

"Onion dip?" Stewart repeated. "I think we can do better than that."

"I like onion dip," Maggie said.

"So do I," Tina added. "Of course, Matt won't kiss me afterward, but that's okay. We'll kiss enough after the wedding."

"When are you getting married?" Maggie asked.

"Not until the end of July," Tina said. "I wanted a June wedding, but evidently you've got to book those two years ahead."

"Wow," Maggie responded. "Two years? That's ridiculous."

Jerry leaned against Maggie's shoulder. "Maybe you should go ahead a book a chapel for two years from now. If Randall isn't out of med school by then, you and I can get married."

I raised my Coke bottle. "You two will make a perfect couple."

Maggie shot me a hurt look.

We finished eating and settled back for a rest. The new couples took paperback books out and began to read, as did Sherry, but Stewart rolled onto his side and fell asleep.

Jerry grabbed his camera and said, "I'm going to take some pictures."

"Can I tag along?" Maggie asked.

"Absolutely. You can be my subject."

He helped her up and off they walked.

She was trying to make me jealous, but with the two of them gone and Stewart asleep, I could talk to Sherry. She looked stunning in her tight turquoise bikini, her hair pulled back and clipped in a flat pony tail, large circular gold earrings dangling from her lobes.

"What are you reading?"

"Probably the saddest book ever written."

"What's it called?"

She showed me the cover, and I recognized it immediately. "*Sophie's Choice*. If I start bawling in a few minutes, it's because of this damn book."

"You're right," I said. "Even I cried when I saw the movie. And I don't cry very often."

She looked over at me. "But you do cry sometimes? Most men wouldn't admit that."

"I'm not most men."

She smiled. "When's the last time you cried? Be honest."

"Just a few days ago," I said, "when I was thinking about my dad."

She took her sunglasses off. "That's the second time you've made a cryptic reference to your father. What's the story?"

"He passed away a few weeks ago. It was pretty sudden. Massive heart attack."

She placed her hand on my forearm. "Oh,

84

Randall, I'm so sorry."

"That's one of the reasons I'm vacationing here instead of California. I wanted to get far away. But the sadness follows you."

She squeezed my arm before releasing it. "How's your mother taking it?"

I looked down at my feet. "You might want to go back to your book."

She chuckled. "Why? She isn't dead, is she?"

I looked over and nodded. "Died of ovarian cancer several years ago."

"Oh, my God. How awful!" She wiped tears from both cheeks. "You've had more than your fair share of tragedy, haven't you?"

"I don't know. What's a fair share?"

Chapter 9

Sherry closed her book and asked me to tell her about my parents, so I spent the next half hour telling her about mother's long battle with cancer and dad's long battle to overcome losing her. "For about a year after she'd died, he ate and drank too much, gained about thirty pounds, but then one day he started jogging again and was back to normal in a few months. Christmases were the hardest times. Dad and I went through the motions, putting up a tree and decorating the house," I told her, "but the effort seemed as hollow as one of those glass ornaments." That's when a look of confusion wrinkled Sherry's face.

"Wait, how long ago was that?"

Without thinking, I answered, "A couple of years ago. Why?"

"Were you still living at home then?"

I realized she was doing the math. "I went home for the holidays."

She peered into my eyes. "How old are you, really?"

I felt myself blush. "Twenty-six," I lied.

"Show me your driver's license."

"I left my wallet in the room."

"Are you really in medical school, or are you still

in college?"

I acted indignant. "Where's this coming from?"

"I don't know. There's something about the way you talk that makes me think you're younger than you say you are."

I shrugged. "Maybe my mother dying when I was a teenager stunted my growth."

It was all I could think to say, and I watched as she scrutinized me. If I admitted the truth about my age, I'd stand no chance with her.

Then I noticed Maggie and Jerry walking back and waved, hoping to distract Sherry. Maggie had a wide smile on her face and trotted over to the towel where she knelt down facing me.

"We had a blast. I felt like a real fashion model. Jerry made me do all these exotic poses, and he's going to send me copies of all the photographs when he gets them developed."

Jerry was beaming. "She really could be a model."

Stewart woke up and rolled onto his back. "What are you prattling on about?"

"Shooting Maggie," he answered. "We found some trails and walked back into the jungle. There were some beautiful butterflies back there."

Stewart sat up. "Butterflies, Jerry? Really?"

Maggie and Jerry exchanged a glance, and then Maggie said, "There was this one butterfly just resting on a tree branch, and it took her forever to open her wings, but once she did, Jerry got some amazing stuff."

Sherry looked at me suddenly, and that's when I realized Maggie and Jerry had fucked. I felt a tremendous wave of humiliation, but tried not to show it.

"I need a beer," I said. "Anybody else?"

"Sure," Stewart said. "I could use a walk, too." He stood and waved for me to join him, saying to the others, "Anyone want us to bring something back for you?"

"I'll take a beer, if it's cold," Maggie said.

"Me, too," Jerry added.

Sherry shook her head, and Stewart asked the other two couples if they wanted anything. The two guys wanted beer, and the girls asked for diet Coke.

Once we were away from the others, Stewart moved a little closer. "I heard you talk about your parents."

"Oh? I thought you were asleep."

"Just dozing on and off." We walked on for a yard or so, when he put his arm over my shoulder and said, "Losing both parents. Man, that's tough."

I looked down at the warm sand, feeling the weight of his arm on my shoulders. It was comforting—like something my older brother had done when I was younger.

"You mind if I ask you a personal question?"

I glanced at him, curious. "No, I guess not."

"How are you fixed for money? I mean, I know you couldn't pay your way today, so…"

"Money's not a problem. I really did leave the room without my wallet."

"So your parents left you with enough to finish college?"

His concern seemed genuine. "My father had a life insurance policy, which my brother and I will split."

He took his arm off my shoulder. "You have a brother? How's he taking it?"

"Richard's quite a bit older. He's married with two kids, so he's pretty caught up in his own busy life."

"Are you two very close?"

"We used to be. But after he got married, he moved to Indiana for a job. That was six years ago. We don't visit each other much anymore."

He patted me on the back like he was a coach and I was one of his players.

Something about our conversation touched me. "You're okay, Stu."

We walked together in silence until we got to the tables and coolers. The crew was setting out face masks with snorkels and fins on the buffet tables, and a few of the other passengers were watching, anxious to get in the water.

"You want to go snorkeling?" I asked.

Stewart nodded. "After a beer."

We grabbed the drinks and headed back. As soon as I saw Maggie's face, I could tell Sherry had told her about our conversation. Maggie could barely look at me, and I wasn't sure if it was because of my parents' death or what she'd done with Jerry.

"What's wrong?" I asked.

Maggie and Jerry exchanged looks again. Then Jerry put his hand on my shoulder. "Sherry told us about your folks, Randy. That's really awful."

He grabbed a couple of bottles from me and handed them out.

"Yeah, Randall," Maggie said, "that's really sad

89

about your mom suffering so long, and then when things are finally getting back to normal, your dad passes away, too. I don't know what to say."

I shrugged. "I shouldn't have said anything. I don't want to be a killjoy."

When I sat down next to Maggie, our arms brushed against each other, and she flinched. I knew then that it was over between us, whatever it had been, so I took a long pull from my beer and stared at the water.

Stewart mercifully changed the subject by talking about the masks and snorkels we'd seen, and everyone seemed excited about getting into the water.

Matt and Tina stood up, and Matt said, "We're going SCUBA diving. Does anyone want to join us?"

I glanced at Maggie, but she shook her head.

"Yeah, I'd like to go," Sherry said.

I stood. "Me, too."

Sherry and I followed Matt and Tina to the boat where the equipment was stored. Sherry told the crew member to put both charges on her credit card since I didn't have my wallet.

"I'll pay you back tonight at the party," I told her.

"You're damn right you will."

The crew members helped us on with the tanks, weight belts and buoyancy compensator vests. Sherry and I sat on the edge of the boat and tugged on our flippers. Then I spit in my mask and smeared the spit on the glass before pulling it on over my head and placing it on my face so it fit tightly.

Sherry pressed the mask onto her face and rolled backward into the water, just as the others had done before us. I followed a minute later, and soon we were paddling away from the boat toward deeper water. The other divers were well ahead of us, so we turned slightly and veered away to be on our own.

After ten minutes or so of hard paddling, we came to a drop where the water suddenly went from about twenty feet deep to more than sixty. We kept our depth at about ten feet and paddled side by side, looking down. The bottom turned from mostly sand to mostly rocks, with some sea grasses and kelp growing between rock clusters. There weren't as many fish as I'd expected, but we paddled on until the bottom fell off more significantly.

I motioned to Sherry to see if she wanted to go deeper and she nodded. We dove downward, the other divers about forty or fifty yards to our left. When we reached the bottom, I stood on a rock and looked around. The current made me sway back and forth gently, and the water was so clear I could see for over a hundred yards.

Sherry motioned for me to join her and she paddled toward a deeper area where the floor dropped off more dramatically. I checked my air—I'd used almost half. I grabbed Sherry's gauge and checked it. She was at exactly half. I took my mouthpiece out and mouthed the words, "Slow your breathing."

She nodded, but suddenly her eyes went wide with terror and she pointed behind me. I turned around and saw a large hammerhead shark swimming toward us. I grabbed Sherry's wrist and held her in place—I knew the worst thing we could do was panic and swim away frantically.

The shark swam lazily around us, went a few yards, and then turned back toward us. We watched as we stood our ground, but I unsnapped the waist belt of my tank so I could pull it over my head and feed it to the shark if he tried to take a bite.

He didn't. Instead, he swam around us again, and then dove into the depths below us and out of sight.

Sherry took her mouthpiece out and said, "Wow," in an explosion of bubbles.

I grinned and pointed in the direction the shark had taken, shrugging my shoulders as if to ask, "Want to follow it?"

She shook her head.

I led us closer to the others, feeling there was safety in numbers, and we found Mike and Tina wearing big smiles. A school of blue and yellow fish seemed fascinated by the other divers—they were swimming right up to people's face masks. We hung in the water watching the show for a while, and then Sherry tapped me on the arm, holding her gauge up. The needle was just on the edge of red, so we headed back to the boat.

On board, we told the crew about spotting the shark as they helped us off with our gear.

"Wow," the female crew member said. "You rarely see hammerheads by themselves. They usually travel in schools. Too bad you didn't have a camera."

On the walk back to our towels, I decided to make my play. "So what's Stewart got that I don't have?"

"What do you mean?"

"I mean, why'd you choose to be with him rather than me?"

She glared at me. "I'm not with Stewart. I'm hanging out with him, but we aren't sleeping together. I'm not like Maggie."

"I like you, Sherry. I'd like to get to know you better."

"You will," she said. "We'll be together tonight at the party, and I'm sure you'll want to hang out with us tomorrow and the next day."

"So you're not really with Stewart?"

"Stewart is the kind of guy I see myself with, eventually. Good job, stable family. I'm at the point in my life where I'm ready to get married. If he pursues me when we're back on the mainland, then who knows?"

We were almost within ear-shot of the others, so I knew I had to go for it.

"I'd like to see you alone, just the two of us. Can we do that?"

"Why? Where do you think that could lead?"

"Maybe to something serious," I said. "Maybe I'm ready to settle down, too."

She stopped and faced me. "Look, Randall, I've seen this before. Summer romances don't last, especially when it's a vacation fling."

I tried to smile. "Maybe this is different."

She took my hand. "You're a great guy, but our lives are much too different. You live on the west coast and I live in the east. You're still in college—or med school, maybe—and I'm a career woman. In a few days, we'll go our separate ways and probably never see each other again."

"Can we have lunch tomorrow? Just the two of us?"

"How? You'll probably be with Maggie."

I glanced in Maggie's direction. She was talking to Jerry in an animated way, pretending not to have noticed us. Stewart was staring right at me, scowling.

"I think Maggie's with Jerry now, don't you?"

She shrugged. "Who knows? I'll talk to her later and see what's really going on."

"So, how about it—lunch tomorrow?"

"Where?"

"The Galleon House terrace?"

She looked down at her feet. "Okay, I'll try, but if I don't make it, please don't take it personally." She looked into my eyes. "I don't want to hurt you, Randall."

"I'd like to kiss you," I whispered.

She let go of my hand and said, "Don't press your luck."

Then she turned and walked over to Stewart, leaning down to kiss him before sitting on the towel next to him.

I kept a stupid grin plastered on my face and walked over. "Did Sherry tell you about our near-death experience?"

Maggie looked up. "What are you talking about?"

"We saw a huge hammerhead shark," I said, sitting on the edge of the towel away from Maggie.

"Really?" Jerry asked.

"Ha, ha," Stewart said.

"Actually, we did," Sherry admitted.

She told the story of our adventure. I watched her lips move and noticed the little creases form at the corner of her eyes whenever she smiled, and the way she played with her hair as she spoke. She possessed a quality that set her apart. There was something regal and graceful in the way she conducted herself. All I could do was stare at her and grin stupidly as if

94

nothing really mattered.

*   *   *

The boat trip back to St. Thomas was strange. Powerful dark thunderheads had built up to the north, and the water was choppy, so several people— including Jerry—went down below to stay close to the toilets. Soon, Maggie said she should check on Jerry, so she went below, too, and Stewart decided to chat with the folks in the back of the boat, and Sherry seemed to feel obliged to join him. I was left on the front deck with Mike and Tina and the other couple. Exhausted from the dive, I simply stretched out on Maggie's towel and slept.

I awoke to a hard rain, the only person still on the front deck. We were in sight of the harbor, but heavy, gray rain clouds created a low ceiling, obscuring the very tops of the mountains in front of us. The wind had come up, and the boat was being tossed a bit. I saw lightning hit the water to my left, miles away, and then heard the slow kettledrum of thunder.

We sailed into the mouth of the bay and made a slow turn to the right. In the rain, Charlotte Amalie looked not like a tropical paradise, but like a French village I might have seen in a movie. I found it terribly depressing and suddenly wished I'd never let Maggie go off with Jerry. I wanted to curl up in my bed with a woman's body next to me, listen to the rain and talk about nothing important.

Once we'd docked, I found the others. Jerry looked terrible—pale and weak—and Maggie wasn't even trying to hide the fact that she was with him now. She had her arm around his waist and was helping him walk. Sherry and Stewart stopped long enough for me to catch up to them.

"We're going to call for a cab," Stewart said. "I want to get Jerry back to the house."

The implication was clear—I was on my own.

"Okay. I can find my way back to the hotel."

Sherry reached for my arm. "Do you want us to get a cab for you, too?"

"No, I think I'll walk. I don't mind the rain. It's not cold."

"It's not that warm, either," Sherry said.

I couldn't tell if it was pity or sympathy in her eyes, but I hated the sad way she was looking at me. "What time's the party?"

Stewart glanced at Sherry as if surprised I still planned to come. "I told people around eight."

"Okay," I said. "See you then."

I started walking from the dock to the road, feeling lonelier with every step, glad my face was covered with raindrops.

It was after five by the time I reached the hotel. I took a hot shower and dressed, then headed for the Galleon House. I knew there were lots of other places to eat and drink, but I wanted to be some place where people knew me.

Mike gave me a salute as I stepped onto the terrace. A few single older men were seated at the bar, and several older couples occupied tables. I went to my usual stool at the far end of the bar and Mike came over, a good honest grin on his face.

"What'll you have? Gin-tonic?"

"No, just a beer. Better take it slow tonight. Got

a party to go to later."

"Oh?" Mike took the top off a bottle of Heineken "So where's the party?"

"Just up the hill. Remember the folks I was with last night?"

"Sure. The one girl was a stunner."

"The two guys are renting a house up the road. They're throwing a party. Invited some folks we met on the catamaran cruise today."

Mike smiled. "Oh? You took my advice and did that trip?"

"Yeah," I said. "It was great."

I told him about different parts of the day whenever he'd come back from making drinks for other folks, and as I drank and talked, the rain clouds behind me drifted away and the sun came out just before setting behind the hill. I walked to the edge of the terrace and looked out over the scenery. The vegetation glimmered like emeralds, the red tiles of the rooftops had a sheen like glass, and the cobblestones of the streets changed from dark brown to almost white as steam rose from them. Birds all around the terrace were going crazy with song, and suddenly I realized how good it was to be alive.

I walked back to the bar, ordered another beer, and told Mike that I had a tentative lunch date with the "stunner."

He raised his coffee mug for a toast. "Here's to the stunner. What's her name?"

"Sherry. Never call her Cherry though. She hates that."

"I'll keep that in mind, if I see her again."

"Just don't make a play for her yourself, okay? I

wouldn't stand a chance against handsome guy like you."

Mike smiled. "You don't have to worry about that."

"Why?" I laughed. "Skinny, beautiful blondes aren't your type?"

He leaned across the bar and said, "Sure. I like skinny blondes as long as they're guys. I'm gay, Randall."

I was surprised. "You don't look gay."

He leaned away. "What do gay men look like, in your opinion?"

"Sorry, Mike. You just don't seem like the stereotypical gay guy."

Still grinning, he said, "I hope this doesn't change how you feel about me, Randall."

"Hell, no, Mike. I've had gay friends before."

His smiled broadened, and he put his hand on top of mine. "Oh? Do tell?"

I laughed. "Not in that way, Mike."

He patted my hand and moved it away. "I'm just yanking your chain. I could tell you were straight the first night we met."

"Really? How could you be so sure?"

"A guy just knows. You didn't put out a gay vibe."

Mike went away to make drinks for other guests, so I nursed my beer, strolled over to the edge of the terrace again and watched night fall over the town. I had to laugh at myself. I'd sort of assumed that Mike and Gillian were together.

People were bringing plates of food down from upstairs, and the aromas made my mouth water.

I checked my watch. I had almost an hour to kill before the party, so I went upstairs and piled my plate with shrimp Creole. It smelled delicious and tasted even better. After stuffing myself with it, I went back upstairs and got a small bowl of lemon sorbet. Then it was time to go up the hill to the "villa" and see how my rivals were doing.

The other couples from the boat trip were already inside the house by the time I got there, and the music was blaring. I found the bar set up on the kitchen counter and made myself a strong gin and tonic. I wandered around. Other people I didn't recognize were milling about, too. Evidently, word had gotten out. I saw Stewart and Sherry standing together in the living room close to the sliding glass door, which was open. Stewart was beaming—couples were actually dancing together out on the patio. Stewart had his arm around Sherry's waist, and when he spotted me, he waved me over. Sherry seemed quite comfortable in Stewart's arm.

"Where's Maggie?" I asked.

"Nursing Jerry back to health," Sherry responded, "in the back bedroom."

"Think I'll say hi." I spun around and walked away.

The door to Jerry's room was slightly ajar. I peeked inside and saw Maggie flipping through a magazine as she reclined on the bed next to Jerry. Jerry was on his side, his back to the door.

I stepped into the room and whispered, "How's he doing?"

Maggie got up slowly and came over. "The boat trip back really took it out of him."

"Can we talk for a minute?" I asked her.

She nodded, and we stepped into the hallway together.

"So, you're with Jerry now?"

She shrugged. "I'm going to stay with him tonight, yes. I doubt we'll do anything."

"You had sex with him today, didn't you?"

She looked at the floor. "It just sort of happened. We got to talking and found out we had some mutual friends—we've actually got a lot in common. Anyway, we were having so much fun, one thing led to another."

I nodded. "Okay. That's what I thought, but I just wanted to make sure."

She put her hand on my shoulder. "You're a terrific guy, Randall. And a great lover. I just think Jerry's a better match for me."

"A match made in paradise," I said. "Well, I wish you guys the best."

"Thanks," she whispered. Then she stood on her toes and kissed my cheek, and I thought of Judas kissing Christ.

I went back to the kitchen and made myself another drink. Then I drifted into the living room, looking for any woman standing alone. All were paired up, so I pushed through the crowd to the patio. Several couples were dancing, but I saw another set of people standing in a circle at the far end of the patio. As I got closer, I could see them passing a joint, and I caught a whiff of grass. Matt and Tina were in the circle, so I nodded and joined them.

"Hey, guys. How's it going?"

Matt handed me the joint. "It's going, man. How

'bout with you?"

Without taking a hit, I passed the joint to the woman standing beside me. "Can't complain," I said. "That diving was fun today, wasn't it?"

He nodded. "It was okay. We didn't see many fish."

Tina perked up, saying, "We heard you guys saw a hammerhead. Is that right?"

"Yeah," I said. "It was little scary."

The woman beside me said, "A hammerhead. Are you sure?"

I looked at her. She was wearing a low-cut black cocktail dress and an expensive- looking gold bracelet. Attractive, but in her mid-thirties.

"There's no mistaking a hammerhead."

"Hard to believe," she responded. "They usually travel is large schools and you rarely see them in the Caribbean."

"Well, we did. You can ask the hostess if you don't believe me."

"Who's the hostess?" she asked.

I looked around but didn't see Sherry or Stewart. "She's the gal with Stu. Her name's Sherry. But whatever you do, don't call her Cherry."

"It's true," Tina said. "Sherry told us about it, too."

The woman shrugged. "Well, that's one for the record books."

"Want to dance?" I asked her.

She looked me up and down. "Maybe later."

I listened to the conversations of the people around me for awhile, feeling the gin and the beer take hold. Tina and Mike drifted away from the circle when the joint was gone, and another couple—one I didn't recognize—took their place. The guys standing across from me pulled another joint out of his shirt pocket and lit it, taking a deep hit before passing it to the new couple.

Before leaving, I leaned over to the woman and said, "Come find me when you want that dance."

In the kitchen, I found Sherry mixing two drinks.

"One of those for me?"

She looked up. "No, sorry."

"That's okay. I'll make my own."

"You're starting to slur your words, Randall," she said, picking up the glasses. "You might want to slow down."

"Slow down, you move too fast," I sang, "got to make the boozing last!"

She pushed in front of me to get back into the living room, but I stopped her. "Don't forget our lunch date tomorrow, 'kay?"

"I said maybe, Randall."

"Maybe, baby," I said. It seemed clever.

After every part of her was gone, except her perfume, I poured myself another drink and moved away from the counter to get out of the way for two guys who'd been standing behind me, waiting patiently.

They looked young, in their early twenties, and one of them couldn't stop staring at me.

"It's you," he said.

"Yep, it's me."

He turned to his friend. "That's the guy who broke Jimmy's nose."

It took a few seconds for that to sink in, but when

it did, I knew I might be in trouble.

"You friends of his?" I asked. "Fellow sea-men?"

"Yeah, I'm the guy who carried him out the other night, remember?"

I took a long pull from my glass, and then shook my head, putting on my meanest grin. "Honestly, I don't remember you at all. That's how much of an impression you made."

"This guy's a prick," his friend said.

I wasn't really afraid, but I wanted to attract attention. So I yelled, "I am a prick, a mean-ass prick! What the fuck are you going to do about it?"

The crowd in the living room quieted and within seconds, Stewart was standing behind the two sailors.

"What the fuck's going on?" he asked.

"Remember that asshole I punched out at the dance club, Stu? These two guys are his friends."

Stewart—a crowd behind him—looked at the two sailors.

"Why don't you guys take your drinks and leave, okay?"

Looking not very happy about it but realizing they were outnumbered, the two skinny twenty-year-olds picked up their plastic glasses of booze and pushed through the crowd toward the front door.

"Say hello to Jimmy for me," I called. They didn't look back.

Chapter 10

Around eleven, I awoke, headache pounding. I'd stayed at the party a while longer, drinking heavily, feeling like a pariah, ignored by everyone. I'd left after midnight and stumbled down the hill to the hotel, somehow making it to my room in one piece.

After showering and shaving, I was tempted to go upstairs and tap on Sherry and Maggie's door, but I didn't have the energy to climb those stairs. Besides, I had a feeling no one would answer. Hoping that Sherry would keep our lunch date, I staggered up the hill to the terrace at the Galleon House.

The terrace was empty—I, the only customer—and one waitress remained, looking annoyed, waiting for me to finish. I figured all the guests were out sight-seeing. I heard footsteps on the stairs and saw, not Sherry, but Maggie climbing the steps. She walked over and sat across from me.

"I wasn't sure you'd still be here," she said.

"Still here," I mumbled. "Want something? Coffee? A beer?"

"No, thanks. I just ate."

The waitress—even more annoyed—started to

come over, but I shook my head.

"Sherry asked me to meet you. She said to tell you that if you're still interested when you've finished med school to look her up. I take it, you made a play for her."

I took a sip of tepid coffee and shrugged. "Yeah, well, after you fucked Jerry, I figured I had nothing to lose. All's fair in love and war, right?"

She took my hand. "Sherry says I owe you more of an explanation about that."

I pulled my hand out from under hers. "You explained it pretty well last night."

"Don't get me wrong, Randall. You're a good-looking guy, and I'm attracted to you. But I'm trying to follow Sherry's example and think more about the future."

That hurt. "So you don't see a future with me?"

She smiled a sweet, sympathetic smile. "Not really. Why? Can you see yourself with me?"

"Maybe," I answered. "We were pretty great together in bed."

She nodded. "There's more to a relationship than good sex."

"But without good sex, there's not much of a relationship."

She laughed.

"Just how serious are you about Jerry?"

Her expression darkened. "Less serious than I was last night, I guess."

"How come?"

She looked around as if debating whether or not to tell me something. "Well, this morning, I was helping Stewart clean up—Jerry was still asleep and

Sherry was preparing brunch. Stu told me that Jerry's practically engaged. This trip is his last hurrah before he pops the question." Her eyes filled with tears, and she wiped one from her cheek. "Sometimes…"

"Sometimes, what?"

She looked at me, her eyes overflowing. "You know how guys say, there are girls you marry, and girls you sleep with? Sometimes I think I'm the kind of girl men don't marry."

She wiped tears away with her left hand, but her right hand was still on the table, so I took it.

"You know what I think? I think there are some women you want to marry and make love to, and I think you're that kind of woman."

She laughed through her tears.

We looked at one another in silence for several minutes. She was hurt, like I was.

"Maybe I will get something," she said. "Maybe a glass of white wine."

I flagged the waitress over. "Can we get some wine?"

She checked her wristwatch. "Got to wait an hour. We don't serve no alcohol before two."

I pulled out a fifty dollar bill and handed it to her, saying, "Well, how about you bring us two glasses and a bottle of good chardonnay. Then you can keep the change."

Her eyes lit up. "You serious, mon? That's like a thirty dollah tip!"

I laughed when she said "dirty dollar" and answered, "I'm serious. You see, we're making plans for the future."

She smiled at Maggie and then hurried to the bar.

A few minutes later, she came back with two glasses and a bottle of chilled wine. She placed the glasses in front if us and made a big display of pouring wine into each glass, rotating the bottle as she finished the pour.

"You want anything else?"

"No, thanks," I told her.

The waitress set the bottle on the table and retreated.

Maggie and I toasted and took a sip.

"That's nice," she said. "Buttery."

I smiled. "Something else you learned in your gourmet class?"

"Yes, and I still don't know why that's so funny."

A memory of Sherry laughing the day we met forced me to change the subject. "Tell me about your family. I mean, you know about me, but I don't know much about you."

She reached across the table and patted my hand as it rested on the bottom of the wine glass. "That's so sad about your parents, Randall. I just can't imagine losing both parents."

A shrug seemed a sufficient response.

She withdrew her hand and sat back. "I guess the worst thing that happened to me along those lines was when my dad was unfaithful. I was ten, and I heard my parents get into a terrible argument. Mother had found out that dad had been cheating with his secretary. I mean, it's so cliché."

I nodded, wondering if my dad had even had a fling with one of the secretaries or nurses in his office after Mom's death. I hoped he had—he deserved some pleasure—but I suspected he hadn't. He'd taken her death hard.

Maggie continued. "They argued on and off about getting a divorce for a year, but they stayed together. It was never the same between them, but they seemed to reconcile. I wouldn't say they have a loveless marriage, but pretty close to it. It's like they're business partners or something. Anyway, it's not the kind of marriage I want."

I listened sympathetically but caught myself wondering what Sherry was doing. I must have seemed distracted because she leaned closer. "What are you thinking?"

"You really want to know?"

She nodded apprehensively.

"I was thinking how much I'd like to make love to you right now." And then, as if the words themselves possessed magic, I suddenly was in the mood to make love to her.

She looked surprised and a bit annoyed. "You know, you're one of those guys that, in old movies, they'd call a cad."

I grinned, dipped my finger into the wine and ran it around the top of my glass, making the crystal sing.

Maggie was smiling, eyelids half closed, when I filled our glasses with the rest of the wine.

I raised my glass. "To Maggie, who will make someone a good wife and a great lover."

She sipped the wine, brought her shoulders forward, deepening the valley between her breasts and smiled. "How can I possibly resist your charms?"

We lingered at the table, smiling at one another with anticipation. A cool breeze was blowing in, carrying scents of jasmine.

Once our glasses we drained, we stood to leave and reached the stairs just as Mike was climbing them. He glanced at Maggie, who nodded as she blushed.

Maggie kept walking while I shook Mike's hand. "Just coming to work?"

"Yep. Two p.m. to two a.m. That's the life of a small-time bartender." He said it with a certain self-deprecation that I found ironic. Then he leaned over and whispered, "That's not the stunner, is it?"

"No," I whispered, "but she has her own charms."

In my room, Maggie and I tore at each other's clothes, almost violently. Once we were naked, she pushed me down on the bed, kissing my mouth—the taste of her lipstick arousing me intensely. She kissed my chest, licking my belly button, and finally taking me inside her mouth until I was hard. Then she rolled me over so I was on top and whispered, "Your turn."

I kissed her mouth, suckled each nipple until it was hard, kissed her belly and moved lower between her open legs. She rocked and writhed with pleasure, and I stayed there until her thighs trembled and she moaned, pushing my head away. I kissed the insides of her thighs until I thought she was ready and then went back to kissing her there until she wriggled and moaned and pushed me away again. I climbed on top and entered her, and we rocked together until I couldn't hold it anymore, and we cried out in unison.

Afterwards, we lay side by side on the cool sheets, and I fell into a deep, dreamless sleep. Movement on the bed woke me up, and I watched Maggie pick up her clothes, go into the bathroom and close the door. The luminous dial of the alarm clock said it was almost five o'clock.

I turned on the lamp and sat up, suddenly feeling famished. Maggie was showering—I could hear the water—but I didn't want to join her. Instead, I pulled the sheet up and waited, wondering what to say to her.

When she came out, she was dressed but her hair was wrapped in a towel.

"I've got to get going," she said. "I'm supposed to meet the others for dinner at Frenchmen's Reef."

"You're leaving?"

"Yeah. I'm going upstairs to change and do my hair." She pulled the towel off her head. "Why?"

Because we just fucked, and it's rude to leave, I wanted to say.

"Are we going to…" I was suddenly at a loss for words.

"Are we going to what, Randall? Drink wine? Have sex?"

"See each other again?"

She leaned down and kissed me gently on the lips. "Let's play it by ear." And with that, she left.

I laughed at what she'd said. *Well, we've played with just about every other body part,* I thought, *so why not the ears?*

After a shower, I dressed and walked down to the waterfront, looking for a new place to eat. Another ocean liner had docked, so there were once again two behemoths rising like upside-down icebergs out of the bay. I found a hamburger stand with outdoor seating and ordered a cheeseburger, fries, and a milkshake—not Caribbean cuisine, but just good old American food.

A young family of four was seated next to me, the dad and mom in their mid-thirties, the boy and girl around ten years old, I guessed. They made a good-looking family and seemed happy, joking and teasing one another as they ate onion rings. The girl would slip an onion ring over her finger, and the dad pretended he wanted to eat the onion ring, finger and all. The girl giggled with delight every time she snatched her finger away from her father's teeth just in time. The mom glanced at me, smiling, and shook her head, as if admitting her husband was a goof, but I smiled an approving grin. The boy laughed, too, but I sensed he was a little jealous that his sister was getting the attention.

They left, and I sat alone looking at the bay, trying to remember something from my childhood before my mother's illness. There must have been times when we'd been as happy and carefree as that family, but I couldn't recall one. I thought about Maggie and Sherry. That's the life they wanted now—a husband and kids. I wasn't ready for that. Not yet. But part of me longed for the time in some not-too-distant future when I would be ready. Ready for the whole scene. Maybe not the white picket fence though. I never liked white picket fences.

Between the cheeseburger and the shake, I was stuffed. I strolled along the shore toward the ships as the sun began to set behind Government Hill. I figured I'd have a few beers at the Galleon House.

To my surprise, the terrace was crowded. Whitey and the other two musicians were warming up, so I found my usual stool and sat at the bar.

Mike came over. "What'll you have?"

"Just a beer."

"Try a San Miguel."

The beer was rich and dark, and I sipped it slowly, listening to Whitey play, watching couples dance, and feeling the night breeze sweep in. The table where I'd sat earlier with Maggie opened up, so I ordered another beer and took the bottle to the table to enjoy the view. After an hour, the band took a break and Whitey joined me.

"Drinking your usual G and T?" I asked him.

He winked. "No G yet, just T. I'll have a real drink when we take our next break."

Gillian, who'd been working the tables, finally walked over.

"May I join you?" she asked, looking at both of us.

"Of course," Whitey told her. "You never have to ask."

She sat down and patted my hand. "Monique told me you gave her a huge tip so she would serve you wine before we usually do."

I felt myself blush. "Yeah, I didn't think you'd mind."

"Well, I'm glad you feel at home here, but please don't undermine our policies. They're in place for a reason."

"I'm really sorry, Gillian. Like I said, I didn't think you'd mind."

She gave me a polite grin and then turned to Whitey, whose disappointed look I couldn't bear. It felt as though I'd let down my own father.

They chatted for a while—about what I couldn't say. I wasn't listening. I was feeling a bit humiliated, so I sipped my beer and gazed out at the rooftops and the lights and the silhouettes of palm trees swaying in the breeze.

A woman's scream pierced the night air.

Everyone on the terrace fell silent.

The guttural, primordial sound of sheer terror grew louder.

Whitey bolted from his chair, yelling, "What the hell?!"

Gillian leapt to her feet so quickly, she knocked her chair over. "Mike, we better check that out."

Mike grabbed the baseball bat, flipped the bar top up, and rushed around to join us. I ran behind Gillian and Whitey down the steps through the courtyard.

When we reached the street, I was shocked to see a naked woman running down the road, arms outstretched, wailing at the top of her lungs. The left side of her face and left breast were covered in something that, in the weird, dim glow of the streetlight, looked like chocolate syrup. But I knew it was blood, and though her face was contorted in fear, her eyes wide with terror, I recognized Maggie running toward us.

Mike and I ran to her, and she fell into our arms, shaking and crying hysterically.

"What happened?"

She shook her head, still screaming.

"Maggie, Maggie, what happened?" I asked again.

She looked up at me, as if recognizing me for the first time, and said, "The villa, the villa."

Mike looked at me, confused.

"I know what she means," I said, ripping off my

113

shirt. I wiped blood from Maggie's face, then pulled the shirt over her, as we guided her down to Gillian.

Gillian took hold of her. "I'll call the police."

"C'mon."

Mike ran behind me, and Whitey sprinted up the sidewalk as fast as he could. When I glanced back, I saw the little silver pistol in Whitey's right hand. Mike was still carrying the bat.

It took less than a minute to run up the steep hill, but it seemed an eternity. I wondered what we would find at Stewart and Jerry's rented house. The lights were off, but the front door was wide open, and when I reached in and turned on the porch light, I noticed drops of blood on the porch and inside the foyer.

Mike rushed up behind me.

"Mind the blood," I told him.

Like me, he looked down, and we carefully side-stepped the blood trail as we followed it down the hall and into Jerry's room. I turned on the light and gasped. Blood was splattered on the wall in several arcing lines, like a macabre rainbow.

I saw Jerry's face—mouth covered by blood, jagged bits of bone or teeth poking through the skin, both eyes swollen shut. Bubbles formed around his mouth and he was gurgling, trying to breathe.

"Dear God," Mike gasped. "We need to roll him over."

Mike handed the bat to me, rushed to Jerry, grabbed his shoulder and pulled him onto his side. I watched from the doorway, frozen. Blood gushed from Jerry's mouth, but then it oozed slowly, and I could tell he was breathing more easily.

I heard a deep, grotesque panting from Stewart's

room. I leaned back to look down the hallway and whispered, "Mike," loud enough for him to join me.

Before stepping into the room, I reached in carefully and switched on the overhead light. The stench of shit hit me first. I saw what should never be seen. Two bodies coated in glistening red liquid lay next to each other on the blood-soaked bed. In the glaring light, my mind would not allow me to recognize them. Above the bed, the wall was covered by dozens of lines of blood splatter—like a sickening Jackson Pollock painting. The odor of urine and feces nearly gagged me.

My eyes followed my ears, and I saw a small creature squatting in the corner like an ape, panting. It, too, was covered in blood.

Standing next to me, Mike yelled, "Jesus Christ!"

The squatting creature looked in our direction, the whites of his eyes showing clearly inside his blood-smeared face.

Watching us, the creature stood slowly, clearly exhausted, and that's when I saw the lead pipe in his right hand. He raised the club over his head and rushed toward us, screaming, but his swing fell between us.

My first swipe with the baseball bat hit his arm and knocked the pipe from his grip, and my second swing caught his temple, sending him back against the foot of the bed.

He was out cold. When we rolled him over, I saw the bandaged nose.

"Oh, my God," I said, looking at Mike. "It's that sailor."

Mike inspected the blood-coated face. "Jesus

Christ!" he said again.

A noise startled us, and we swung around to see Whitey rushing down the hall, the little silver gun in his hand.

"What the hell's going on?"

"Bloody murder," Mike said.

That's when I looked back at the two bodies. I stepped closer, sure the bare-chested man was Stewart, but his face was so badly smashed in, it was impossible to tell. The slender woman lying next to him was topless, her small breasts covered in blood. Her head looked like a smashed grapefruit.

I wonder who that is? I thought. My mind did not allow me to grasp the obvious.

Then I heard the weird whine of a police siren—or maybe it was an ambulance—and I turned to Mike. The look on his face was strange, like he felt sorry for me,

"Come on, Randy," he said, putting his arm around me. "There's nothing we can do for them."

He guided me toward the door.

"I'll check for a pulse," Whitey whispered.

"Let the police do that," Mike told him. "They're gone."

Mike guided me down the hall, around the corner, into the kitchen where he turned on the overhead light and sat me down in a chair at the table. I noticed that most of the liquor bottles were still on the counter.

Then two black men in white police uniforms rushed in, and Whitey motioned for them to follow him. I heard voices and the crackling of police radios, and soon two other men—one white and the other black—rushed in. They were dressed all in white, and
116

I thought, *Oh, good, the paramedics are here.*
And then I passed out.

The Caribbean Prisoner

Chapter 11

When I came to, I lay on the cool tile floor, a cold cloth on my forehead, Mike kneeling over me. The concern in his eyes reminded me of my mother's face whenever I'd been sick as a child.

"What's going on?"

"You fainted."

"But why?" I asked. "I've been eating."

Mike smiled. I was confused. Then a policeman leaned over, and I remembered what I'd seen.

"Is he okay?" the cop asked.

"He's coming around," Mike told him.

And the police officer stood and walked away.

"Think you can stand?"

"I don't see why not," I said. But he had to help me up.

I was surprised by how limp I felt. Mike guided me into the chair. When I saw the little forest of liquor bottles on the counter, I understood who had been in the bed next to Stewart.

"Oh, my God! Was that who I think it is?"

Mike knelt down in front of me, putting his hands on my shoulders. "Yeah, Randall, I think it probably was."

Tears fell from my eyes. "Why? Why? Why?"

Two cops escorted the blood-smeared sailor out the front door, his hands cuffed behind his back. He was naked, except for his boxers, almost entirely covered in red.

I turned and vomited on the very spot where I'd just been lying. Whitey came into the kitchen and held my shoulder, while Mike cleaned up the mess and handed me a glass of cold water.

While I was sipping the water, the paramedics went by with someone on a gurney.

"Who's that?" I asked.

The white paramedic glanced in my direction. "The lone victim in the first bedroom."

"Will he be alright?"

"He's got a chance."

"What about the other two?" I called. But they had disappeared. I looked up at Whitey. "I want to see them."

"You can't, son," he said, patting my shoulder. "It's a crime scene now."

I put my head in my hands and studied the floor. "Why did it smell like shit in there? Wasn't it enough to kill them? Did he have to shit on them, too?"

Whitey gripped my shoulder. "They probably lost control of their bowels, Randall. That usually happens when someone dies."

I shook my head. "It's just so… vulgar."

We stayed in that little kitchen for hours, watching as more people arrived—police detectives and investigators, I was told. One of them—a man in his fifties, I suspected—asked me a series of questions, and I tried to answer each one as clearly as I could. I had no idea what time it was, but Mike finally asked one of the cops if we could go. After checking with a couple of the older men, he nodded.

Mike and Whitey helped me walk. My legs felt like rubber. With my arms over their shoulders, we staggered down the middle of the road, under dim street lamps that obscured the deep, deep blue night sky with its smattering of stars.

They deposited me at my hotel room where collapsed on the bed and cried myself to sleep. I awoke a few times, and buried my head under the covers, only to be lurched awake later by nightmares—smashed faces, unrecognizable bodies. Sometimes my mind imagined the sailor swinging the lead pipe, grimacing, blood spraying over him.

Around nine in the morning, there was a knock on my door. I tried to ignore it, assuming it was the maid, but there was a second, louder knock, followed by a man's deep voice. "This is Detective Granger. I need to ask you some questions."

I threw off the covers, tugged on the shorts I'd worn the previous night and a clean shirt—suddenly recalling that I'd given my other shirt to Maggie.

When I opened the door, he filled the space, blocking the light. His face was in darkness, but I could tell he was sizing me up.

After clearing my throat, I asked, "Any news about Maggie—the woman who ran down the hill screaming?"

"She's in the hospital," he said. He reeked of nicotine. "Has a mild concussion, but the doc told me she'll be okay. Her friend wasn't so fortunate."

120

"Jerry? Is he dead or alive?"

"Alive. Barely. Doc says he'll probably have brain damage."

I felt awful for Jerry, but then thought about Sherry and crumbled inside. I tried to hide that I was ready to start crying again, but I couldn't. I put my hand up to my eyes and pressed against them, even as tears spilled out.

"I'm sorry," I said, coughing. I couldn't stop the tears, so I stepped back and sat at the foot of the bed. "Can this wait? I—I don't know if I can think straight right now."

"Try to answer just a few questions now, and I'll follow up later, okay?"

"Okay," I whimpered.

"Now we know your connection to the victims, but I understand you also knew the perpetrator. Is that correct?"

"The sailor?"

"Yeah. Seaman James Collins. Tell me how you knew him."

"Collins." I nodded. "Right. Yeah. His friends called him Jimmy."

"How did you know him?"

"Well, let me think." I closed my eyes, first picturing him as the bloody creature huddled in the corner, then as the smart-ass punk we'd thrown off the terrace the first night I was on St. Thomas. "My first run-in with him was a few nights ago at the Galleon House. He and three of his friends were causing trouble, and Mike, the bartender, told them to leave."

He'd started to write notes in a little notebook
121

and, without looking up, asked, "Were you involved in that altercation?"

I shrugged. "I guess you could say that."

"How?" he asked, again without looking at me.

"I don't remember exactly. I helped Mike and the others stand up to those guys, I guess. Whitey and the other musicians were there, too."

"Yeah, I got that," he said.

"And Gillian, the owner," I added. "In fact, one of them—I think it was Collins—grabbed her by the arm, and that's when Mike and everyone else told them to leave."

He finished writing something before looking at me.

"Did you see Seaman Collins again a night or two ago?"

I nodded, realizing he was gathering as much evidence as he could against this maniac. "Yeah, that's correct. The five of us—Sherry, Stewart, Maggie, Jerry and I—ran into him and his buddies at some dance club. They were drunk and obnoxious, and Jimmy—or, Seaman Collins—took a swing at me."

"Did he connect?"

Did he connect? I thought. *Like a love connection?* "What?"

"Did he hit you?"

"Oh. No, I managed to duck."

Granger looked at me. "Did you land a blow?"

"Yeah," I said. "I landed a couple."

"Did you know you broke his nose?"

"I wasn't sure."

He looked down and wrote in his pad again,

flipping the page.

"Look, it was self-defense," I said. "He swung at me first."

The big cop nodded but kept writing.

"I'm not going to be charged with assault, or something, am I?"

He shook his head. "Doubt it."

"I mean, he was looking for trouble that night and the night before."

He kept writing, and I wondered what.

"It was almost like he wanted something to happen, you know?"

He closed his notepad, saying, "And something did. Last night, you broke his wrist with that baseball bat, and fractured his skull."

"I don't care. He was ready to attack us."

"That's what your pal, Mike, said."

"Where's Collins now?"

"In jail."

"Inside that big red building?"

"The Fort. It's what we call our police station. Used to be a fortress."

I wiped my cheeks and nose, realizing my face was still wet. "Any chance he could escape?"

Granger chuckled. "No escape for him. Confessed to everything."

I huffed. "Good. I'm glad. Fucking punk."

"He's a pretty disturbed kid. Got some serious problems."

"You can say that again."

"How long you plan to stay here on St. Thomas?"

I shrugged. "I leave Sunday."

"Could you stay longer, if you had to?"

"I guess so," I said. "Why?"

"Just in case we need to tie up some loose ends."

"For how much longer?" I asked. "I was actually thinking about leaving sooner." It was a lie. I hadn't until that very moment given any thought to leaving early, but it suddenly seemed like a good idea.

The big man scratched the top of his head. "Well, another week or so, if it's possible."

"I'll think about it."

He dug a business card out of his shirt pocket and handed it to me. He'd been sweating, so the card was damp.

"Give me a call if you think of something I should know, or if you change your travel plans, okay?"

His name was Det. Adam Granger.

Grabbing the door handle, he turned to go but stopped. "You want to hear something funny?"

I looked up.

His back was to me. "Collins said he went there looking for you. Said he thought it was you in the bed next to the blonde."

It didn't take long for the implication to sink in. I was the target of the killer's rage. I was responsible for Sherry's murder. Blood drained from my head, and it was all I could do not to collapse as I watched the large man pull my door closed.

Then I rushed to the sink and vomited. I splashed cold water on my face a few times. I needed a shower and a shave, but I didn't give a damn. I slipped on my sandals, grabbed my room key and left.

The only place I could think to go was the Galleon House, but when I got there, I found the gate to the courtyard locked, a hand-printed note saying,

"Closed until further notice."

Glancing around, I was surprised to see how normal everything looked. The sun was up, brightly illuminating the colorful houses, and tourists dressed in absurdly bright clothing were strolling toward town, idiotic smiles on their faces.

I stumbled down the road to find a bar, but found a liquor store instead. The young, black clerk eyed me suspiciously. I looked awful.

"A bottle of Cutty Sark," I told him. He reached for the pint. "No, the big one."

He reached for the bigger bottle but turned. "Can you pay?"

I pulled out my wallet and opened it, showing him the twenties and fifties inside. "In fact, give me two."

He put two bottles inside a paper bag while I was grabbing some potato chips, and I paid him. He inspected the fifty dollar bill closely, shrugged, and gave me my change.

"You need a bath," he said.

I nodded. "I could take thousand baths, but it won't help."

Inside the sanctuary of my stuffy little room, with the air conditioner blowing full blast, I went through the ritual of pouring the scotch slowly over ice cubes in a glass. After a while, it was too much trouble to grab ice out of the bucket, and before long, it was easier just to drink out of the bottle.

I don't remember finishing the first bottle, but sometime during the night, I decided the whole thing must have been a bad dream. I climbed the stairs, pulling myself up by the railing until I'd reached the third floor. I staggered to room 22 and knocked. No

125

one answered, so I pounded, yelling, "Sherry! Maggie!"

The door to room 24 opened, and a skinny, older woman looked out.

"You're drunk."

I stumbled in the woman's direction, and she closed the door, but not all the way, peeking at me through the slit.

"You know where Sherry and Maggie are?"

"The young gals next door? No. Haven't seen them."

Her breath reeked of cigarette smoke. I was spinning. I was going to be sick. I somehow managed to stagger to the railing where I hurled over the side. I heard the watery splatter hit the courtyard below.

When I turned around, the door was closed. Clinging to the cold metal railing, I descended into the darkness below.

Chapter 12

I must have made it back downstairs in one piece because I awoke lying on the bedspread inside my room. My head throbbed and I couldn't move without feeling like I would vomit again.

Eventually, I felt strong enough to shower and shave. I needed something on my stomach—soup, crackers, Seven-Up—and I was just about to leave when someone knocked on my door.

I opened it guardedly, expecting either Detective Granger or the sailor's angry friends. Instead, Maggie was standing there, about to cry, the left side of her face swollen and bruised.

"Oh, God, Randall," she said, collapsing into my arms.

All I could do was hold her and let her cry. She sobbed fiercely, in deep, guttural tones that shook her whole body.

"She's dead, Randall, dead."

"I know, I know."

"My best friend is dead."

"It's horrible," I whispered, "horrible."

"I can't believe it," she cried. "Sherry's gone."

Her crying grew weaker, and she seemed to be

getting control of herself.

"Does her family know?"

She nodded, still in my arms. "They're flying down tomorrow to stay with the body until the police release it."

"Good," was all I could say. It seemed so feeble.

"They want me to pack up her things and leave her bags at the police station."

Maggie drew away from me, looking into my eyes. "Will you help? I'm not sure I can do it alone."

"Of course, I will," I told her. "When?"

"Now, I guess. I changed my flight. I'm leaving in a few hours on the last flight off the island tonight."

As sick as I felt, I followed her up the stairs. She took each step slowly, as if her legs were heavy, and I wondered if it was just the dread of seeing Sherry's clothes or if Maggie had suffered some brain damage.

When we reached the third floor, the two teachers were just coming out of their room. The slender one with the bad skin had a freshly lit cigarette between her fingers and the other one was holding a wine cooler.

The skinny smoker gasped when she saw Maggie's face. "What happened to you?"

Maggie glanced at me as if to say, *I don't want to talk about it.*

The woman scowled at me. "Did you do this?"

Maggie said nothing, but shook her head.

The smoker rushed over and forced Maggie to look her in the eyes. "You can tell us if he hurt you. We'll protect you, I promise."

"It's not what you think," I told the woman.

The woman grabbed Maggie's arm, but she

128

yanked away, saying, "Leave me alone. I don't know you."

The heavier woman said to Maggie, "Would you like us to call the police, dear?"

Maggie tried to ignore them as she fumbled to get the key inside the lock.

"She and her friend were attacked," I explained. "Not by me, by someone else."

Maggie finally got the door unlocked and opened it, saying, "Please leave us alone. Randall's here to help me."

I followed Maggie into the room and closed the door slowly, looking at the two women who eyed me with suspicion.

"Wow," I said, exhaling. "Talk about leaping to conclusions."

"I don't have the patience to deal with... with anything."

She started to cry again, so I wrapped my arms around her and let her cry all she wanted. The room smelled of perfume. They must have used a lot of it the last time they were there. Finally, Maggie settled down enough for us to get to work.

"Let me get my things out of the bathroom first, and then would you mind packing up everything that's left in Sherry's bag for me? I just know if I start handling her things, I'll lose it."

"Sure," I said. "No problem."

While Maggie was gathering up her things in the bathroom, I looked at the two dressers, one on each side of the bed. One was strewn with blouses and under garments while the other one was tidy—only a hair brush and a lipstick on the surface.

Maggie came out carrying her small bag, her eyes filled with tears. She opened the closet and handed me two yellow suitcases without saying a word. Then she began folding the clothes on her dresser as if in a trance.

I took the smaller yellow bag into the bathroom and filled it with the makeup and perfume bottles. I checked the shower stall and found a bottle of Herbal Essence shampoo. When I looked under the sink, I found a box of tampons and tossed it in the bag as well. I tried not to think about Sherry, but images of her—laughing at the café the first time we'd met, sleeping on the beach, her body stretched out and glistening in the sun—kept popping into my head.

Maggie was sitting on the bed crying when I came out. I sat down next to her and put my arm over her shoulder.

"It's not fair," she said, trying to catch her breath. "What happened to Sherry—it's not fair. She was so good, so decent, so beautiful and smart."

"I know, I know."

"I wish it had been me instead. Sherry deserved to live more than me."

"Don't say that, Maggie. Neither of you deserved what happened."

"But Sherry was better than me."

"Why would you say something like that?"

"Be honest, Randall. You liked her better. Everyone did. She had a special quality."

I grabbed Maggie by the shoulders and looked into her blood-shot eyes. "Maggie, you're beautiful, too, and caring, and warm. You're a lot friendlier than she was. And more loving, I think. The two of you

130

were different that's all."

She cried again softly, resting her face against my shoulder, her tears dampening my shirt. I put my hand on the back of her head and stroked her hair. Then she pushed away. "We'd better finish packing. Besides, you really need a bath."

Maggie grabbed her other suitcase from the closet and began filling it, so I opened the larger yellow suitcase on the bed and started to put the hairbrush and tube of lipstick into it.

"Better put those with her bathroom stuff."

I did that and then opened the top dresser drawer. A neat stack of folded tops sat beside an equally neat stack of folded bras and panties. I picked up the undergarments first and stacked them in the corner of the suitcase. Then I picked up the blouses and tee shirts, and Sherry's fragrance rose from them. I started to hold them up to my nose, but stopped myself, realizing how weird that would be with Maggie standing behind me.

The second drawer held two neat stacks of shorts and two folded bikinis. I packed them, too, before opening the bottom drawer which was empty.

"That's it, I think."

"No," Maggie said. "She has three dresses hanging here in the closet."

I looked at Maggie, who was staring at the short dresses as if they were ghosts.

"Want to hand them to me?" I asked her.

She shook her head. "I can't touch them. If I touch them, I'll go to pieces."

I stepped around the foot of the bed and reached in to grab the dresses. Maggie stepped away, looking out the window above the bed.

"It's so beautiful here," she said. "I used to think it was the most beautiful and peaceful place on earth." She shook her head. "But now... I'll never come back to this island. Not ever."

I didn't know what to say, so I folded the dresses without speaking, put them inside the suitcase and closed the lid. Then I stacked the bags by the door and sat in a chair in the corner of the room to watch Maggie finish. She worked very slowly, very deliberately, and again I wondered if she had brain damage.

When she finished, she turned to me. "Will you ride to the airport with me? I'm afraid to be alone."

"Of course," I said. "Do you have everything?"

She glanced around the room. "I think so. I don't care if I don't, I just need to get out of here."

I stood, saying, "We need to call for a cab, don't we?"

She screwed up her face in despair, saying, "I forgot to call, didn't I?"

Walking to the nightstand on Sherry's side of the bed, I told Maggie, "No problem. I'll call the desk."

She looked from the phone to me and back again. "Oh, that's a good idea."

I picked up the phone and dialed. "Front desk? We need a taxi to take us to the airport right away, please." The woman said okay and hung up.

By the time we'd lugged the bags down three flights of stair, the cab was waiting. Maggie stepped into the office while I loaded the bags. We were driven through the low, late-afternoon sunlight to the airport. I'd agreed to drop off Sherry's suitcases at the police station on the way back to the hotel.

"Give them to Detective Granger, if he's there," Maggie instructed.

"You've spoken to him?"

She nodded. "Smokey, the bear? Yeah. He interrogated me at the hospital."

"Why do you call him that?" I asked.

She laughed a little. "He's as big as a bear and smells like smoke."

"What did he tell you? I mean, did he tell you why they think Collins did it?"

She looked at me, confused. "Because he was found at the scene covered in blood. You should know that—you found him."

"No, I don't mean that."

"I can't remember the attack at all. The only thing I remember is coming to next to Jerry and seeing all the blood. Even though it was dark, I knew there was blood all over the place. And I'll never forget the awful gurgle noise Jerry was making."

"Did Granger say anything about why Collins did it?"

"Oh," Maggie said. She looked down at her feet. "He said Jimmy was drunk and high on drugs and wanted to get back at us for—I don't know— humiliating him, or something. Can you believe that? I mean, he makes a couple of crude passes at us, and we're to blame because we didn't fall in love with him or something? He's as crazy as Jeffrey Dahmer."

I nodded, feeling somewhat relieved. Maybe it wasn't just my fault that Collins had targeted Sherry and the others. Still, I remembered how good it had felt to smash my fist into his face, and I felt guilty.

133

We rode the rest of the way in silence, both of us alone in our dark thoughts, I suspected. Finally, we arrived at the airport and Maggie reached for her wallet.

"I'll pay," I said. "It's the least I can do."

Standing on the sidewalk in front of the terminal, Maggie hugged me, putting her lips to my earlobe. "Thank you for everything," she whispered. "You were there when I needed you."

"I wish I could have done more."

She kissed my cheek, then grabbed her bags and walked inside the terminal. I waved to my own reflection in the dark glass as the door closed behind her. When I got back inside the cab, I wondered if I'd ever see her again.

Chapter 13

B y the time the taxi reached the police station, the sun was disappearing behind Government Hill, its yellow rays splayed in all directions above the horizon. I paid the driver, grabbed Sherry's suitcases and climbed the stone steps of the massive red fortress. The lobby was small and dark and smelled of cigarette smoke and Lysol. I went to the counter and asked for Detective Granger.

"What's it concerning?" the clerk asked. He was a slender black man in a white uniform.

"The murders from the other night. I've got one of the victim's luggage."

He picked up the phone. "Your name?"

I told him and he called Granger.

"Wait over there," he said, pointing to a row of old, wooden chairs.

While I waited, I thought about the fact that Jimmy Collins was inside this very building. What did he look like now? Was he cleaned up? What was he doing? Sitting in his cell, regretting what he'd done? *Was he even capable of feeling regret?*

I was so lost in thought, I didn't notice the big

detective until he was standing in front of me.

In his gravely voice, he said, "You look better than you did yesterday."

"Brought you Sherry's suitcases."

He sat down next to me. "Did the other gal make it to the airport?"

"Yeah. Just came back from dropping her off."

"How's she doin'?"

"Pretty sad—the loss of her best friend. I'm worried about her injury."

"Oh?" He seemed genuinely concerned. "How come?"

"She's moving a little slower. I wonder if she has some brain damage."

"You're going into medicine or something, right?"

"I'm thinking about it," I said. "My dad was a doctor."

"I've seen a lot of head injuries. Takes a little time to get back to normal."

That made me feel better.

"So," I said, "is he here? Jimmy Collins?"

Granger nodded. "In my office right now, bein' questioned by the D.A., before the military police can take him into custody."

"He's back there?" I glanced at the door that I assumed led to his office. "Could I see him?" I'm not sure why I asked, but I did.

Granger's stare made me nervous. "Why would you want to see him?"

"I don't know. To get some answers, I guess."

He inspected my face. If the eyes are windows on the soul, I wondered what he saw in mine. Maybe he could see the guilt I felt, knowing that I had, in some way, contributed to the death and mayhem the sailor had caused.

"That's an interesting idea," he said. "Let me check with the D.A. and Jimmy's attorney. Wait here."

He pushed his large body up out of the chair, grabbed the handles of Sherry's luggage and started walking toward the door. I felt a sudden impulse to bolt. Something told me that once I stepped into the back offices, I'd never escape, or if I did, I'd never be the same.

While I waited, a few odd people straggled into the lobby—some to pay fines, some to ask about court dates, some who spoke in such soft whispers I couldn't guess what they were saying. Finally, Granger opened the door and waved me inside.

I wasn't sure what to expect. *Would Collins be in chains? How would he react to seeing me?*

When I walked through the door to Granger's office, the first thing I noticed was the gray cigarette smoke that hung in layers over the heads of the three people seated around a table. The next thing I noticed was how small and young Jimmy Collins was, sitting next to two older men. One man—his lawyer, I assumed—was dressed in a light brown military uniform and looked about thirty years old. He sat up straight, short-dark hair framing a stern, rugged face.

The other man was a striking, older black man with hair graying at the temples. He wore a crisp, neatly pressed white shirt and a maroon tie. Despite his age—probably mid-fifties—his eyes were eager and intelligent. He was fit—his muscular chest and

137

arms filling his tailored shirt.

He stood first and shook hands with me. His grip was firm and the way he looked at me made me feel as nervous and guilty as Granger had earlier.

"You're Randall Wake," he said. "I've already heard a good deal about you. My name is Thurgood Whitaker, the Prosecutor for St. Thomas." His voice was deep and clear, and he had a slight British accent.

"Are you sure this is okay?" I asked him. "I mean, I don't want to jeopardize your case."

"Your presence here cannot possibly jeopardize the case against Mr. Collins. He's already signed his full confession with his lawyer present. Your being here might, however, shine light on this entire matter and help me know what recommendation to make to the judge."

"In terms of punishment?" I asked.

"In terms of justice," he answered.

That's when I first really saw Jimmy Collins. He slouched in his chair, both arms resting on the table in front of him, as if he'd just lifted his head from a nap. His right hand and arm were in a clean white cast. A large padded bandage was taped to his right temple and a smaller Band aid covered the bridge of his swollen nose. The flesh around his eyes was black and blue. An orange prison jumpsuit hung off his shoulders like loose skin from someone who'd lost a hundred pounds too quickly.

He glanced at me, and his expression gave me a chill. His eyes were cold and blank, but also sad and desperate, as if pleading with me to say something—anything—that might assuage his guilt. Frankly, he looked pitiful—nothing like the blood-smeared

138

monster I'd imagined—and I knew I was responsible for his injuries. Part of me was glad he seemed so utterly defeated; another part felt a sense of guilt.

The man sitting next to him stood and reached across the table. "I'm Lieutenant Matt Daniels, Jimmy's lawyer."

Like the Prosecutor's strong, confident grip, Daniels' handshake was firm.

"Nice to meet you," was all I could manage. *Nice? What in God's name is nice about any of this?*

Jimmy looked at his lawyer and asked, "Should I shake his hand?"

His voice was thin and flat, nothing like the loud, obnoxious braggart he'd been before. I wondered if this was the real Jimmy Collins, or if he was faking weakness to get sympathy.

"No, Mr. Collins," Thurgood Whitaker said. "That's not needed here." The Prosecutor motioned toward a chair. "Please, Mr. Wake. Have a seat."

Standing behind me, Granger literally pulled the chair out for me as one might for a woman. The gesture made me feel odd, suspicious, but I sat down anyway.

The office itself was larger than I'd expected. Granger's desk was at an angle in the corner, piled with papers, a lamp with a green shade on one side, an over-flowing set of in-out trays on the other. An old telephone sat on the right and an overflowing ashtray on the left. On the wall behind his chair hung certificates, awards, and photos.

The table where we were sitting was in the middle of the room. On it were two ashtrays—also overflowing—and an old cassette tape recorder. Two briefcases sat on the table as well, an old, worn leather one in front of Jimmy's lawyer and a new, black briefcase in front of Whitaker.

"So, tell us, Mr. Wake," Whitaker asked, "why did you wish to see Jimmy Collins?"

Thurgood Whitaker's eyes—though stern—seemed kind and wise, and I felt as if I was in the company of someone who possessed a spiritual quality, like a priest, perhaps.

"I—I'm not sure," I admitted. I turned my gaze toward Collins. "I guess I just want to know why he did it. Why he killed my friends."

The twenty-year-old's face crumbled. He started to cry, dropping his head onto his arms as though utterly exhausted.

After a few minutes of crying while we looked away, Jimmy finally stopped, maybe more from sheer exhaustion than anything else. He raised his head and glowered at me, blood-laced snot hanging from his nostrils. His lawyer pulled a handkerchief from his hip pocket and handed it to him.

"You want to know why I did it, huh?" he asked, wiping his nose. "You want the short answer or the whole story?"

I wasn't sure how to respond. "Tell me why you went to that house," I said. "How'd you even know about it?"

"Like I told Mr. Granger, I went there looking for you, to get back at you for breaking my nose."

"But why go there?" I asked, bewildered.

"My buddies told me they'd seen you there the night before. I figured that's where you were staying."

140

"But that wasn't me in the bed next to Sherry."

"I didn't know that. It was dark, and I was really messed up. I thought that guy was you."

"But why the others?" I asked, my voice cracking. "Why the women, for God's sakes?"

He shrugged. "Like I said, I was totally messed up. Been drinking all day, anything I could get my hands on, and I'd smoked some weed and done a little coke. And I was pissed. You and your pals acted like you was way too good for me. When you broke my nose in front of my shipmates, it was—it was humiliating. Couldn't look them guys in the face after that. Not without getting drunk."

He stared at me. Maybe he was looking for sympathy or just some measure of understanding, but I felt nothing but anger and hatred toward him.

Lieutenant Daniels patted Jimmy's shoulder. "Tell him about your past."

He shrugged, looking down at his hands. "Can I have another smoke first?"

Granger shook a cigarette from his pack of Pall Malls and Jimmy tweezed it between his thumb and finger. Daniels lit it for him with a match. After he'd inhaled deeply, he blew out a long stream of gray smoke.

"These guys think my past is important. I guess because my Ma died when I was pretty young and my dad used to slap me around. He's a piece of work, my old man. Called me a pussy most every day of my life. Hell, that's why I enlisted right out of high school—to get away from that old bastard."

Daniels took a Camel from his pack and lit it while we watched. After exhaling, he said, "Tell Mr.

141

Wake what happened to you in boot camp."

Jimmy took a quick, nervous drag from his cigarette and shook his head. "Nah. It ain't important."

"Actually," the Prosecutor said, "I think it's the most important piece of the puzzle. What happened to you in Orlando was, I believe, the motivation for your actions. What Mr. Wake did was merely act as a catalyst, if you will, the match that ignited the fuse."

Jimmy took another long drag of his cigarette before crushing it out. "They want me to tell you what my CO did to me. Like it matters now."

Daniels' face contorted with disgust. When I glanced at Detective Granger, he looked away.

"Okay," I said, "what the hell happened to you?"

Jimmy shrugged again. "Let these guys tell you, if they think it's so goddamned important."

Daniels said, "Jimmy was molested by his commanding officer. Repeatedly. This is something we're going to have to investigate, and I know my CO will not be pleased."

"Molested how?" I asked.

"The guy was queer for me, okay!" he blurted. "Caught me jerkin' off in the latrine one night. Said I could be court marshaled for doin' that. He'd been drinkin—I could smell it on him—and he made me suck it at first. Told me he'd put me in the brig if I didn't do what he wanted."

I felt sick.

"Tell him the rest," Daniels said.

"Nah, he don't care."

Thurgood Whitaker's expression told me I had to care.

"Go on, Jimmy," I said. "You've told me this much. Might as well tell me the rest."

Chapter 14

The windows were dark. Night had fallen. Jimmy's swollen nose and black and blue eyes showed complete despair. His face seemed fragile as if his skin were as thin and vulnerable as an egg shell. I thought that, at any moment, if he cried again too hard, his face would shatter into a thousand fleshy pieces.

He caught me staring at him and scowled. "I don't need your goddamned pity."

Thurgood and Daniels gave me reassuring nods.

"I don't pity you," I said. "I just feel bad. Like the whole thing could have gone differently if…"

"If, what? You and your girlfriends had been nicer to me? If you hadn't busted my nose?"

Something caught inside my chest. I was to blame, wasn't I? At least, in part.

Jimmy looked up through the clouds of gray smoke at the dark ceiling and then down at his hands on the table. He closed his eyes and hung his head, his chin almost resting on his chest.

"Nah, it was all me. I got so much hate inside, it just boils out sometimes. It was bad enough, what my father done to me all those years. Then that guy at boot camp. I should have fought back against that guy. Ubel. I just couldn't do it. I was afraid of him. His skin was weird—too shiny, like fish scales or something. Like he wasn't exactly human and if I didn't do what he made me do, then—I dunno—something terrible would happen."

I didn't want to, but a whisper escaped my lips. "What'd he make you do?"

Jimmy shook his head back and forth slowly, over and over, before saying a word. Then, as if he couldn't stop himself, he said, "Ubel bent me over and made me take it up the ass. He pounded me like I was a goddamned girl, so hard, it hurt. Three times, he did that. Three different nights he made me go with him to the latrine. I couldn't stop him. It was like I was walkin' in my sleep, when he'd come and get me."

Then, as if all his strength had finally ebbed, Jimmy Collins dropped the side of his face on the table and stared at me with deadened eyes, like a fish taking its last gasps of air.

Daniels patted him on the back, but it didn't help. Jimmy was dead inside.

"I can't tell you why I killed them people," he said, his voice hardly above a whisper. "Like I said before, I was messed up. Drunk, stoned, so full of hate I couldn't see straight. I woulda killed you and that other guy if I'd had any strength left. Hell, I woulda murdered everyone on this whole fuckin' island, if I coulda."

With his head still at rest on the table, he closed his eyes. "Can I go back to my cell now? I wanna sleep. I need to sleep real bad."

145

Thurgood reached over as if to pat Jimmy's head but stopped himself, his hand hovering over the prisoner like a bishop blessing a child. "Sure," he said. "Get some rest. You've got a long trip ahead of you tomorrow."

Jimmy looked from Thurgood to Lieutenant Daniels. "What trip?"

"I've got to take you back to base for questioning and to stand trial," Daniels explained.

"I thought I was gonna be tried here. On the island."

"No, son," Thurgood said. "We can't try in a civilian court. You have to have a military trial."

"Where?"

"Probably Miami," Daniels said, "but you might have to go back to the base in Orlando. I'll get my orders in the morning."

Jimmy looked panicked. "But I don't want to go back to that base. I can't go back there."

The lawyer helped Jimmy to his feet and guided him toward the door. Detective Granger opened the door and waved in an officer who took Jimmy's arm.

Jimmy wouldn't leave at first. He pulled the officer back inside the room. "Please don't take me back to Orlando. You can't take me back to Ubel."

"It's not up to me," Daniels said.

Jimmy staggered away, and I wondered if he'd look back at me. I expected him to say one more thing, but he just let himself be herded down the hallway and out of sight.

"That boy needs a good psychiatrist," Thurgood said.

Daniels nodded. "Maybe the Navy can arrange

one for him once I get him back to the states."

Granger shook out a cigarette and lit it. As he blew out a stream of smoke, he said, "He won't ever be right, though. He'll always be fucked up. No doctor in the world can cure that... that rage. It's inside his bones."

Daniels closed his briefcase. "I need a good, stiff drink. Anyone want to join me?"

The Prosecutor shook his head, as did Granger before saying, "I don't drink with the enemy." He intended the comment to sound funny, I think, but it fell flat.

"I could use a drink," I said. "Want to join me at the Galleon House?"

Once we'd left The Fort, we walked up the hill in the darkness. Dim street lights shone feebly, and the air felt thick and steamy. No breeze came up from the water. I realized my shirt was damp and wondered if I'd been sweating the whole time, while listening to Jimmy Collins, or if I'd just started as we climbed the hill. I was relieved to find the gate open, and the "Closed" sign gone.

Daniels sighed. "That was pretty rough."

I nodded as we walked under the archway. "Yeah," I admitted. "On everyone. Can we change the subject?"

"Sure." We climbed the steps in silence, until he asked, "How'd you find this place?"

I pointed at the Midtown Hotel. "I'm staying right down there. This is convenient."

When we got to the terrace, I was surprised to see how empty it was. Two couples sat near the railing, and one guy sat at the bar keeping Mike company.

Daniels and I sat at the far end of the bar, close to where Jimmy and his three buddies had sat the first night I'd seen them. I nodded to Mike, and he wandered down, wiping a wine glass with a white dish towel.

"How you holding up, Randall?"

"So, so. How 'bout you?"

He shook his head. "I'll never forget that horror as long as I live. Had the worst nightmares last night I've ever had."

I nodded. "Mine would have been worse, but I got too drunk to dream."

Mike grinned a little. "Who's your friend?"

"This is Lieutenant Matt Daniels," I said. They shook hands across the bar. "He's Jimmy Collins's lawyer."

Mike drew his hand back as if from a flame. "How the hell did you run into him?"

"I dropped off Sherry's suitcase at the police station. Detective Granger and I got to talking, and he introduced us."

Mike looked puzzled. "Isn't that some kind of breech of legal ethics or something? I mean, should you be talking to him before the trial?"

"There's not going to be a trial," Daniels said. "Jimmy gave a confession and will plead guilty at the arraignment."

"Oh?" Mike gave me a skeptical look. "What's he going to do, plead insanity or something?"

"He is a pretty troubled kid," Daniels said. "But I'm not sure where he'll end up. The Navy will have something to say about that."

Mike shook his head in disgust. "Well, I hope he
148

never sees the light of day, wherever he winds up."

I wanted to change the subject. "I could use a stiff drink, Mike. Will you get me a double gin-tonic?"

"Sure. And you, Mr. Daniels?"

"Vodka and tonic sounds good."

"Comin' right up." Mike stepped away.

"I don't think your friend likes me," Daniels whispered.

"If I hadn't seen how good you were in there, I probably wouldn't like you either, Lieutenant Daniels. A few hours ago, I wanted Jimmy Collins to go to the gas chamber. Part of me still does."

"Call me Matt. I understand how you feel. My job requires me to represent people who are accused of crimes and to be the best legal advocate for them I can be. Of course, in a situation like this, where there's no question of guilt, I think I'm doing the right thing for everyone by helping Jimmy resolve it as quickly and fairly as possible."

Mike came back with our drinks. "There you go, gentlemen."

I took my glass and glanced around. "Pretty slow tonight."

"The whole Island's talking about the murders. Even though they've got the killer locked up, people are spooked, I guess."

Daniels picked up his drink. "Or maybe the Islanders feel it would be disrespectful to go out and celebrate in light of what's happened."

Mike nodded. "Yeah. That's probably true, too."

My stomach gurgled. "Is the buffet set up, Mike?"

"No, but I can get you a plate of cheese and fruit, if you want."

"That'd be great. I haven't eaten much today."

Mike walked back down to the far end of the bar, patting the single guy on the hand and saying something before lifting up the flap and disappearing upstairs.

"Want to move to a table?" Daniels asked. "I hate barstools."

He started for the same table Jimmy and his friends had occupied, but before he grabbed a chair, I said, "Let's get closer to the banister, to catch the breeze."

He huffed, asking, "What breeze?" But he followed me to the edge of the terrace.

Somehow the streets and the houses seemed darker, the moon, smaller and the stars, duller. Maybe there was a little fog in the air, or maybe the humidity had created a steamy veil, obscuring the stars.

Matt Daniels and I sipped our drinks in silence, hoping, I suppose, that the alcohol would cleanse us. My glass was almost empty when Mike arrived carrying a platter piled with various cheeses, crackers, and sliced mangoes. It was a beautiful platter, filled with color, but looking at it, I wanted to vomit. Something about it made me imagine Sherry's bashed-in face.

"A refill, gentlemen?" Mike asked.

"I'll have another," Daniels said.

"Me, too."

After Mike left, Daniels picked up a piece of cheese and put it on a cracker. "Looks pretty damn good." He chewed heartily, and I realized he hadn't actually seen the victims. Then he picked up another cracker and piled a different wedge of cheese on it.

150

"Thought you were hungry?"

"Need another drink first."

He shrugged and popped a piece of fruit into his mouth.

I'd finished my second drink and waved at Mike. He was leaning across the bar talking with his friend, but he nodded and went to work on another round of drinks.

The two couples got up to leave, and I realized it was just the four of us on the terrace. I ate a few crackers and a piece of cheese as I told Daniels about myself. The gin was beginning to help—I wasn't thinking about Sherry's face every few seconds.

Mike and his friend walked over, each carrying two glasses, and joined us.

"This is my friend Bob," Mike told me. "He comes down from Miami Beach about every four months."

I shook Bob's hand and introduced him to Matt Daniels.

Bob looked like a movie star—short, curly blonde hair, blue eyes and smooth, tanned skin.

"Mike's been filling me in on your gruesome adventure." He looked straight at me. "Sounds absolutely horrible."

I took a long pull from my fresh drink.

"And you." Bob turned toward Daniels. "How can you defend that monster?"

Daniels grinned and took a sip before answering. "Even monsters are entitled to their day in court. But the more you learn about Jimmy Collins, the more you find out about the other monsters in his life."

"Oh? Please enlighten us."

Daniels gave a good summation of Jimmy's background and finished by saying, "so part of Jimmy's state of mind was the confusion he felt about his homosexual encounter with Commander Ubel."

Mike shook his head. "What Ubel did can't be called a homosexual encounter. It was rape, pure and simple."

"He abused that poor boy," Bob added. "Used his power to force Jimmy to do things he didn't want to do. It's a crime of sadistic violence."

"Yeah," Mike agreed. "It's more about being a sadist than anything else. He gets off on complete domination. That's not love."

Bob made a cutting motion at his neck. "Just like a man holding a knife to a woman's throat and making her have sex."

"Only in this case," Mike said, "Ubel's weapon was his rank and the threat of imprisonment, if the kid didn't comply."

I winced and sipped my drink. "We don't think about men getting raped, do we? But I guess it happens."

"Only in prisons, usually," Daniels added.

Bob glared at him. "It happens in the real world. More than people care to admit."

Mike nodded. "You know how hard it is for a woman who's been raped to come forward?"

"Sure," Daniels said. "They know they're going to be grilled about their own sex lives. I've never tried to discredit a victim that way when I've defended someone accused of rape. Fortunately, haven't had to do it very often here."

"Well," Mike said, "it can be even harder for

152

men."

He looked at Bob with such sympathy in his eyes that I suddenly understood their relationship as well as Bob's sad history.

"You speak from experience?" Daniels asked.

"No, not me personally," Mike admitted.

"I was raped," Bob said. "The summer before I went to high school, some older boys grabbed me on the beach and took me under a dock. Three of them did to me what was done to your client. The other had a conscience, evidently. He couldn't get a hard-on, so he just watched."

I didn't want to, but I suddenly visualized Jimmy Collins bent over, being raped by some blurry, indistinct figure.

"What happened to those boys?" Daniels asked.

"Nothing. I didn't tell anyone."

"Why not?" I asked.

He turned in my direction, and I was struck by his penetrating blue eyes. "Because, my friend, to tell on those boys would mean admitting I was gay. And I simply wasn't ready to admit that. Not even to myself. Not at thirteen."

"Did you ever see them again?" Daniels asked.

"Almost every day. We went to the same high school, you see."

"Jesus," I said. "That must have been hell."

"A special kind of hell I wouldn't wish on anyone. But it got better over time. They left me alone. I avoided them. A few years later, one of them—the leader—was killed in a car accident. Another one got arrested before he graduated. And the one who couldn't go through with it eventually transferred to a different school."

We fell silent. I drained my glass and was about to ask for another drink, but I saw Detective Granger climb the stairs and head straight for our table. He looked so serious, I thought he was going to arrest someone. Maybe me.

Chapter 15

G ranger was a large and tough-looking guy anyway, but the way he lumbered toward us made me nervous. Matt hadn't noticed him yet, so I nodded in Granger's direction.

"Detective Granger's here," I said. "Looks like he means business."

Daniels turned and started to stand, but Granger motioned for him to stay in his seat.

"You're gonna want to sit down, Lieutenant," he said. He stood beside the table and looked down at the attorney's face, as if inspecting it. "I have to tell you something, but maybe this isn't a good time."

"Something happen to Jimmy?"

Granger nodded, took a deep breath, and exhaled slowly. "It's about the worst news I could give you about your client."

The blood drained from the Lieutenant's face.

"What—what happened?"

Granger put his hand on the attorney's shoulder. "He hanged himself."

Matt's face screwed up in pain. "How?"

"Used his t-shirt. Ripped it into pieces and made a short rope. There's a small metal cage over the light in the ceiling. He managed to work the rope through one of the bars."

Daniels shook his head and looked down at the table. "I, I should have known he was suicidal. Should have insisted you put a watch on him."

"It isn't your fault, no more than it's ours."

Daniels shook his head again. "Yeah, it is. I'm supposed to be my clients' advocate. I'm supposed to keep them safe when they're in the system."

Mike asked, "Has this ever happened before? I don't recall anyone in the police station jail killing himself before."

Granger leveled his gaze at Mike. "We've had a couple of attempts, but, you're right. No one's ever been successful."

"Well," Bob said, "it'll save the taxpayers a load of money."

Daniels shot him a hateful look, and Mike laughed nervously, saying, "Christ, Bob, that's pretty cold."

"Sorry," said Bob. "I know what happened to Jimmy was awful, but what he did was worse. The sins committed against him don't excuse the sins he committed."

Lieutenant Daniels leaped to his feet and lurched across the table, trying to grab Bob's shirt, but Granger stopped him.

"Let's go, Counselor," the detective said. "We've got some paperwork to do before this night's over."

Detective Granger kept his large paws on Lieutenant's shoulder and guided him toward the stairs.

I sat quite still, trying to make sense out of

everything. Dizzy, I thought I might pass out. Was this death my fault, too? If I hadn't challenged Jimmy Collins that first night, and if I hadn't punched him in the face the next, he might have gone on his merry way.

The image of Sherry's battered face filled my head, and I felt like throwing up. Then Jimmy Collins—his face blue, eyes bulging from the sockets, tongue hanging out.

"It's too much," I said. "It's all too much."

With tunnel vision and my chest feeling crushed, I stood and staggered toward the stairs. I made it back to my hotel room and opened the other bottle of scotch. Sitting on the bed, I drank from the bottle, a few gulps at a time, until it was empty and I let it drop. The last thing I remember was watching the green bottle roll into the bathroom, clinking across the tiles.

Hours later someone was banging on my door. I stared at the clock. Seven in the morning.

"Who's there?" I yelled.

"It's the manager, Mister Randall. Today's the day you got to check out."

"Give me a few hours."

"Okay, okay, but you get out by ten o'clock, okay?"

I rolled over and saw that I'd thrown up on the bedspread that covered the pillow next to my head. The vomit stank. I managed to stand, and, though wobbly, I pulled the bedspread off the bed, balled it up and tossed it onto the floor of the shower. When I climbed back onto the bed, I saw that the vomit had soaked through, wetting the pillow, so I tossed it into

157

the bathroom as well.

A few hours later, more banging on the door.

"Mr. Randall, you got to go, okay?"

"Yeah, yeah," I yelled. "Just gettin' in the shower."

"See that you do!" the manager yelled. Her deep smoker's voice sounded phlegmy. "I'm callin' da taxi for you right away. Understand? Right away!"

I dragged myself into the bathroom and showered, and after dressing, threw my clothes into the suitcase.

Sure enough, the taxi was waiting for me at the curb.

"Lady says you're goin' to the airport. Is that right, mon?"

"Yeah. The airport," I managed.

*   *   *

The American Airlines counter was busy. The first flight out was going to Miami by way of San Juan. On the plane, I managed to sleep until we landed on San Juan, which from the window, looked flat, dull, hazy.

A few passengers disembarked, but a dozen more came aboard. Shortly after we took off, the stewardess came down the aisle pushing a drink cart. I got a Seven-up, the only thing I felt I could keep down. By the time we reached Florida, I was starting to feel better, and the view of Miami from the window of the plane got me thinking about something other than Jimmy Collins and Sherry.

I followed people through the terminal toward the baggage claim and taxi stands, unsure where I was going to go. I'd almost convinced myself to turn around and buy another ticket back to California when I felt a tap on my shoulder. I recognized the guy from the plane as one of the passengers who'd boarded in San Juan.

"You headin' into Miami Beach?" he asked.

"Maybe. Why?"

"You want to split a cab? Save a little dough?"

I'm not sure why, but I agreed. As I followed him to the cab stand, I looked him over, uncertain what I was getting into. He was about my height, maybe in his mid-thirties, dressed in expensive-looking vacation clothes, a clean short-sleeved shirt with epaulets on the shoulders and creased tan slacks. His brown loafers looked new. Even the tassels seemed polished. On his left wrist was a gold watch, and after we'd climbed into the back seat, I noticed the brand name when he slipped his briefcase behind the passenger's seat. It was a Rolex. A gold band was on his left ring finger.

The driver leaned back as he pulled away from the curb and asked, "Where to?"

"I'm staying at the Fontainebleau," my companion said. "How 'bout you?"

"What a coincidence," I lied. "That's where I'm going, too."

I'd never been to Miami and had no idea where to stay, so following his lead seemed as good a plan as any. After the cab pulled onto the freeway and we settled in for the drive, the stranger reached over to shake my hand.

"My name's Jason Fienes," he said, "but everyone calls me Jay."

159

I shook his hand, saying, "I'm Randall."

He had a good, strong.

"What brings you to Miami, Randall?"

I shrugged. "Takin' some time off from school."

"On spring break?"

"In a way." I didn't feel like saying much. "I'm actually taking a semester off."

He chuckled. "School getting too tough for you?"

I looked at him. "My dad died a few weeks ago."

His expression changed from bemused superiority to sympathy. "Oh, I'm sorry. Was it a long illness?"

"No. He had a heart attack."

Jay frowned. "That's got to be tough."

"Hasn't been easy," I admitted. I changed the subject. "What brings you here?"

"A dental conference," he said matter-of-factly. "I'm a dentist. Got my own practice in Iowa."

"Iowa?" I was surprised. "Didn't you get on the plane in San Juan?"

"Yeah. Went down there with my family for a vacation before heading to the conference."

"How was it?"

"Humid. Even at the beach. And expensive. Spent more than I'd planned."

"You should've come to St. Thomas," I said.

"We went there last spring. Thought we'd do a different island this year."

"We?" I asked.

"My wife and daughter were with me. In fact, they were supposed to join me here in Miami, but my daughter got sick."

I nodded but kept my face pointed toward the glass. Tall hotel buildings appeared, and the sky was
160

blue between large white clouds. On one side of the boulevard was a canal, and on the other, rows of resort hotels.

We rode in silence until we reached the Fontainebleau, an enormous white structure that curved like a crescent moon. I wasn't sure what architectural style it was, maybe art d éco or post-modern, but it was impressive—and a little intimidating—a far cry from the little Midtown Hotel on St. Thomas. After paying the cabbie, we walked into the spacious, white lobby together, carrying our bags. I felt out of my league, having never stayed at a resort hotel that looked so ritzy.

Two clerks at the counter waived us forward, and I heard Jay give the clerk his name. He clicked away at his computer and said, "Yes, Mr. Fienes. We have you in a room with two double beds, is that correct?"

"Actually my wife and daughter won't be joining me after all, so can I switch to a room with a king?"

"Oh, I'm sorry," the clerk said. "We're booked solid with the conference."

My clerk, who'd been writing something on a notepad, finally looked up. "Name?"

"Randall Wake," I told him, hoping someone named Randall or Randy anything had made a reservation.

The clerk clicked away on the keyboard, scowled, then clicked on something with the mouse, but shook his head before asking, "Did you make a reservation?"

Feigning bewilderment, I nodded. "Certainly did. Weeks ago."

From the corner of my eye, I noticed Jay glancing

over.

Still staring at his computer monitor while typing away, my clerk said, "Well, I'm terribly sorry, Mr. Wake, but I don't seem to have a reservation for you now. Do you have your reservation number by any chance?"

My face burned, but I tried to make it appear that I was angry, not embarrassed. "No, I didn't expect I'd need a confirmation number at this hotel."

Then I looked at Jay, pretending to be annoyed.

"Is there a problem?" he asked.

"They lost my reservation."

"Bummer," he replied. His clerk held out some forms for him to sign.

"Do you have a room for me or not?" I asked the clerk.

He frowned politely and shook his head. "I'm so sorry, but the hotel is completely booked. We're hosting two different conventions this weekend."

I looked down at my shoes. Still groggy and hung over, I couldn't think.

"I can call other hotels for you, sir," the clerk offered. "To see if they have a vacancy."

"That would help."

The clerk picked up the phone and started to punch in a number, turning away from me as he waited for someone to talk to. I just wanted to climb into a bed and sleep.

Jay tapped my shoulder again. "I've got an extra bed in my room, if you want to bunk with me."

"Thanks, but I couldn't impose like that."

"We can split the cost. Save me a little cash."

I shrugged, inspecting Jay's expression.

"Hey, you'd be doing me a favor," he added. "Like I told you, I splurged in San Juan, so I wouldn't mind saving money."

By that time, my clerk had hung up and was looking at me. "The first place I tried is all booked up. Do you want me to try someplace else, or…"

Jay's clerk seemed to be awaiting my decision, too.

"Well," I said, "if it's really okay with you, then, sure."

After the formalities, Jay and I were inside an elevator riding up to our room. Under normal circumstances, I would have felt uncomfortable, but Jay seemed like a decent guy, and I just wanted a place to crash.

"You feelin' okay?" he asked.

"Actually, I'm a little hung over."

Jay grinned. "Yeah, you look a little green around the gills."

"Think I'll take a nap before dinner."

He nodded. "I could use one myself, but I've got to check into the conference and then there's a banquet."

When we got inside the room, Jay stopped between the two beds. "Which one would you like?"

"I don't care."

"Well, I'd prefer the one closer to the door, if that's okay."

The room was plush. I tossed my bag on the other bed and opened the curtains. Our window faced west, so sunlight streamed in—the sun was just over the rooftops of the buildings across the street.

Jay unzipped his bag and started unpacking, and I

163

kicked off my shoes and lay down on the bed with my head propped on the pillows. Staring out the window at the endless blue sky, I could feel myself drifting off.

"Don't want to seem rude," I said, "but I'm falling asleep, so have a great time at your conference."

Jay chuckled. "We all get hammered the first night, so we can just settle in and take the rest of the conference seriously."

I grimaced, imagining a banquet room filled with dentists chasing each other around with pliers in their hands, trying to pull out each other's teeth.

Chapter 16

Of course, I would dream.

Two bloodied corpses lay beside each other on a blood-drenched bed, their nude bodies glistening under the light of a full moon outside an opened sliding glass door. People were standing on the patio, cocktail glasses in their hands, whispering to one another as they peered inside. A man dressed in a white smock was struggling to pull teeth from Sherry's mouth. He was obviously frustrated and kept looking over his shoulder at me as if silently pleading for help. Sherry's eyes bulged with fear, but she seemed paralyzed, unable to move, except for her darting eyes.

Finally, the nightmare dentist ripped a molar from Sherry's mouth and held it up for all to see. "Got it!" he declared, and the folks outside cheered.

The gleaming white tooth was disproportionately large, and bloody roots splayed from the end of it like the legs of a red squid squirming to get free of the pliers.

The dentist handed me the pliers, saying, "Your turn."

That's when I woke up sweating, my heart

pounding so hard I thought I was having a heart attack.

I couldn't remember where I was. The room was dark, except for city lights streaming in through the window. When I stood and looked outside, I recalled how I'd arrived in Florida. I missed my father painfully just then. He wasn't always an affectionate man, but once a few years ago when we were decorating the Christmas tree, I turned to him with tears welling up in my eyes and said, "I sure miss Mom."

He put his arm on my shoulder and said, "I do, too, son. I do too."

Above the rooftops, the sky was dark enough that the first stars were showing. Looking at them, I said, "I miss you, Dad." But, of course, there was no answer, and the darkness made me gloomier, so I turned on the lamp beside the bed. Its light painted a wide orange fan on the wall.

It was almost nine. I knew I should eat, so I showered, dressed and went to the restaurant off the lobby.

It was packed. The maître d' told me I could eat at the bar. So I found myself once again sitting at a long bar, waiting to be served. The bartender was a tall, fit, well-dressed man in his mid-thirties. He looked like he was in the military. I ordered a scotch and soda and asked for a menu.

While he made my drink, I scanned the room. Most of the customers looked like professional men in their mid-thirties or late forties, and even though they were dressed in different clothes, all wore variations of the same yuppy uniforms—loose-fitting

Hawaiian shirts, cream-colored slacks and leather sandals. At some tables, one or two attractive women sat, surrounded by adoring men, soaking up the attention.

My drink came, along with a menu, so I ordered a steak and French fries, with a small salad on the side. I could watch the crowd in the mirror behind the bar, the images broken by glass shelves lined with various colored liquor bottles. *This place probably does more business in one night than the Galleon House did in a week.*

Thinking about the Galleon House brought back a flood of memories. I pictured Mike and Whitey and Gillian smiling and laughing, which made me feel better. Memories of making love to Maggie popped into my mind, too, and whenever a bloody image tried to squirm in, I pushed it out.

My father would have asked me to describe my best memory, and it was easy. I replayed as much of the scuba dive with Sherry as I could. Seeing her eyes behind the glass of her facemask go wide with fear when she saw the shark swim toward us. Seeing the bubbles rush out of her mouth when she laughed. Being alone with her in the quiet calm of the sea water was the happiest memory of all.

I picked at the food. It was delicious, but I was afraid I'd get sick if I ate too much. I ordered another drink and sipped it while trying to decide what the hell to do next with my life.

Part of me wanted to go to the roof and let myself fall off. I just saw no point in going on. I closed my eyes and imagined falling off the edge of the roof, my body plummeting through the night air, weightless

167

until it struck the pavement. My father would be furious if he were alive and knew I was thinking that way, and my brother would be angry—he'd probably blame himself for not being there for me.

I felt an arm on my shoulder and for a second I thought it was dad. When I opened my eyes, I saw my roommate Jay reflected in the mirror behind the bar, a goofy grin on his face.

"What you doin' all by yer-self here, buddy?" He was hammered.

"Got hungry," I said, nodding toward the platter. The gristle I'd cut from the steak lay like a question mark on the plate.

"Food's pretty good here, huh?"

"Yeah. Have you eaten?"

"We ate hours ago," Jay said. "Now we're just drinkin' and tellin' lies." He pointed to a table in the far corner. "C'mon. I'll introduce you to my comrades. One's an oral surgeon, and he's been buyin' us his favorite scotch. Is very 'spensive."

I picked up my glass and followed Jay to the table that held his five friends. All of them were pretty drunk middle-aged men with their shirts open too low and tufts of chest hair spilling out, as if this was their idea of cutting loose.

Jay introduced me to everyone, but I couldn't really hear their names. I pulled a chair away from another table. Soon they were telling dirty jokes and laughing too loud, and I sat there next to Jay, wondering why I was there.

After a while, an attractive young waitress in a low-cut dress came over and took their drink orders. They all order Glen Levitz scotch. Jay told me I had to try it. When the waitress leaned over to pick up the empty glasses, the men sitting across from her hooped and hollered.

"Thanks for the peep show, Ginger!" one yelled.

"Oh, baby, do I want to go to Gilligan's Island with you!" another said. "I bet I could make those volcanoes erupt."

She grinned, aware she was giving them an eyeful.

When Ginger left, Jay leaned over and said, "I'd like to impact those molars!" Then he leaned away and laughed like it was the funniest joke he'd ever heard.

I watched the waitress weave between the tables. Everyone in the bar was in their mid-thirties or older. As far as I could tell, only the waitress and I were in our early twenties.

When the drinks came, I tried to pay for mine but the dentist sitting across the table waved me off. "This round's on me." He held out a hundred dollar bill, requiring the waitress to lean across the table to reach it, which brought on a fresh round of whistles and hollers. She took the hundred and tucked it into her cleavage, smiling the whole time.

"Thanks for the tip," she said. "Now who's paying for the drinks?"

It took the others at the table a few seconds, but then they burst into laughter and the scotch drinker pulled out another hundred dollar bill. "Keep 'em comin', honey," he said.

She smiled at me. "I always do."

That line brought on another round of hollers and whistles, and I felt myself blush, though I knew the

169

room was too dark for anyone to notice.

For the next hour, I vaguely listened to the conversations. At times, the men talked seriously about their profession, but most of the time they made lewd jokes about the ways they would pleasure the waitress or what they'd like to do with all the college girls who were in Miami for spring break.

Jay said loudly, "Why you think I got Randy here to room with me? He's my wing man. Gonna introduce me to all the hot young coeds, aren't you, Randy?"

"Sure," I said. "That's a perfect job for me."

"What's a perfect job?"

"Pimp," I answered.

He laughed, but I think he knew I was annoyed.

"Where's the restroom?" I asked.

Jay looked at me, as if repeating the question in his mind, then he pointed to the far end of the bar.

"Back in a few minutes," I said.

"You want another drink?"

"No, I don't think so."

"You sure? It's on me."

I walked away without answering and headed to the bathroom. The men's room was spacious but poorly lit. I washed up after relieving myself and studied my face in the mirror. I needed a shave. The nap hadn't done much to reduce the bags under my eyes.

The waitress stood at the corner of the bar, counting bills on her tray.

"You don't look old enough to be a dentist," she said without looking up.

"I'm not."

"Oh?" She folded the bills and tucked them into her bra. "What are you doing hanging out with those guys?"

I shrugged. "Flew back from Puerto Rico with that one guy, Jay."

She looked me up and down. "What were you two doing in Puerto Rico?"

"No, no, we weren't there together. I was flying back from St. Thomas, and we wound up on the same plane, that's all."

"So you two aren't together, together?"

I laughed. "No, not at all. I'm straight and he's married, so I'm pretty sure he's straight, too."

"You'd be surprised," she said. "A lot of married men come to Miami Beach and wind up with another man. It's sort of a thing here."

I held out my hand. "I'm Randall."

"I'm Marion."

We shook hands, and I held hers a bit too long. "But your nametag says Ginger?"

"That's my stage name.

So you're an actress?"

She grinned. "Haven't you heard, honey? All the world is a stage, so of course I'm an actress. Especially in my line of work."

"You do have a lot of stage presence."

"If you mean I have big tits, I already know that."

I frowned. "That's not what I meant. Not at all."

I started to walk away, but she grabbed my arm.

"Sorry. I'm used to a lot of crass comments working here, wearing this outfit."

"No problem," I said, starting to walk away again.

"I get off in about an hour. If you're still around, you want to have breakfast?"

"Breakfast? At two in the morning?"

"Takes me a while to wind down."

"Maybe another time," I said. "Kind of tired tonight."

"C'mon. Keep me company."

I glanced around the room. It was well after midnight and the crowd was thinning out. I really didn't want to get involved with another girl. It just seemed weird so soon after what had happened.

"Hey, I'm not asking you to marry me or anything," she said, sounding a bit embarrassed. "I just like a little conversation with my meal."

"Sure," I said. "Get me when you're ready. I'll be over there with the tooth fairies."

Chapter 17

As I walked back to the table, seeing all those drunken men in their loud shirts, I had the eerie feeling I was back in St. Thomas. Jay was Mike, the bartender, and Marion, Maggie. *Who among this crowd would be Jimmy Collins?* Maybe I was in a kind of hell or purgatory where, no matter where I traveled, I'd end up with a new group of fast friends, some of whom would be killed.

Jay pointed to a glass as I sat down.

"Ordered you another drink anyway."

His eyelids were sagging.

"Thanks, but I really didn't want one."

"Oh, don't be a fuckin' pussy. Drink up."

"Hey, I appreciate the gesture, but don't get belligerent, okay?"

He glared at me with glazed eyes, and for a second, I thought he might take a swing at me. Instead, he threw his arm over my shoulder.

"Sorry, man. Guess I've had too much to drink."

"You want to head back to the room?"

Pulling his arm off my shoulder, he nodded. "Probably should." Jay pushed his chair back and tried to stand, but plopped back down, laughing.

"Geez, I'm hammered."

I looked at his friends for help, but they were swapping stories and ignoring us. Besides, they all seemed equally hammered.

"Here," I said, "let me help."

Jay stood up with me and put his arm over my shoulder.

"See guys later," he said to the table.

I managed to steer him out of the restaurant to the elevator, and after a short ride, I got him into the room.

"Gotta pee," he said.

I turned him toward the bathroom and watched as he held himself up by holding onto the sink. When he had finished, he zipped up and walked toward me, grinning stupidly.

"Like a race horse," he said.

Jay staggered to his bed, slipped off his shoes, and climbed under the covers. Lying on his back, he said to the ceiling, "Thanks for getting me here."

"No problem, pal." I couldn't help but smile at him.

Downstairs. the table where we'd been sitting was empty, and it had been cleared. The rest of the bar was almost empty, too, and Marion strolled over to me, smiling.

"Get your friend settled in okay?"

"Yeah. He's plastered."

She nodded for me to follow and she led me to the bar. "I thought you might come back, so I saved your drink."

"Thanks," I said, climbing onto a barstool. "How soon do you get off?"

She smiled a coy little grin. "Well, I clock out in five minutes, if that's what you mean? As for getting off, we'll have to wait and see."

I held her gaze, but my heart wasn't it.

"Finish your drink while I change."

She walked away, and I picked up the drink and sipped it. The ice had watered it down, which was okay with me.

When Marion came back, her hair was in a pony tail and her makeup was more subtle. The low-cut dress had been replaced by a tight-fitting white cotton tee-shirt and faded blue jeans.

"Wow," I said. "You look... different."

"Less like a hooker, right?"

"You didn't look like a hooker before."

"Sure, I did. Part of the job. Get the guys hot so they want to impress you, and they leave bigger tips." She waved goodbye to the bartender and nodded for me to follow. "Are you hungry?"

"No, not really. You?"

"Starving."

We walked out of the lobby and turned down the street. Even though it was almost two in the morning, it was still warm and a bit humid. When we crossed the street, I felt the breeze blowing in off the Atlantic and smelled the salty air. It reminded me of St. Thomas and a chill went down my back.

"So what fancy café are you taking me to?" I asked, trying to get my mind off of images of Sherry.

"Oh, it's a charming little out of the way spot that only the locals know of."

We turned the corner and came to a Denny's. Marion held the door open for me, grinning.

"Very classy," I said. "I'm amazed the tourists haven't discovered it."

"Quaint, huh?"

She led me to a booth in the back and I slid in beside her. The waitress—a lanky lady wearing too much red lipstick—strolled over with a coffee pot.

"Who's your handsome friend?"

"This is Randall. Randall, meet Paula Fox."

She held out her hand. "Everyone calls me Foxy."

"That's because you are," Marion said.

"Hello, Foxy," I said, shaking her hand.

"For an old gal, I'm not too shabby. You want the usual, hon?"

"You know I do," Marion answered.

"How 'bout you, hon. What'll you have?"

"Just a couple of eggs over easy and some wheat toast."

Foxy stared down at me. "Oh, a health nut, huh?" She poured two cups of coffee and walked away.

"She used to work at the Carnage Delicatessen in Manhattan," Marion told me. "Moved down here about ten years ago when she caught her dirt bag husband cheating on her, and she's been one of my best friends ever since."

I nodded, sipping my coffee.

"So what's your story, Randall? What brings you to Miami Beach?"

Setting the cup down carefully, I said, "Honestly, I got on the first flight I could out of St. Thomas. I just wanted to get off that island as fast as possible."

Marion pulled her leg up and sat on it. "Ooo, this sounds intriguing. Tell me more."

"Can we talk about something else? I'm trying to

176

leave all that business behind."

"Sure. Yeah. Let's talk about the weather."

"Tell me about your job," I said. "You love it or hate it?"

"Both. I love meeting interesting people, but I hate it when someone treats me like an airhead just because I show a little cleavage. The money's good, and the job gives me a workout, so I keep in good shape."

"How long have you been there?"

"About three years. Foxy helped me land that job."

Our food came, my small plate with two perfectly cooked eggs, and her platter of French toast, scrambled eggs, four sausage links and hash browns.

"You're going to eat all that?" I asked.

She picked up a sausage link and put it between her lips, nodding.

We ate in silence—I nibbling my food, while Marion ate ravenously. She finished her food almost as soon as I'd finished mine.

"Where do you put it all?"

"I only eat two meals a day, so I need my fuel."

Pushing her platter aside, she said, "Now you've stalled long enough. Tell me what happened on the island. Why did you have to leave in a hurry?"

I looked at her, feeling like I might cry, and she must have read my expression because the smile left her lips.

"Something pretty awful happened down there, didn't it?"

I nodded. "Are you sure you want to hear it?"

She touched my hand, which was still resting on

the table near my coffee cup.

"Maybe telling someone will help."

"Maybe I should talk to a priest or a psychiatrist instead."

"I'm getting my Master's in behavioral psychology," she said, "so maybe I can be of some help."

I looked at her clear, brown eyes.

"It's a pretty sad story. A young couple about our age was murdered in their sleep, and another couple badly injured."

"And you cared about them, didn't you?"

I shrugged, feeling a tear roll down my cheek.

Marion listened to the whole tale with a sympathetic expression. I told her about my crush on Sherry and lying about my age, the fights with Jimmy Collins and then talking to him in jail later. I didn't tell her about my parents though. Nor did I describe how Sherry looked with her face caved in, nor about the Jackson Pollack painting in blood on the walls.

When I'd finished, she closed her eyes, took a deep breath and exhaled slowly. "Those people meant something to you," she whispered. "More than you'll admit, I suspect." Her voice was soft as if we were whispering in church.

"Maybe."

She peered into my eyes as if she were looking for a soul. "The question is, why do you push your feelings down the way you do? Did some other terrible tragedy happen earlier in your life?"

"A tragedy?" I repeated. I looked to the ceiling, taking a deep breath. "I learned somewhere that it's only a tragedy if someone of great status falls from
178

grace and dies. You know, like Oedipus or Hamlet. I'm neither."

"Now you're avoiding answering the question. That's classic."

"Well, my mother died when I was pretty young, after a long battle with cancer."

Marion nodded.

"So, Doctor Freud," I said, "are you going to tell me that I suppress my emotions because of the loss of my mother's love?"

She stared at me blankly. "What do you think?"

"Oh my God, you really are studying to be a psychiatrist."

"No, not a psychiatrist. A psychologist."

"What's the difference?"

"About three more years of college and a hundred grand in student loans."

I sipped the tepid coffee.

"Funny you mentioned Oedipus," she said. "Freud would have a field day with your situation."

"Oh? What might the good doctor say?"

"He'd probably say, since your mom died when you were young, your feelings toward her were stunted and, as a result, you idealized her. You were denied the opportunity to grow out of the early romantic attraction toward her, which stunted your emotional maturation."

"Very interesting," I said, yawning. "So I'm in love with my dead mother and I'll never have a normal relationship with other women—is that your diagnosis?"

"Something along those lines."

"Great. Thanks. What do I owe you for this

session?"

"Seriously, though, Randall, at some point you'll need to deal with the loss of your mother. You should spend some time with a good therapist and sort out your feelings. Otherwise, you'll go through life unable to feel and express honest emotions in a healthy way. Especially toward women."

Her voice was soft and sincere and utterly condescending. "What makes you think I haven't already dealt with the loss of my mother? I've dealt with it every fucking day of my life."

She pulled away, frowning. "By that outburst, you're proving me right."

"Am I?"

"Yes. You aren't in control of your emotions. Too quick to anger."

I stared at her, the coffee churning inside my stomach. "You want an honest expression of my emotions? I honestly want to slap your smug face."

She didn't seem shocked. "That's an interesting response, Randall. I express concern for you and offer advice, and your reaction is anger and a threat of violence. You might want to think about that."

I slid out of the booth and stood. "You can pay for my meal out of the tip I left you." From the corner of my eye, I saw her waitress friend heading over and I knew it was time to leave.

Chapter 18

Inside the hotel room, the bathroom smelled of vomit. Jay had gotten sick while I was out, but he was snoring away under the covers, so I knew he was alive. I tried to sleep, but the conversation with Marion replayed in my head. I knew she was right, that I should probably talk to someone about all the emptiness I was feeling, but it was still embarrassing to hear it. I lay in the darkness wondering if my pathetic condition was somehow plastered on my face for all to see. In a way, I was as pathetic as the Caribbean prisoner, Jimmy Collins, drifting through life, damaging everyone I met.

Jay's electric shaver woke me up. It was almost eight in the morning, but the room was still dark, though I could see a sliver of sunlight between the heavy curtains.

Wearing only a pair of light-brown slacks, Jay popped out of the bathroom. "You're awake?"

"My eyes are open."

He chuckled. "That's a start." He pulled a shirt off a hanger and put it on, asking, "Do you know how I got to my room last night?"

I sat up against the headboard. "I helped you."

"Man, I really overdid it. I barely remember

asking you to join us. What happened after that?"

"I joined you. We drank and joked around, and then I helped you back to the room."

"Well, thanks. Guess I owe you one." He pulled out a tie and put it on, tying a Windsor knot while watching himself in the closet mirror. "I have to give a paper at ten-thirty, so got to look the part. What do you have planned for today?"

My mind was blank. The question made me realize how empty and pointless my life was. "Might look for a job," I lied.

"A job? Here? I thought you lived in California?"

"Nothing's really holding me there."

Jay shrugged while tugging on a dark blue blazer. "Well, good luck." He grabbed a leather valise and opened the door. "If you're not busy, come find me at about five- thirty for dinner."

"Will do," I called, watching the door close as he left.

Then I was alone in the dark room.

If I had had a straight razor, I would have slit my wrists.

I lay there visualizing red blood spurting from the open wounds, knowing I'd drift toward dim unconsciousness and then into serene eternal sleep.

But the maid might come in.

She'd scream, upon seeing my bed sheets soak with blood.

And maybe I'd be saved. But to what end?

I'd be sent to a mental hospital, and who knows how long they'd keep there, poking at me with their insulting questions the way Marion had.

No. Bleeding to death in a hotel room bed before room service showed up was not an answer. If I really wanted to do it, then falling off the roof was the best way.

That was enough reason to drag myself out of bed and take a shower. I laughed at myself in the shower, thinking, *Why do I need to be clean to fall off the roof?*

Nevertheless, I showered and shampooed my hair and shaved my face. I opened the curtains and looked out at the sunshine on the buildings across the street. Then I dressed and left the room with my wallet in my hip pocket and the room key in the front pocket of my shorts.

As I waited for the elevator, I wondered, *Why did I take the room key?*

That's when I knew I didn't really want to die yet. It could wait. Maybe later in the day. Maybe tomorrow. Maybe next week. *What's my hurry?*

When the elevator doors opened, I stepped inside. A young family of four was on board, a clean-cut man about Jay's age, with an attractive, if plump, wife and two kids, a boy who looked about five and a girl who looked at least seven.

"Are you here for the conference?" I asked.

"He is," the wife answered. "We just tagged along to play."

"We might go to Disneyland," the little girl said.

"Disneyworld," the father corrected. "Disneyland's in California."

We reached the lobby, and I got away from them as soon as I could. Heat radiated from the sidewalk. I started walking south toward the sun, having no idea where I was going or what I was doing. But walking gave me a sense of purpose.

There's something about being in a city you've never seen before that makes you feel alive. I studied the facades of the buildings, the fire escapes in the alleys, the pigeons roosting on the telephone lines, the palm trees holding the fronds up to the sky like offerings. I walked by an older apartment building painted pink and observed old men sitting on the veranda reading newspapers. *How had they wound up here? Were they alone? Had their wives died or divorced them? What kept them going? Is it enough to wake up each day, just to drink a cup of coffee and read the paper?*

Finally, I reached a part of the road where the buildings looked so run down that I thought it might not be safe to go on, so I turned around and headed back. I wasn't hungry exactly, but my stomach was churning, so I looked for a decent restaurant. I found one with a Help Wanted sign in the window.

Most of the customers were older couples. I found an empty table near the back. The place was about the same size as the Denny's I'd been in the previous night, but it was much older. Clean but dreary. A heavy-set middle-aged guy dressed like a short-order cook brought a menu over.

"Coffee?" he asked, handing me the menu.

"Sure."

He grabbed a coffee pot, walked back, turned over my cup and filled it.

"Is it too early for a BLT?"

"Nope. What kind of bread?"

"Wheat toast, I guess."

"Comin' right up."

Sure enough, he stepped around the corner and started cooking in the kitchen. He obviously needed a waiter.

I imagined working in this place. I studied the faces of the old men and women, some of whom were carefully lifting food to their mouths. I watched one couple in particular. The man looked comatose. He stared blankly out the window while sipping his coffee as if he was bored to tears and just waiting for the grim reaper to stroll in and snatch him up.

The skin of the woman's face was deeply wrinkled, especially around her mouth, and her skin was coated with makeup, her lips painted bright red. She wore too much blue eye shadow and her hair was almost as blue as her eye shadow. Watching her chew turned my stomach.

She must have sensed that I was staring at her, for she turned and grinned, revealing flecks of lipstick on her perfect white teeth that had to be dentures.

I nodded, trying not to be rude, but looked away. Yesterday's newspaper was on the chair behind me, so I grabbed it. The day-old paper was full of interesting, horrible stories; reading it was like reading a murder mystery. All the horror and death seemed completely unrelated, but somehow I sensed a master plan at work.

I was startled when the cook put the sandwich down in front of me.

"Anything else?" he asked. "Juice? Soda?"

I looked into his exhausted eyes. "No, thanks."

The sandwich looked okay though the lettuce seemed wilted and brown around the edges. The bacon was under-cooked, and the tomato was without flavor. The mayonnaise tasted fishy. I ate half of it before pushing it away.

If the food had been good, I might have asked about the job. And though I didn't want to work in this place, the Help Wanted sign had given me the idea that maybe working as a waiter in a nicer restaurant might be fun. For awhile.

With a new sense of purpose, I strolled back toward the hotel, stopping at each business that looked promising, filling out applications. I went into a florist shop, a dozen different restaurants, even a few medical offices. All of the people were polite and gave me the applications. Most said they weren't hiring, but they'd keep my application on file. I gave them my room number at the hotel for an address, which made a few of the secretaries smile. I wondered if they thought I was advertising myself as ready, willing and able to date them.

The thing is, I didn't care. I didn't care if I got a job, or if one of those horny gals called me for a date, or if I stayed in that hotel until I was finally ready to jump off the roof. I figured I was now living on borrowed time. One more day of life or twelve more days—what did it matter?

Both the temperature and the humidity were in the 90s that afternoon, so by the time I got back to the hotel room, I was hot and exhausted.

"Man, you look like hell!" the dentist said when he came in.

"I just got in from hell. It's insane out there."

"What'd you do all day?"

"Looked for a job."

"Any work?"

I laughed and told him what folks had told me—that Miami Beach would virtually shut down after college students were finished with spring break

He offered to buy me dinner, and I accepted because I had not eaten much all day. Inside the restaurant, the gabbing of people and clatter of dishes drowned out the soft radio music. We sat by the window with a view of the Atlantic. The ocean mirrored the sky, and there was no visible horizon between them. *How could life suddenly seem so hopeless? Days and nights and days rolling into each other like formless gray clouds.* An attractive waitress came, took our orders and left.

"You look like you're lost in thought. Or just exhausted?"

"Both, I guess. Feeling a little…"

"Restless?"

"More like lost."

"I know the feeling. That changes once you get tied down and have kids."

I nodded, but looked away, and Jay let me dwell inside my own thoughts.

The waitress came with two platters of New York steaks and baked potatoes on her arm, nonchalantly balancing them as if part of a floor show. We'd ordered beer, and I was almost done with my bottle before I zeroed in on the label.

SAINT ELMO

Bottled and Distilled in the Virgin Islands

"Why in the hell did you order this beer?"

Jay shrugged. "I thought you'd want something to remind you of your holiday on St. Thomas."

187

I pushed the bottle away. "I'd rather forget most of it."

"Why? What happened?"

I ignored him and he didn't press me. I switched to scotch and soda, and Jay ordered rum and coke. After our second drink, Jay spoke up. "Want to talk about it?"

"I think I'm just burned out on school. Maybe I should take a year off and work."

Jay nodded. "You okay for money?"

"My dad's life insurance will keep me afloat for a few years, I guess."

"You know how I became a dentist? Got trained by the Air Force. Best decision I ever made. Six years of training on Uncle Sam's dime, and when I got out, I joined a lucrative practice. Now I'm set for life."

I laughed. "You think I should join the Air Force?"

"Doesn't have to be the Air Force. You like the ocean, right? Maybe the Navy?"

I pictured Jimmy Collins and his friends in their brilliant white uniforms, and then imagined the commanding officer he'd described, doing what he'd done to Jimmy. It made me sick.

But it also made me think.

We had another round and drank in relative silence until Jay suggested we walk down the boulevard.

"Let's check out some other bars."

Traffic was thick. Double lanes of cars reflected roadside signs and lights, shiny mirrors of all shapes and designs. Streetlights pushed against the night-blueness of the sky. The sun had gone completely down, but it threw orange fire on the storm clouds moving east. The stifling humidity made my shirt cling to my sweaty back.

I watched the twin rivers of light from the traffic that moved in contrary directions, and I wished I could be carried away. I wanted to jump on one of those massive ocean liners I'd seen inside the bay of Charlotte Amalie and cruise away, far from the continent that held the decaying bodies of both my parents, knowing the earth would soon swallow Sherry's mangled body as well.

Chapter 19

The farther we walked, the closer we came to brightly lit bars and clubs where loud music vibrated the windows and people of all sorts danced and laughed on the patios just off the sidewalk. The colors, the noise, the laughter and music were contagious. Soon I couldn't help but get caught up in the scene. Jay steered me into a club packed with people closer to my age than his, and as he paid the cover charge for both of us, he leaned over and yelled above the Latin music, "You gotta be my wing man, okay?"

We pushed through the sweaty, perfumed bodies to the bar and ordered. I switched to gin and tonic and ordered a double. Jay stuck with rum and coke, yelling, "Me and the Captain make it happen!"

Grabbing my drink, I turned around to scan the crowd. Most of the guys wore tight black jeans and even tighter shirts, and the girls wore tight, low-cut sundresses or tight tee-shirts and tighter shorts. The music infected everyone—we were all dancing in place, rocking and swaying and bumping up against each other's bodies because it was unavoidable. Sex was in the air so thick I thought everyone might bust into an orgy.

Jay's smile told me he was in heaven. A cute Latino girl with long jet black hair looked up at me smiling as she sipped the straw in her drink. She rubbed against me like a Salsa dancer, so I moved against her in unison and felt myself get hard for the first time in days. She felt it too, laughed and spun around so her butt was against me, grinding so hard I was afraid I'd climax. But she knew when to stop, I guess, and moved away. My eyes were closed, so I didn't see where she went at first, but then she put her hand inside the open shirt of a body builder who'd evidently just come back from the bathroom. Maybe he'd been dancing with her before me and had to clean himself up.

"C'mon," Jay yelled. "I see a table opening up."

He pushed between bodies toward the patio where two young couples were gathering up their things. As soon as they slid off the stools, Jay pounced and pushed away another couple who'd been eyeing the same spot. I sat down across from him and looked out the open windows to the packed patio.

"Who was that girl you were dancing with?" Jay yelled.

"I have no idea."

"She was a hot little thing, though, wasn't she?"

I nodded and sipped my drink.

"We've got to find two more like her," he yelled.

"You're a married man, Jay."

"Not tonight," he yelled, holding up his left hand. His wedding ring was off, but the impression of it was still on his finger.

"It's that easy?" I asked him.

He smile and nodded. "Now flash that great smile of yours and get some women over here."

I glanced around the room. It didn't look promising. All the ladies seemed paired up. Then a new song that was more techno than Latin started and the crowd went wild, rocking in unison to the heavy beat.

We sipped our drinks, scanning the room, nodding our heads to the rhythm of the loud music like a couple of stupid teenagers. A tall muscular guy standing next to us leaned over and asked if the empty chairs were available.

"We're saving them for our dates," Jay yelled.

The guy looked skeptical but didn't challenge us.

I was just about done with my drink, so I leaned across the table and yelled, "If you think you can hold these chairs, I'll go to the bar and get us two more."

"It's a deal," he yelled.

I pushed back toward the bar and waited until I could get one of the bartender's attention. Once I'd ordered, I turned around to see if my Salsa dancer was nearby, hoping her Sylvester Stallone-looking boyfriend had gone to the men's room again.

Instead, I saw an attractive young woman who looked familiar, and when she noticed me, she grinned and nodded. It was Ginger—or Marion—the waitress who'd psychoanalyzed me the night before.

She pushed between some people and came over. She had on a low-cut red dress with spaghetti straps on her shoulders and her face was made up like a fashion model's.

"You look different," I told her. "All dolled up."

"Got my groove on tonight. My night off."

"Are you here alone?"

"My friend Erica is with me. She went to the bathroom."

The bartender came back with the drinks, so I paid him, saying, "Keep the change," loud enough for Marion to hear. Then I glanced at her nearly empty glass.

"Can I get you something?"

"Sure. Two pina coladas."

I looked at the bartender who nodded and went off to make the drinks.

Setting her now empty glass on the bar, Marion leaned in to whisper in my ear. "I'm sorry I upset you the other night. That wasn't my intention."

"I know. You were absolutely right. My emotions are out of whack."

"Friends?"

Her perfume was strong and arousing, so I smiled and nodded. She kissed my earlobe, and her soft lips left an impression. Though I couldn't see it, I knew her lipstick was on me, and I found that arousing.

The drinks arrived, so I paid again and handed one of the cold glasses to Marion. She took a sip and rolled her eyes, grinning. "They make the best drinks here."

A tall slender blonde in a silky white sundress tapped Marion on the shoulder. "Who's your friend?"

Marion spun around taking the glass away from her lips.

"This is Randall. He's from California."

"I'm Erica," she said, holding out her slender

hand. "What brings you to Miami Beach?"

I shook her hand and said, "Beautiful women like you and Marion."

She threw her head back and laughed. "No beautiful women in California?"

"Sure, but variety is the spice of life."

"Good looking and witty to boot," Erica said, a bit sarcastically.

"I'm not trying to be witty," I said, handing her the other drink. "I'm going for urbane."

"Urbane! I like that."

"Here's to being urbane," I said, raising my glass.

The three of us toasted, the tension was gone.

"My friend and I have a table," I said. "You want to join us?"

"Sure," Erica answered.

They followed me through the crowd. When we got to the table, Jay's eyes lit up.

"Man, I'm glad to see you. I almost got into a fist fight trying to hold this table."

As we sat on the stools at the tall table, I said, "You remember Marion?"

Jay studied her face as he shook her hand. "You look familiar."

"I waited on your table the other night."

"Wait," he said. "I thought your name was Ginger."

"That's her stage name," I said. "Her real name's Marion, you know, like Maid Marion from Robin Hood, and she's going to be a psychiatrist."

"No, not a psychiatrist, Randall. A behavioral psychologist."

"I predict you won't be able to stop," I explained.

194

"You'll go back for your medical degree and become a psychiatrist, eventually."

Erica leaned closer. "Are you being urbane now?"

I laughed. "Yes. Yes I am."

Jay looked confused. "What's your name?"

Erica held out her hand and told him.

"Erica," he repeated. "That's one of the loveliest names in the English language."

"If you like that," Marion said, "you should hear her nickname."

"What's your nickname?" Jay asked.

She sipped her drink, batted her eyelashes and pretended to be embarrassed.

"It's Erotica," Marion said. "That's what we called her in the sorority."

Jay grinned broadly. "I'd love to hear the story behind that."

"After another drink or two," Erica said. "It wouldn't be urbane of me to confess everything right now, since we've just met."

"What's all this 'urbane' business?" Jay asked.

Marion patted his arm. "It's Randall's word. He's trying to be urbane tonight."

"I'm not sure what that means?" Jay admitted.

Erica leaned over to speak into his ear. "It means he's trying to be debonair."

"Suave," Marion added. "Like the shampoo."

"That's me," I said. "Put a little dab in your hand, massage until there's a nice lather, then rinse and repeat."

Erica laughed. "Will you leave me with split ends or full of lustrous body?"

"You already have a lustrous body," Jay told her.

195

She smiled. "How urbane of you to notice."

"Okay," I said. "Enough with the urbane. It's getting old."

"Want to dance?" Jay asked Erica.

She put her drink down and nodded, so the two of them pushed toward the crowded dance floor, disappearing beyond a wall of people.

"Your friend's beautiful," I said.

"She actually does a little modeling in Miami, but she majored in broadcast journalism and wants to get on a TV news show."

"Well, she's got the looks for it."

"But the competition is tremendous. She just had a small part in a commercial, so she's hoping something will come from that."

"Here's to Erica's big break," I said, raising my glass.

Marion touched her glass to mine and took a sip. "It's fun being out with her. She attracts men like moths to a bonfire."

"I'm sure you attract your fair share of me, too."

"Oh, it's not that I'm jealous. Not at all. I like to observe the different ways men behave around her. I'm thinking of writing a paper on the six typical strategies men use when attempting to seduce attractive women."

"Six typical strategies? There're that many?"

Marion eyed me. "How would you describe the ways men try to seduce women? What are some of the typical ploys you and your friends have used?"

"I can't tell you. The guys will kick me out of the man club if I do."

"Well, I'll tell you my theories and you just nod if

you agree, okay?"

I nodded.

"First, the oldest ploy in the world is the one you've used two or three times with me."

"Oh?"

"The bribe. You buy ladies drinks and other trinkets with the hope that we'll feel so obligated that we'll give in and let you have sex with us."

I nodded.

"Second is flattery. You think that we so crave attention that if you flatter us enough, we'll give in and let you have sex with us."

I nodded again, smiling.

"Third is playing the alpha male. You want us to believe that you're better in almost every way than any of the competition, so our natural primitive instinct to mate with the most dominant male kicks in and we let you have sex with us."

Again I nodded, but I was feeling a little apprehensive.

"The fourth strategy is playing for sympathy. You confess some sad secret about yourself that makes us feel sorry for you, which brings out our maternal instincts, you believe, and then we'll give in and—"

"Have sex with us. I get it. What's the fifth strategy?"

"Ah, now we're delving into the really devious tactics."

"Do tell."

"The fifth strategy is the perfect mate ploy. You let us believe that you're not only ready to settle down, but we're the perfect match for you—the gal of your dreams—and you want nothing more than to

197

make a good living at your well-paying job, buy a nice house in a good neighborhood and raise a family. Sound about right?"

"Scary how right you are." I recalled telling Sherry that maybe I was ready to settle down. It made me a little sick, so I sipped my drink.

"Making you nervous, am I?" Marion asked, grinning.

I nodded.

"Ready to hear about the sixth strategy? It's the coup de grâce."

I nodded once again.

Before she could speak, Erica and Jay returned, sweaty and panting. Erica's nipples were as hard as pencil erasers and she was smiling seductively at Jay.

"He's a great dancer," Erica told Marion. "You should have seen us out there. People actually made room for us so they could watch. It was incredible."

Jay smiled and shrugged, so pleased with himself he almost exploded.

"It takes two to Tango," he said.

"You should dance with him, Marion. He's got amazing hands."

"I bet he does," Marion said, smiling at Jay.

A pang of jealousy jabbed my heart. "Marion was just telling me all the ways men seduce women."

"Oh, yeah," Erica said, after gulping from her glass. "Her Six Strategies of Seduction. I've heard all about it."

"Only six?" Jay asked. "I thought we had dozens of tricks up our sleeves."

"You do," Marion replied, "but they can all be categorized under six basic headings."
198

"Oh, really," Jay said. "You think we men are that simple-minded?"

Marion nodded, taking a sip from her glass.

Our glasses were almost empty. "I'm going to the bar. Can I get everyone another round?"

"Oh, strategy number two," Erica said. "The bribe."

"I thought it was number one," I said.

"The first three aren't ranked," Marion explained. "They're interchangeable."

"Whatever. You guys want another round or not? I mean, would you most beautiful women like me to provide more expensive beverages since I seem to be the best man for the job?"

Smiling coyly, both Erica and Marion nodded.

Chapter 20

We drank and danced for another hour until Jay proposed moving the party to our hotel room. To my surprise, Marion and Erica accepted the offer. The club we were at had started to fill with a different clientele, a hard-looking crowd that made me nervous.

We staggered back to the hotel in each other's arms. Marion rubbed my back as we walked. Erica held onto Jay like they were old friends. We were a little drunk, but not so drunk that we didn't know Jay married.

Marion didn't seem concerned about being seen as we walked through the hotel lobby. Inside the elevator, Jay grabbed Erica and kissed her for the duration of the ride while Marion and I stood by watching. Part of me wanted to protest, but Marion's perfume was sweet and strong, and the glistening skin of her cleavage, smooth and tanned.

We left the lights off when we pushed inside the room. Jay and Erica waltzed to his bed where they fell on their sides still in each other's arms. I closed the drapes, which plunged us into complete darkness. Only the sounds of the other couple's struggle to disrobe each other disturbed the quiet.

Marion's hand cupped the back of my neck as she pulled my mouth down to hers. We kissed passionately, standing only a couple of feet away from the other bed where Jay must have entered Erica because she moaned so tenderly, it aroused me even more. Marion unbuttoned my shirt, and I dropped my shorts. Her hand found my erection, and she pushed me onto my bed. I couldn't see her—not even an outline—but I could tell she was letting her dress drop to the floor.

I tugged the bedspread down and climbed under the sheet, and Marion's body slipped in next to me. We embraced and kissed, lying on our sides. Her back was bare, but she still had on her panties. She reached down and tugged at my briefs, and I pushed them down and pulled my legs free.

"Do you have protection?" she whispered.

"No," I whispered.

She paused, but her breathing was heavy and her skin was warm. "Promise me you're clean," she whispered. "No diseases, right?"

"No, of course not," I whispered. But then I thought about Maggie and wondered if she had given me anything.

"I'm on the pill," Marion whispered, her breath hot against my cheek, "so I won't get pregnant, but if you give me something, I'll cut your balls off,."

Her words should have made me go limp, but they had the opposite effect. I rolled on top of her, pushed her legs apart and then slipped inside her. She was so wet it thrilled me. Her hands clutched my buttocks, and she pulled me toward her again and again. Our

201

passion cries drowned out the other couple, and I exploded inside her in blinding ecstasy.

I collapsed, but she held me on top of her tightly, rocking her pelvis ever so slightly, as if enjoying the feeling of my softening penis inside her. She kissed my temple and stroked my back, whispering, "You feel so good in me. You feel so good."

Before long, I was getting aroused again. I pushed up and began rocking in and out of her. This time was for her pleasure. I moved rhythmically in and out, in and out, getting harder with each stroke.

When she began to moan with pleasure, I stroked faster and harder. Her moans grew louder, which only fueled my desire to please—I could feel every centimeter of her vagina contracting around my penis.

Suddenly, she screamed, "Oh God! Oh God!"

Exhausted and sweaty, I rolled off and lay next to her—both of us panting.

I'd completely forgotten that Jay and Erica were in the bed next to us. Whether or not their experience had been as intense as ours, I couldn't say. But soon I fell into the deepest sleep I'd known in days.

*   *   *

I awoke with Marion's arm across my chest. Someone had parted the drapes slightly, and daylight streamed in through the slit. I lifted my head to see the other bed. Erica was asleep on her side facing us, but Jay was gone. I glanced at the bathroom. The door was open, and the light was off, so I deduced that he'd gotten up some time earlier, showered, dressed and left for his convention.

Honestly, I didn't care. I felt rested—even restored.

Marion groggily opened her eyes, stared at me for a few seconds, as if trying to remember who I was, and then said, "You're a great lay," before rolling onto her side away from me and going back to sleep.

I rolled over, kissed the nape of her neck and whispered, "So are you." Then I fell asleep again.

Sometime later a noise awoke me. Erica walked to the bathroom naked and closed the door. She came out a few minutes later wrapped in a towel. Seeing that my eyes were open, she smiled. I smiled sheepishly back, my arm still wrapped around Marion under the sheet.

Marion stirred and then sat up, pulling the sheet around her breasts before resting her back against the headboard.

I sat up and scooted back against the headboard, too.

"Can we order room service?" Erica asked. "I feel like eating a big breakfast in bed."

Marion smiled at me. "How'd you sleep?"

"Best night's sleep I've had in a long time."

"It was lovely. Last night, I mean."

"I agree completely."

"Okay, okay," Erica chimed. "Enough pillow talk. I'm hungry."

I leaned forward to look at Erica. The tight towel made her breasts bulge.

"Sure. Order whatever you want."

She picked up the phone and dialed. "Yes, I'd like an order of eggs Benedict, some fruit, orange juice and coffee."

"Make that two orders," I said.

"Make it three, if it's okay with you?" Marion asked me.

"Yes, three orders, please," Erica repeated. She hung up. "They said twenty minutes."

"I've got to pee," Marion said. She threw the covers off and walked to the bathroom unashamed.

"I guess you two have seen each other naked before," I said.

"A few times. Hey, Randall, do you have a clean tee-shirt I can wear? I don't feel like getting dressed yet."

"Sure." I reached under the covers and found my briefs. After tugging them on, I got up and went to my suitcase. "White, yellow or light blue?"

"The yellow one please."

I tossed her the shirt. She pulled it on, carelessly letting the towel drop away, giving me a pleasant show.

"Thanks. Offer Marion the blue one."

I grabbed the shirt and went to the bathroom door. "Erica thought you might like a tee-shirt."

Marion opened the door, standing in front of me naked, smiling, seeming to enjoy my eyes roaming over her body. She took the shirt and stood on her toes to kiss me. "Did I tell you that you're a great lover?"

"I think so, but I could hear it again."

I put my arm around her and pulled her body against mine to kiss her more deeply, but she pulled away. "I haven't brushed my teeth yet, and neither have you."

I stepped into the bathroom and closed the door,

grabbing my toothbrush from my toiletry case. "Want to use my brush?"

"No, just squeeze some toothpaste on my finger."

We brushed our teeth together, watching each other in the mirror. After rinsing out our mouths, we face one another and embraced, and I kissed her as well as I could. Her body seemed to respond as she writhed in my arms.

She extracted herself from me, saying, "We'd better not start again, with breakfast on the way."

"Okay, but I do want to make love to you again."

She finally pulled the tee-shirt over her body and then went out, leaving me some privacy. I relieved myself, splashed water on my face and rolled deodorant under my arms before going back out.

Erica held the TV remote and was watching a talk show. "Bill Clinton won the Democratic nomination for President."

"Yeah. So?" I asked. Politics bored me.

"I think he's sexy," Erica answered.

"He's kinda chubby," Marion said.

Erica shrugged and turned off the TV. "So what should we do today, boys and girls?"

"I've got no plans," I admitted.

"I have to be at work at seven, but other than that, I'm free."

"Let's go to the beach," Erica suggested. "We can go home after breakfast and freshen up, then meet Randall back here at noon or so."

Marion looked at me.

I nodded. "Sounds good."

"Great," Erica said. "Maybe your pal Jay can join us after his meetings."

"Maybe," I said. "You do know Jay's married, don't you?"

"I don't judge, I just enjoy."

"We're existentialists," Marion added.

I looked at her. "Which means what?"

"That people are completely responsible for themselves, for their own actions. If Jay accepts the responsibility for cheating on his wife, then that's on him, not us."

"Life's too short," Erica added, "to constantly second guess other people's choices. I say, follow your gut. Besides, when men cheat on their wives, it usually means they aren't that committed to begin with. Who knows? Maybe something good will come out of his little tryst with me."

"Sometimes it's through our indiscretions that we truly learn who we are, Randall. I'm sure you'd agree with that, wouldn't you?"

I didn't answer. Somehow speaking of such matters would utterly annihilate the joy I was feeling. "I'll leave a note in the room for Jay," I said. "What beach?"

"One of the best sections of Miami Beach is right behind the hotel. Plus we can get snacks cheap, with Marion's discount."

There was a knock on the door and Erica sprang to her feet, clapping her hands. "Yippee! The food is here, the food is here!.

She sounded so childlike that the weight of the previous words evaporated.

Soon the three of us were eating in silence, having satiated almost all of our appetites.

Chapter 21

The three of us rendezvoused at the beach around two in the afternoon. The air was humid, but a strong breeze blew in from the water, and I noticed storm clouds on the horizon to the south. Rows of wooden lounge chairs with thick cushions were reserved for hotel guests. I showed my room key to the Cuban cabana boy, and he handed us towels and took drink orders.

Once we'd settled back to soak up the rays, each of us with closed eyes behind our sunglasses, I asked Erica to tell me about herself.

"What do you do for a living?"

"I'm a part-time bank teller and a full-time college student, like Marion."

"A psychology major?"

She laughed. "No, no, no. Business. But I met Marion when she and her professor were doing an experiment. They needed volunteers."

"Subjects," Marion corrected. "And you were paid."

"I was one of her guinea pigs."

"What was the experiment?" I asked.

"It was a variation of Milgram's experiment on

obedience," Marion explained. "We wanted to see how far someone would go to force a subject to consume a substance that might make him sick, as long as they would be rewarded monetarily."

"It was really cool," Erica said. "Dr. Jacobson told me that I would earn an extra fifty dollars for every cup of cherry juice I made the girl drink. The girl was Marion and supposedly she was allergic to cherries, so she pretended to get sicker and sicker the more she drank. So I coaxed her to drink because Dr. Jacobson told me they were experimenting on ways to cure people of their allergies, but that was just a ruse."

"How many cups did she drink?"

"I got her to down five before she started acting so sick. I thought she might die, even though Jacobson kept saying the risk of death was minimal. But I really wanted to make five hundred bucks, so I would've kept going."

"It wasn't real cherry juice, just water with red food coloring."

"But I didn't know that," Erica said indignantly. "And you were acting all disoriented and weak, so I thought I should stop."

"What was the point?" I asked.

"To see how far someone might go just to make money, even if they thought they might be harming another human being."

I sat up and looked at Marion. "Again, what was the point?"

Marion sat up and pulled off her sunglasses to look at me. "These days, a lot of people are pushing products that are either unhealthy or downright harmful for consumers. We were studying just how far someone might go if encouraged by someone in a position of authority."

"And your results?"

"Similar to Stanley Milgram's. The vast majority of people will harm others if two conditions are met: they personally profit and someone in authority gives them permission. It has all sorts of applications to sales, marketing and business, especially in areas like pesticides and pharmaceuticals. We got a good-sized grant for that research. Or Dr. Jacobson did, I should say."

I laughed. "So he was motivated by money to do cruel things to others, just like the experiment he was setting up."

Erica burst out laughing. "I never thought about it like that, but I guess Randall's right. That kinda makes Jacobson a guinea pig, too, in a way, doesn't it, Marion?"

Marion scowled. "No, not at all. This was valuable research. Dr. Jacobson is motivated by science, not grant money."

"Still," I said, "I'm sure the money helped."

The young Cuban arrived with our pina coladas, so I signed for them and we all took sips of the cold drinks. Erica seemed oblivious to how annoyed Marion was, but I could see it in the way she stared straight ahead and avoided looking at either of us.

"I wonder if your roommate will show up?" Erica said.

"I left a note and a phone message telling him we'd be down here."

Without looking at us, Marion said, "Maybe he's

finding the conference interesting."

Erica cupped her right breast. "More interesting than these?"

I chuckled, but Marion wasn't amused. "There's more to life than sex."

"True," Erica answered. "There's drinking and money and good food."

"And the beach," I added. "Don't forget the beach and the sunshine."

"Yeah, we sort of take that for granted, living here."

"What about you, Randall?" Marion asked. "What motivates you these days? I mean, you've dropped out of school and you don't have a job, and apparently you have all the money you need. So what keeps you going?"

I shook my head. "Honestly, I don't know. I'll probably return to school in the fall and then go on to medical school, eventually. Like my father."

"Oh, I think you'll be a great doctor," Erica chimed. "I mean, you've already got a good grip on anatomy." She nudged Marion's shoulder.

"What's your immediate goal?"

I held out my glass. "To get drunk and have sex."

"Woo-hoo!" Erica yelled. "I'll toast to that!"

"Seriously, Randall," Marion said. "Be honest. Close your eyes and think about what you'd like to do, if you could do anything you wanted."

"Ooo, that sounds fun. Can I play, too?" Erica asked.

She looked at me intensely. "This means something to me, Randall. It's sort of a test to see whether or not you're someone I want to spend more time with."

I took a long pull of my drink and stared at Marion, wondering whether or not I wanted to have any more to do with her. But this was the closest thing to a real relationship I'd had in a week, so I played along.

I closed my eyes and tried to clear my thoughts. Images of Sherry and the others kept popping into my head—bloody, brutal images that made me queasy. Then I saw the face of Jimmy Collins—his laughing, arrogant expression the first time I saw him, the angry, hateful expression after I'd socked him, and his utterly defeated look in the blood-red building on St. Thomas.

With my eyelids clamped closed, I said, "I'd like to find the cause of Jimmy Collins' madness and do something about it."

"Good," Marion whispered. "What was the cause of Jimmy's madness, as you call it?"

I opened my eyes and smiled. "You'll love this. It's absolutely Freudian. His father abused him. Treated him like shit."

"Wait, am I missing something?" Erica asked.

"Not now, Erica. Go on, Randall."

Man, I thought, *she really is going to be a psychologist.*

"From what I can tell, what really pushed him over the edge was this officer in the Navy who also abused him. Sexually."

"Wow," Erica said. "That's so weird. I knew a guy in high school who was sexually abused."

"Erica, let me deal with Randall first, okay?"

"Geez, okay, okay. It's like we're all so serious
211

now."

"This is serious. Who was this abusive officer, Randall? Do you know his name?"

"Um, it's a weird name. Sounds like evil." I closed my eyes and tried to recall the conversation with Jimmy in Detective Granger's office. "Ubel. Commander Ubel."

"Good, good," Marion cooed. I wasn't sure why it mattered to her. "Now where did all this happen?"

"You mean the sex stuff in the Navy?"

"Yes. Where did this happen?"

"The base in Orlando, I think."

"Orlando?" Erica repeated. "I dated a guy who went to boot camp there. Now he's on a submarine somewhere. Wouldn't you hate to be stuck on a submarine?"

"You know, Randall, Orlando's not far from here. If you wanted to, you could go to the base and report what happened."

I laughed. "Why the hell would I want to do that?"

"Well, why do you think?"

I snorted. "Stop playing shrink and just tell me."

Erica chuckled. "Don't you just hate it when she does that?"

"Do you really want me to answer you, Randall?"

I nodded, sipping my drink.

She put her sunglasses back on. "It would be good therapy for you, for one thing. I mean, you're carrying a lot of guilt for your friends' deaths and injuries, so if you do something about it, you'll probably feel better. Don't you think so?"

I nodded, but I badly wanted another drink.

"Maybe. Probably. I don't know." I caught the cabana boy's eye and waved him over.

"And there's another reason," Marion added.

"Oh? What's that?"

The young Cuban hurried over and flashed a toothy smile. "Si, senor?"

"Another round, please."

"Would you like a pitcher instead?"

I glanced at Erica, who smiled and nodded.

"Sure. That'd be great."

"Do you want to hear what I have to say or not?" Marion asked after the Cuban left.

"Yes, of course."

"I know I do," Erica said. "I find all this stuff fascinating, even though I don't know the whole story."

"If this man Ubel is really abusing the young men in his command, then he should be stopped. It's a crime, what he's doing, and you have knowledge of it."

I shrugged. "I'm sure Jimmy's lawyer and the detective down in St. Thomas already informed the proper authorities at the base."

"Are you? Are you really sure?"

"They must have. I mean, like you said, what he did was a crime, so…"

She reclined against the cushion and sipped her drink. "I hope you're right. Because if they didn't, then this man will continue to victimize other young men, and that might lead to another Jimmy Collins. You have the power to stop that from happening, Randall."

I stared at her for a few seconds. "Is this just a

213

variation of the Milgram experiment? Maybe you want to see how far you can push me."

"Maybe. Or maybe you just don't want to take responsibility. I mean, your knowledge of this horrible crime makes you responsible in a way. You now have a duty to stop this cycle of abuse. Or at least try."

I sat back and scanned the horizon, contemplating Marion's words. She was right. But the thought of confronting someone—actually going onto a Navy base and talking to that man's superior officer—it scared the hell out of me.

The Cuban placed the pitcher of drinks on the table between Marion's chair and mine, and I signed the bill, adding a thirty percent tip, unsure why I wanted to be that generous.

"Muchos gracias, senor!" he gushed. He refilled our glasses before going to another customer.

The wind had picked up and the storm clouds were closer though we still had a few hours of sunlight. The satisfaction I'd felt that morning had vanished.

Chapter 22

R aindrops pelting my bare chest woke me. I'd
fallen asleep after we'd finished the pitcher
of drinks. The girls had gone, and the beach was all
but empty. Gray clouds blanketed the sky in all
directions, and the horizon had disappeared into a
watercolor of dark blue mixed with dark gray.

When I tried to sit up, I realized how drunk I was.
Wobbly, I managed to grab my damp shirt, tugging it
over my wet hair. I checked my watch—it was after
five, and I was hungry. I stood up to make the walk
back to the hotel, but just held the top of the lounge
chair until the world stopped spinning.

Staggering isn't fun. You'd think it would be,
because it looks funny in movies, but when you're
trying to plant one foot in front of the other without
falling on your face, staggering isn't fun.

I managed to get back into my room and cleaned
up. Eventually, I felt sober enough to dress and go
downstairs to eat. Marion was working, so I found a
small table in a corner and waited for her to come
over.

"Are you okay? We didn't know whether or not

we should wake you up."

"Yeah, I felt a little abandoned."

She scrunched up her face in a sympathetic frown.

"It's my fault. Erica said we should wake you, but I thought you needed the sleep. Forgive me?"

"I forgive you. But I'm starved. Can you take my food order?"

"Of course. Do you know what you want?"

"New York steak, medium, baked potato with the works and a green salad with bleu cheese dressing."

"Isn't that what you had the other night?"

"Yeah, so?"

"You're going to get fat, eating all that."

"I'll work it off later."

"Maybe I can help. Want me to come to your room when I get off?"

That caught me off guard. I wasn't thinking about sleeping with her again. All I could think about was taking the first bite of that juicy steak. But I nodded and smiled, and Marion, dressed in her low-cut "Ginger" outfit, smiled back at me, her eyes glistening.

"You want something to drink with your dinner? A pina colada, maybe?"

"No! No more alcohol for a while. Just a Seven-up on ice."

"You got it, darlin'"

She spun around and walked away slowly, knowing I was watching her. I had to admit, seeing those legs and knowing what it felt like to be between them perked me up.

The restaurant was filling with men dressed in slacks and Hawaiian shirts. A group of four men and one very attractive woman sat down at the table next to mine, and after ordering drinks, they seemed to hunker down. The men listened to the woman, who pulled out brochures and handed them to everyone at the table. The woman, whose dress was a size or two too tight, seemed to be a sales rep from a medical supply company, and she spoke very precisely about improvements in instruments whose names I didn't recognize. Meanwhile, the men—all of them dentists, I guessed—seemed to listen intently, though I suspected they just enjoyed looking at her while she spoke.

The whole little scene depressed me. My father used to complain about being pestered by sales reps at his office. "Used car salesmen in pretty dresses," he called them. It made me realize that, in reality practicing medicine was a business like everything else. Dad complained about many aspects of running a doctor's office. Patients who didn't pay their bills, fights with insurance companies who questioned his orders for tests, and the ever-rising cost of liability insurance.

My father had been a good doctor. I'd heard from many of his patients over the years how much they liked him. Sometimes one of his patients would say, "Your father saved my life," or words to that effect. I'd always been proud of him, even late at night when sometimes he'd had too much to drink and moaned about his problems.

At any rate, I did not have a false idealistic view of the medical profession—not since I was thirteen— and being with Jay, who seemed more interested in getting laid than learning the latest procedure for extracting a tooth, only reinforced my cynicism.

I was happy when Marion brought my food. She leaned over when she set the plate down, showing off her cleavage. "Hope everything is to your liking, sir."

The wry smile on her face made me laugh. "I'm sure it's all delicious."

The food was good, but the place got busy, so I didn't have a chance to talk to Marion again. I finally paid the bill and went back to the room. Jay was getting dressed when I walked in.

"Guess what?"

"What?" I asked, as if I cared.

"Erica's picking me up and taking me to her favorite spot for dinner."

"She's quite a girl."

Buttoning his shirt, he walked past me into the bathroom. "You can say that again." He combed his hair, slicking it down with some kind of gel, then inspected his teeth, turning his head from side to side.

"Vivacious," I said.

"What?"

"Erica. She's full of life."

"You're tellin' me." He flashed a toothy smile.

"Talked to your wife and kids lately?"

The smile faded. "Just a few minutes ago."

"How are they?"

He shot me an angry look. "My daughter's still a little sick. What's it to you?"

I stepped out of the way as he walked to the dresser and grabbed his watch.

"I guess I don't understand how marriage works."

Sliding his watch over his hand, he turned around and shot a cold expression at me. "No one plans to cheat when they get married. Sometimes things get stale. I have an occasional fling and it keeps me... fresh."

"Fresh?"

"It's hard to explain. I can go back to my life refreshed, I guess. Believe it or not, it helps me stay committed to my family and my practice, knowing I can have a little vacation from all the stress once in awhile."

I nodded as he walked by me toward the door.

"Do you think your wife has little vacations like that, too, sometimes?"

He spun around, and I thought he might slug me, but standing so close, he must have realized that I was taller and in better shape.

He grabbed the handle and opened the door. With his back to me, he said, "Maybe it's time for you to find a room of your own." With that, he left.

I stood in the little hallway staring at the closed door.

In bed, the gristle of the steak and the dressing of the salad conspired to make my stomach churn, so I had trouble falling to sleep. Maybe the conversation with Jay had soured my stomach, too.

* * *

Someone was knocking. I was inside my stuffy little hotel room in Charlotte Amalie on St. Thomas. The persistent knocking scared me. Was it Detective Granger coming to arrest me? I glanced into the tile bathroom. Walls smeared with blood. A woman's bare and bloody legs on the floor. How had Sherry's dead body gotten in my bathroom?

The knocking grew louder. Any minute Granger would shoot the lock and the door would crash open! When I glanced at the bathroom again, Sherry was standing in the doorway, her face covered in blood.

I lurched out of my dream and sat up. I might have screamed.

Someone really was knocking on the door of my hotel room.

The clock showed 2:10 a.m. Was it Jay? Had he forgotten his room key in his rush to get out?

"Randall?" a woman's voiced called from outside the door. "Are you awake? It's me, Marion."

Marion?

The vision of Sherry still vivid in my mind faded as the events of the last day or so became clearer. I went to the door. Marion stood there in her waitress outfit.

"I was about to give up on you," she said. Then she stood on her tiptoes and kissed my chin. "You must have been sleeping the sleep of the dead."

That made me laugh. "You have no idea how right you are."

"Well go back to bed, but don't go back to sleep. I need to shower, so stay awake until I'm done, okay?"

"Okay," I said.

She smiled and patted my cheek. "You feel kinda hot. Do you have a fever?"

I felt my face. "Probably just sunburned."

She turned her back to me. "Unzip me, would you?"

I tugged the zipper of her uniform down, exposing her back and bra strap. The sight should have aroused

220

me, but I was still dizzy from my dream. She let her dress drop, and I turned and climbed back into bed.

By the time she climbed into bed with me, I'd fallen asleep, but feeling her body slid up against mine woke me.

"Are you too tired to make love?" she asked.

I rolled onto my side facing her and nodded.

She kissed me lightly and said, "We can wait until morning."

"Thanks," I whispered. "Just hope Jay doesn't come back too early."

"I don't think we have to worry about Jay. Erica plans to keep him with her all day tomorrow."

I shut my eyes. Sleep overtook me immediately.

* * *

The telephone rang early the next morning, startling both of us. I answered in a panic. "Hello!?"

"Jay?" It was a woman's voice.

"No, this is Randall."

"Randall? Oh, they must have given me the wrong room."

Before she hung up, I said, "No, this is Jay's room. We're just sharing it."

"Sharing it? I don't understand."

"Jay wanted to save money, and the hotel didn't have a room for me, so we decided to share a room."

"Oh." There was a long, uncomfortable pause. "He didn't tell me anything about sharing a room with anyone."

"Who is this?" I finally thought to ask.

"I'm Jay's wife. Is he there? I need to speak to

him."

I glanced at the other bed, which was neatly made. "No, he's not here right now. Can I take a message?"

"Do you know where he is?"

I glanced at Marion, who only frowned and rolled over. "Downstairs at the conference, I guess."

"At seven in the morning?"

I looked at the clock. It was indeed a few minutes after seven. "Maybe he went to breakfast. Or to work out or something. I don't know. We were asleep."

"We? Who's we?"

"I had a girlfriend stay the night."

"Oh, really. You have a girl in the room that you're sharing with my husband?"

"That's right." I didn't want to talk to her anymore because she sounded so suspicious. "Look, I don't mean to be rude, but we were asleep when you called, so…"

"So, you want to go back to sleep. How old are you? You sound young."

Unsure why, I felt myself blush. "I'm twenty-five," I fibbed. "So what?"

"And your girlfriend? Is she in her twenties, too?"

"What difference does that make?"

"Does my husband have a twenty-something girlfriend, too?"

I tried to think of something to say. "You need to talk to him about that," I managed. "Now do you want me to give him a message or not?"

"Tell him his daughter has appendicitis and is going into surgery."

I looked at the back of Marion's head. "Oh. I'm sorry. Look, I'll try to track him down for you, okay?"

She mumbled something and then the phone went dead.

I nudged Marion. "Do you know Erica's phone number?"

She rolled over. "Of course. Why?"

"That was Jay's wife. His daughter's in the hospital. We should let him know."

She sat up and rubbed her temples with her fingers. "I guess we should." She pushed me out of the way, so I climbed out of bed and walked to the bathroom as she dialed the bed-side phone.

When I came out, Marion was almost dressed. "She didn't answer. I'm going to her place and bang on the door. Want to come?"

I started to say yes, but then remembered the exchange Jay and I'd had. "No, I don't think so. Before Jay left last night, we had a little row."

"Oh? What about?"

"Let's just say, I don't think he wants to share a room with me anymore."

She grabbed her purse and hurried by me. "Well, he'll probably check out and go back home to be with his family, so I don't think you have to look for a new place."

I shrugged. "Guess not."

"You want to come with me or not?"

"Think I'll shower and dress so I'm alert when Jay gets back."

"Suit yourself," she said, brushing by me.

The door to the hotel room once again opened and

223

closed in my face. *Suit myself?* Something in the way she'd said depressed me. A wave of utter loneliness swept over me, and I did not know what else to do except to perform the morning rituals of a normal life.

Chapter 23

"It's enough to make you believe in Karma," Jay said as he packed.

I sat at the desk watching. Marion and Erica sat side by side on my bed looking at the floor.

"You try to have a little fun, and God smacks you down for it."

Marion looked up. "I don't believe in God," she said. "I think we find meaning in mere coincidences."

Jay looked at her as if she were speaking a different language. "Mere coincidences? Huh. You know, I really don't want to hear psycho-babble from a cocktail waitress."

"Hey," Erica said. "That's uncalled for."

"Sorry. I'm just upset."

"You feel guilty," Marion added. "It's perfectly understandable."

Jay zipped his bag closed and scowled at Marion. "Oh? And what's your prognosis, doctor?"

Marion put her hand on Jay's, saying, "I'm not judging you, I'm just trying to show you that I understand what you're feeling."

He pulled his hand away, but his expression

softened.

Erica stood and hugged him. "Go home to your wife and daughter. Tell them you love them. That's the truth, isn't it?"

Jay nodded. I thought he might cry. "Of course, I love them. I just…" He shook his head and closed his eyes.

"You'll be fine," Erica said softly. "By the time you get home, your daughter will be out of surgery and everyone will feel better."

"I know, I know," Jay said. "I just hate the idea of someone cutting my little girl open."

His voice stabbed me. I thought about Sherry's parents—what must they be feeling?

Erica left with Jay, and Marion lingered at the door asking if I'd be all right.

"I'm fine," I told her.

"What are your plans now?"

I shrugged. "Honestly, I don't know." I looked at her as I got up and walked around the bed to the nightstand to grab my watch. She had her hand on the door handle and seemed eager to leave. "What are your plans for the day?"

"I've actually got to get some schoolwork done. Got a class this afternoon."

I slid my watch on. "What are you doing after class? Want to get some dinner?"

She studied the carpet, and I sensed that, for whatever reason, the attraction she had felt before was gone. "Well, I have to work tonight, so I don't think I'll have time."

"Okay," I said softly. "Well, you know where to find me."

She nodded, opened the door and left. Perplexed, I went over and watched her through the peep hole. She didn't look back as she walked to the elevator, nor did she glance at my door while she waited. Only her perfume lingered like a ghost in the little hallway.

I decided to walk for a while before lunch, to clear my mind. So much had happened. Dad's death, then the inheritance, then the island romance—the sad crush I'd on Sherry and the good sex I'd had with Maggie, and then the murders—the bloody, bloody murders. And now—what?

I headed south on the sidewalk, and for the first time I noticed the name of the road the Fontainebleau Hotel was on—Collins Avenue. Collins Avenue! I'd flown hundreds of miles to escape what had happened with Jimmy Collins, yet here I was staying on a street bearing his name. I couldn't help but laugh, thinking, *truth is stranger than fiction!*

It was a cool morning. A gentle breeze rustled palm fronds overhead. Had I been a typical tourist, I might have felt happy. But so many emotions and memories churned inside me that I couldn't think straight. I desperately wanted to sort things out, to make sense of everything that had happened. *Was some grand scheme governing it all?*

My thoughts turned to Jimmy Collins again. What had caused that young sailor in the crisp white uniform I'd seen for the first time at the Galleon House to transform into the heaving, blood-coated jackal I'd seen crouching in the corner of the bedroom where Sherry had been beaten to death? It was *Jekyll and Hyde*. Well, almost. From his own account, Jimmy hadn't had a privileged upbringing like the good Dr. Jekyll. No—that was more like my background. But something had so twisted Jimmy that he'd utterly lost his humanity and brutally bashed in the faces of four people. What had pushed him over the edge?

Maybe Marion was right. Maybe I should go to the naval base in Orlando to tell someone what Jimmy Collins had told me about that officer who'd abused him—raped him, really, by his account. I had knowledge of a crime and a duty to act on it, didn't I? But surely Jimmy's lawyer would make sure the authorities knew. Besides, how could I be sure Jimmy had told me the truth? Maybe it was all a pack of lies.

Part of me wanted to investigate and find out what really happened to that poor, stupid kid. But another part of me found it all meaningless. *What difference could it make?*

As I strolled down the avenue, thinking my dark thoughts, passing the occasional stranger preoccupied with his own life, I began to feel queasy—not from hunger or too much to drink, just from an acidic emptiness that hollowed out my gut.

Then I saw it.

A poster. Inside one of those black metal frames. Standing on the edge of the sidewalk between the buildings and the street.

A gray aircraft carrier with a fighter jet taking off, the massive ship surrounded by blue white-capped waves. It could have been a poster for the movie *Top Gun*. Written in large white letters against a deep blue sky were the words, "Find Adventure!" At the bottom in bright red letters, "Join the Navy!"

I stood before that sign for several minutes,

staring at it the way Moses must have stared at the burning bush.

Finally, I glanced around and saw the recruiter's office. A good-looking black guy in uniform was sitting behind a desk watching me, an expectant grin on his face. Then I noticed an attractive woman with short blonde hair—also in uniform—staring at me. Her expression was harder to read, but she smiled and gestured for me to come inside.

And so I did.

"Tell me about the base in Orlando," I said. "What goes on there?"

They sat me down, poured me a cup of coffee, smiled and showed me pictures of the base.

"One of the finest training facilities in the country," said the handsome black guy enthusiastically.

"I did my basic training there and loved it," gushed the blonde. "Made some great friends there, too."

"You'll love it. Good looking young guys and gals working together during the day and hanging out together at night."

The blonde nodded. "Yeah, there's a bar on the base with music and dancing. Once you get through the first five weeks or so, it's just like being at college."

"And trust me when I say, you will party hard."

I was reminded of Jimmy Collins and his buddies at the Calypso bar the night I broke his nose. Had they been ready to party hard?

"What about the officers?" I asked. "I heard some of them can be real assholes."

The black guy nodded, grinning. "Oh, sure, they act bad ass at first. But that's just to scare you into obeying their orders. It's mostly a bluff."

A plan was taking shape. "What if I wanted to be under the command of a specific officer? Is that possible?"

They glanced at each other, looking a little confused.

"Never heard a request like that," the black officer said. "Do you know some of the commanding officers or something?"

"Only by reputation," I said. If I could get close to this guy Ubel, maybe I could expose him. That wouldn't bring back Jimmy or Sherry, but I might be able to stop something as horrible from happening again.

"Are you in college now?" the blonde asked.

"Yeah. Fourth year pre-med."

The black officer rocked back in his chair and flashed a grin. "Wow! Going to be a doctor! What do you know about that, Lieutenant?"

The blonde fanned herself. "I think I'm in love!"

They told me I'd be eligible for officers' school with my years of college. Said I'd go in as an "E-3" and earn higher pay than most other recruits right away. They told me that I could become an orderly and later go to medical school "on the government's dime."

"An orderly?" I said. "Isn't that just a fancy name for nurse?"

"Think of the job more like a physician's assistant," the female recruiter said.

I knew they were playing me, doing their job,

telling me what I wanted to hear. But I didn't care. I signed the paperwork and hoped I'd be able to track down the man who'd raped Jimmy Collins.

* * *

A few days later, I was on a bus with twenty other guys headed to Orlando. It was like living inside a dream. I didn't say goodbye to Marion. Just packed and checked out the day I boarded the bus. I didn't even call my brother to let him know. He would have tried to talk me out of it anyway, or ridicule me for making a bad decision.

As I rode the bus that evening, watching daylight bleed from the sky, I thought about Jimmy Collins. As if in a fevered dream, I felt compelled to see what he had seen, to learn why he had become a monster. Even then, I wasn't exactly sure why. But a nagging sense of purpose gnawed at me. It was as if invisible hands were pushing me, pushing me—toward what, exactly, I did not know.

Chapter 24

The Recruit Training Center in Orlando, Florida, was like a barren college campus, sprawling across sandy soil, spotted with haphazard tufts of grass and shaded in random places by a few struggling trees. Each U-shaped three-story building, constructed with a façade of tan bricks, housed several companies of new recruits, and the barracks were connected by commanders' offices at the junction of the two wings.

Processing us took several days. Our heads were shaved, our civilian clothes boxed up and mailed home, and new RIF uniforms assigned. We spent an entire hot and humid afternoon inside a sweatbox of a room, standing at rows of tall wooden tables, stenciling our names inside our clothes so they could be returned to us after going to the laundry. We learned to march two by two everywhere we went. We hurried to the mess hall for meals, only to stand in formation for twenty or thirty minutes, until it was our company's turn to enter. We were awakened each morning at five to the pleasant sound of tin garbage can lids being pounded together like cymbals.

Inside, the barracks were long, bland dorms with two rows of metal bunk beds divided by a line of tables in the middle of the room. The harsh fluorescent lighting only made the room seem more sterile. One night I sat in my stenciled white boxers at a table in Battalion 4, oiling a fifty-year-old drill rifle. I was trying to remember the beauty of the beaches in St. Thomas and St. John when Hagen, a scrawny twenty-year-old who stuttered, stepped between two bunk beds carrying his rifle. He sat down next to me and put the Remington on the table.

"Wha-what do you think of these old pieces of sh-shit?"

I shrugged. "Pretty useless."

He opened the chamber and pulled the bolt clear of his rifle. "Look here," he said, putting his finger inside the chamber. "They b-blocked the b-barrel with a plug!"

I worked the action. "Mine, too."

He slid the bolt back into the chamber. "I'll be g-glad when they g-give us the real thing."

The fuzzy boom of rap music rocked from the glass-enclosed smoking room.

"Hey," Hagen said, jumping to his feet. "They g-got the stereo working! Are you c-coming?"

I shook my head as I wiped the rusted metal and worn wood a last time and stood, feeling jabbing pain dig into my back. Hagen jogged to the smoke-filled room where most of the other recruits were laughing. When he opened the door, loud music and cigarette smoke billowed out.

The clock above the Commander's office showed me that taps would come over the P.A. system in fifteen minutes, so I carried the old rifle to the rack and slid the cable through its trigger guard. Then I

233

went back to the table a sat down next to two other recruits who were playing checkers.

Behind the glass of the Chief's office, Commander Reed was talking to the Yeoman, both moving their lips like the characters of a silent film.

The Yeoman stepped out of the office ahead of Chief Reed.

"Attention on deck!" he screamed.

Within seconds, the other sixty-five recruits throughout the barracks jelled into position.

Fit and trim in his uniform, Chief Reed looked us over. The stereo had been turned off, and the barracks were noiseless, except for the steady hum of the air conditioner.

Reed smiled a fatherly smile that made me miss my dad. "I'll bet you guys are glad to have some tunes."

"Yes, Chief!" we shouted.

"We're going to become a Flag Company, men. It's a special honor. We'll be responsible for parading in front of the other companies. By the way, that's the reason you guys get those decommissioned rifles. No other recruits get those. Anyway, once I finally have seventy-six men, I can start your training as a flag company. Hopefully, it will only take a few more days. But understand, it's worth the wait. It's a great honor, boys, and I know you'll do me proud."

"Yes, Chief!"

Then Chief Ubel entered the barracks through the door that led to Battalion Command Headquarters. My heart pounded so hard when I first gazed upon him that I worried if others could hear it. Ubel was shorter than Reed, his hair and complexion darker.

His Mediterranean skin had the sheen of fish-scales that Jimmy Collins had described. Standing at attention, I glared at Ubel.

Chief Reed spoke sharply: "Will you please dismiss the men now, RCPO?"

"Yes, chief!" He took a few steps forward, shook himself down like a rooster before belching its cry, and yelled, "Comp'ny, Diss-mist!"

Chief Ubel grinned. He seemed to enjoy seeing us in our skivvies, standing at ease. Our eyes met, and I shuddered. Then Reed grabbed Ubel's shoulder, turning him away from us, and the two officers left.

The P.A. System crackled, and the same bored voice I'd heard for six nights said, "Taps, taps. Lights out in five minutes. Taps, taps." Like the other recruits, I climbed onto my bunk and rested my head on the pillow.

A black kid named Freddy Ferguson was my bunk mate. Sporting a wide, friendly smile, he'd introduced himself to me and several other recruits the day we arrived. When we were told to find a bunk, I saw he'd claimed a lower one and asked if he'd mind if I grabbed the one above.

"Hell, no," he'd said, laughing. "Better you than one of them fat guys. I don't want some fatso fallin' on me in the middle of the night, that's fer sure."

Now Ferguson whispered, "Hey, Wake. You asleep yet?"

"No."

"Man, I hate this waiting around, don't you?"

"It sucks,"

"Man, I never thought I'd say this, but I'm actually lookin' forward to startin' school."

"Yeah, me too," I whispered. "What are you going to train for?"

"Radioman. I'll be knowin' all that's happenin' without bein' right in the middle of the shit, if you know what I mean. How 'bout you?"

"Medic," I said. "My dad was a doctor, so…"

Someone banged the frame of our bunk. "Knock it off, you two. It's lights out. No more talking."

It was only one of the other recruits who'd been assigned sentry duty for two hours, but still, we'd been told any guard could write us up and we'd be on report. I wasn't sure what that meant, but it didn't sound good.

The guard walked on and in fifteen minutes or so, I heard Ferguson snoring away. Despite long days of doing nothing, everyone seemed exhausted by the time we were finally allowed to hit the rack.

But I lay in the dark, unable to sleep. After a while I broke into a cold sweat, pain burning my side. My stomach and back had been growing more painful each day. It didn't seem like the flu or food poisoning. More like I'd been punched in the side. I decided to stretch and walk it off, so I quietly climbed down from the bunk and went to the Head.

At the urinal, I checked to see if there was blood in my piss. There wasn't, but relieving myself did reduce the pain in my back and sides.

Back on my bunk, I wished I could sleep. The nights seemed as long as the hot Florida days in the training center. From four bunks away, I could hear Paul Dowdy praying in a hushed voice. "Deliver us from evil. Pray for us sinners, now and at the hour of our death."

Dowdy was strange. Everyone in the barracks avoided him. He seemed obsessed with religion. It was all he talked about. Why he hadn't joined a seminary instead of the Navy puzzled me. I'd had a conversation with the tall, blonde recruit earlier in the day. He quoted Bible verses and readily admitted that he's joined the Navy to atone for getting his girlfriend pregnant before "entering into wedlock."

I'd laughed when he said the word wedlock. I almost said, "If you have to be locked in anything, you probably shouldn't do it." But his serious, sincere expression told me to keep my comment to myself. That night, I fell asleep listening to the hushed prayer, repeating *pray for us sinners, now and at the hour of our death*.

* * *

The next morning, I woke up sweating. Easing off the bunk, I tried to stretch as I walked slowly to the bathroom where I shaved and brushed my teeth, a little concerned about the haggard face staring back at me in the mirror. After I got dressed, I joined the other and waited to go to breakfast. I looked out a window at "The Grinder"—a seemingly endless expanse of black asphalt. Under the rising sun, the grinder looked glossy with simmering neon puddles of heat.

Inside, I grew more aware of the steady hum of the air-conditioning. The noise made it seem as if we were already on a ship that was slowly slicing through the water—headed where, I couldn't imagine. But my kidneys ached and throbbed, so the steady background hum annoyed me more than it should have.

We were ordered outside and ambled out of the air-conditioned barracks to face the blast-furnace heat outside. Someone in a uniform screamed "Fall-in," and we recruits stumbled together on a sidewalk. We walked together, an irregular platoon of newbies tripping over ourselves, trying to keep up with the cadence being yelled. We marched to a sprawling building, and then waited outside the mess hall, from which odors of burnt toast and bacon came.

After we were finally admitted to the cafeteria in slow-moving, single file lines, I suddenly felt out of place inside a mess hall with hundreds of uniformed recruits. All of them seemed dazed or exhausted, moving robotically in the lines, picking up their trays one-by-one like zombies.

Breakfast was flavorless—rubbery scrambled eggs, bland white toast, under-cooked bacon. I was amazed at how quiet the other new recruits were. Some who'd been in longer were talking and laughing, but everyone seemed guarded. I drank my cup of stale coffee and then followed the others to turn in my tray at a window.

Too soon, we were lined up on the sidewalk again, the sun already beating down on us, hot and high. We marched along neat, clean cement sidewalks that reminded me of the white sand beaches of St. Thomas.

In the barracks later, we had nothing to do but wait. Chief Reed had told us that we were going to be a flag company, and therefore we needed exactly seventy-six men. There were only sixty-six of us so far.

"When we get ten more suitable recruits, we can start your training," he told us. "Until then, get to know each other."

Books weren't allowed, but games were, so quite a few guys played chess or checkers. We weren't allowed to lie on our bunks either, so some guys stretched out on the floor and slept.

The tedium of waiting just to march to lunch was excruciating.

Finally, we were told to line up, and it was such a relief to have something—anything—to do.

We'd barely settled into our caterpillar-like stroll when something stopped us so suddenly that the men in the rear collided into the ranks in front of them.

"What the fuck?" Ferguson asked.

"Hell if I know," I answered.

"This dude behind me pisses me off! He's steppin' on my heels!" Ferguson turned to the recruit behind him. "You're steppin' on my act, dude!"

Someone yelled, "Eyes right, and shut up!"

On the grass stood a trembling recruit, and an officer whose back was to us.

"Holy fuck!" Ferguson said.

"What?" I asked.

"Brother, I ain't sure, but if Ubel has anything to do with it, you can bet your ass it's gonna be bad!"

Ubel bellowed at us. "This recruit did not salute me, men. Now he must do penance."

The recruit was on his hands and knees and put himself in the push-up position on the grass. He started strong, shouting out "Sir, one, sir, sir, two, sir," as if he could go on forever, but after twenty or

239

so, he strained to keep going while Ubel leaned over him, yelling for him to count louder.

The sun was too hot. Sweat dripped into my eyes. I knew the other kid must have been drenched in sweat. I thought I was going to pass out, but then a strange laughter pulled my attention away from Ferguson's boots. The recruit lay face-down in the grass, breathing hard, wheezing, almost crying. Chief Ubel laughed at him.

"You're too weak, son. You got to get tougher!"

"Yes, sir!" the kid yelled. But his face was still on the ground, and his sweat and tears were watering the dry grass.

We were ordered to look to the front and marched past the recruit to the mess hall. I wondered what would happen to him. His face was still buried in the ground, and Ubel stood over him, grinning.

Inside the mess hall, I asked Ferguson what he'd heard about Ubel.

"He's a faggot," Ferguson said, shoveling food in his mouth. "He tried to make me when I was in the stencil room, but someone came in and told Ubel he had to go to a meeting or some damn thing."

"What do you mean, he tried to make you?"

"You know how we had to stencil our names in our clothes? He made me do mine over, after everyone else had gone, and then he stood real close behind me, pretending to help me do it right. His stinkin' breath was right on my neck."

Someone walked by, telling us we had to hurry up. Ferguson stared across the table at me.

"Let me lay this on you. The dude who came into the stencil room was a brother, see, and he told me that Ubel's men are made to stand for hours in the afternoon, and just watch the sun go down!"

"What for?"

"Punishment, I guess."

"Punishment? For what?"

"Who the hell knows?" Ferguson said. "Maybe he just gets off on havin' the power."

I thought about Marion just then and wondered what her diagnosis would be. *Sado-masochistic tendencies fueled by an inferiority complex*, I suspected. Or maybe he was just a prick.

Chapter 25

Around three the next morning, I awoke feeling sick. From somewhere in the dim red glow of the safety light came the guard's shuffle, moving closer until it was the sound of breathing. The guard walked by, apparently sleepwalking. After he'd moved away, I slipped off my bunk and went to the head.

I crouched at a toilet feeling hot and dizzy. The floor felt cool on my legs, and I rested my head on my arms, feeling like I might pass out. I may have drifted off for a few minutes, but then I felt a hand on my shoulder.

When I looked up, I saw only a wrinkled forehead, and a soft voice asked, "What's wrong?"

"I'm alright."

Paul Dowdy looked down at me with sympathy in his eyes

"Look, I'm really all right," I said again.

"Did you get sick?" Dowdy asked. His voice had a light, feminine sound.

"I thought I might."

He tried to put his palm on my forehead, but I

jerked away. "What the hell?"

"Let me see if you have a fever."

"No." I pushed him away. "Leave me alone, faggot."

Paul closed his eyes, looking truly wounded. I'd used that word before—in fact, it made me recall the night I'd broken Jimmy's nose—but hearing Ferguson say it earlier had planted it in my head. I regretted it at once.

"You don't have to be a homosexual to care about another person," Paul whispered. "Would you like me to pray for you?"

My laugh echoed off the tile walls. "Seriously? You want to pray for me?"

"Prayers can heal. I've seen it."

"Okay, Dowdy. Say a prayer for me. It couldn't hurt, I guess." I laughed again sarcastically. But part of me hoped he would.

*　*　*

The next morning between breakfast and lunch, I noticed Paul standing at one of the tall, narrow windows, his head down and his fingers interlaced at his waist. He looked serene. He'd probably taken ridicule all his life for his beliefs.

Movement outside the window caught my attention in time to see Chief Ubel herd a group of recruits onto the grinder. I watched the men march in rigid formation until halted by a command that I could not hear. Heat reflected up from the black grinder, giving me the impression that what I saw was a desert mirage.

The men all faced the mid-morning sun, and Ubel strode among their ranks grinning. Sometimes he stopped and straightened the shoulders of a recruit or made him arch his back to stand taller. At other times, he shoved one who was slightly out of alignment back a few inches. There was nothing better to do than watch the company commander's performance, so I stood there for half an hour.

Later, Hagen stepped beside me and looked at whatever I was watching.

"Is that Ubel's c-company?"

"Yeah. Poor guys have been on the grinder for almost an hour."

"He's a s-sadistic bastard, isn't he?"

"Enjoys putting his hands on those guys every chance he gets," I said.

Hagen leaned closer to the window and watched for a few seconds. Ubel put a finger under one recruit's chin and pushed his face higher.

"Sh-sure seems that w-way."

Eventually, Ubel's men marched away—where to, I had no idea—so I started a game of checkers with Hagen, once one of the game sets became available. We played four times, and I let him win the last time.

I was so bored, all I wanted to do was sleep, but we weren't allowed on our bunks. All we could do was wander around the barracks and talk. Seeing over sixty dazed and bored men milling about as if they were in a zombie movie depressed me to no end.

Sweat stung my eyes. I felt my cheek and realized I did have a fever, so I went to the bathroom to splash cold water on my face.

244

When I looked up from the cold water, Ferguson was standing behind me

"Hey, man. You don't look so good."

Suddenly, like a gunshot, a hoarse voice roared, "attention on deck!" Ferguson and I jumped both ways, leaping away from each other at first, then into each other, as we scrambled to stand at attention

"Attention on deck!" the voice ordered again.

We stood absolutely still.

In his beige uniform, wearing his hat, Commander Reed stepped from behind the white-uniformed sailor and smiled.

"We now have enough recruits to begin our real training."

Cheers erupted from the recruits, but faded just as quickly when Reed held up his hands for silence. Finally, the monotony of waiting was replaced by the less monotonous training in how to carry flags while marching in one direction, then turning sharply, only to march in another direction. A slightly more interesting tedium…

* * *

One afternoon, we were commanded to form up outside again. The sun burned through my blue utility cap. We marched to a large circular building and were halted outside its doors. Everything was beige: the grass, the brick building, the trees in the distance, even the sky. I shut my eyes against the heat as if the darkness of the mind made the body cooler. I visualized Sherry's bronze body that day on Morning Star Beach. Her smiling lips moist and red. "Where are you going?" she asked.

I jerked and my eyes opened. The building wobbled in front of me. So did the distant trees. I felt dizzy. Pain throbbed again in my back.

Someone pushed from behind. Everyone was stepping into the round beige building. We pulled the hot caps off our sweaty heads and tucked them into our belts as we entered. It was mercifully dim and cool inside.

An officer wearing more glitter on his chest than the others came on stage as someone yelled, "attention!" We jumped to our feet. The officer introduced himself as the Base Commander and told us this was our official Commissioning Ceremony. The pomp was intended to impress, but the hypnotic noise of the air-conditioner and the speaker drugged me to sleep—for how long, I couldn't be sure. My head bobbed, jerking me awake several times. I looked around to see if anyone had noticed, but half of the others were asleep, too. Then I saw Ubel. He sat stiffly on the edge of the stage at the end of one row of chairs. Under the lights, his face looked like a lump of putty. One of his eyebrows kept twitching. Puffy sacks under his eyes made them deep and dark.

Ubel turned his gaze in my direction. There were a couple of hundred recruits sitting in the audience, so I couldn't be sure he was actually looking at me, but I held his stare for several seconds before a smirk spread across his mouth and he winked. I had to look away. When I glanced back, Ubel's eyes were targeting a different section of the audience.

Even though Ubel was dressed like the other officers on the stage, to me at least, he seemed to stick out. I couldn't explain it, but I wondered if others noticed. Did the other officers know about Ubel? Did they know he did sadistic things to recruits? Did they know he had raped Jimmy Collins?

I was tempted to stand up and yell what I knew about Ubel to everyone in the room. I imagined how that would play out and realized I'd probably be taken into custody and wind up in the brig.

If what Jimmy Collins had told me was true—and I remembered vividly how credible his story had seemed in that jail cell on St. Thomas—then Ubel had to be stopped. That's when it hit me that I was here for a reason. I had a mission. I had to destroy Ubel.

A calming sense of satisfaction settled over me. I sat back and closed my eyes, grinning, even as the pain caught in my spine.

The rest of the day was a blur of pain. Mail arrived for some of the men, but of course I didn't get a letter. No one knew where I was. I tried to play checkers with Hagen, but halfway through the game, I lowered my head to the table and slept until it was time to go to the mess hall again.

Food made the pain worse. The walk back to the barracks made me wince, and Ferguson ran up behind me, putting his arm over my shoulder.

"How's it hangin', man? You're walkin' with a limp."

"My back is killing me. My sides feel like they're in a vice."

"You got a fever, man?"

"Who the hell can tell in this frickin heat?"

He pulled his arm off my shoulders. "You are kinda sweaty, man. Tell the Chief tonight. He'll send you to see a doc. Maybe some gorgeous-ass nurse will take your temperature, man."

"Yeah. Maybe."

Ferguson stopped me. "Back and sides hurt, huh?"

"Yeah. Pretty bad at times."

"You know, that sounds like what I had last year. A kidney infection."

I shrugged, recalling one of my dad's favorite gripes: *Everyone thinks he's a doctor.* "That explains the pain in my sides, but not the back."

"No, no, check it out. It's all connected."

He looked so earnest, I wanted to go along. "So what did the doctor do?"

"Gave me some pills, of course. Antibiotics."

I turned and started walking again. "Great. You wouldn't happen to have any left, would you?"

Ferguson stayed beside me. "Course not, but he also told me to cut some shit out of my diet. Coffee, bread, and salt. Especially salt."

"No more coffee, bread or salt. Got it."

"Seriously, man. I was feelin' better just a day later."

"I'll give that a try tomorrow."

Back in the barracks, most of the men headed into the smoking lounge, so I just sat at one of the picnic tables with my back against the table's edge, trying to find a comfortable position.

Later, I had to push the laundry bin around, which actually helped take my mind off the pain for a while. The best part was pushing it outside, into the night air. It was still muggy but not as hot, and I stood under the steamy, dark sky, wondering what Marion might be doing. She was probably waitressing. I visualized her in her sexy, low-cut dress and smiled at the memory of making love to her.

Of course, thinking of her brought back a flood of other memories—making love to Maggie, Sherry's horrible bloodied face, then Jimmy Collins crouched in the corner, covered in blood. I wondered if I'd ever get those images out of my head.

*   *   *

I could hardly wait to go to bed. But once I fell asleep, after tossing and turning, I had strange dreams about the Commissioning ceremony. In one dream, Ubel's body began to grow as he sat on the stage. It grew and grew like a snake, stretching from the stage out into the audience, squirming up the aisle, filling the auditorium, until his head—part human and part serpent—arched in my direction and his slimy tongue tested the air. The snake's lips twisted into a grin as he lurched toward me to strike like a cobra.

That dream caused me to jerk awake, which sent a jabbing pain down my back. I pulled myself off the bunk and started for the bathroom. After urinating, which seemed to lessen the pain a little, I went to the sink and splashed cold water on my face. When I looked up, Paul Dowdy standing behind me.

"You should see a doctor."

"Probably."

"Maybe what you have is contagious. Have you thought about that?"

I shook my head as I turned around to face him.

He started to reach for my forehead, but stopped

himself.

"I have been praying for you."

"It's not working."

"You have to help. You've got to pray, too."

With his fair complexion and bald head, Paul had seemed like an old man in a way, but suddenly I saw how young he really was. "How old are you?"

He looked at his feet. "Twenty. But the Bible has provided me with wisdom beyond my age, I believe. And so has…"

"What?" I asked.

"Sue." Paul said, turning away.

"Is that your girlfriend?"

He lowered his head, but nodded. "She was. She's…"

I didn't really want to know, but I asked anyway. "She's what?"

He faced me. "She's a bit older. She's the only woman I've ever… you know, been with. She got pregnant."

I wanted to be sympathetic, but my sides hurt and I felt dizzy. I sat on the edge of the sink, feeling obliged to hear more.

"So you got your girlfriend pregnant and then what? Ran off to join the Navy?"

He shook his head violently and took a step toward me. "No, no. I begged her to marry me, but she said I was too young to get married, and besides…"

"What?"

"I didn't have a job. I couldn't support her and a kid, she said."

Tears spilled from his eyes. If we'd been long-time friends, I might have put an arm around him. But we were both standing in the bathroom in our white boxers.

"So what did she do?" I asked, trying to sound sympathetic. "Marry someone else?"

He dropped his head into his hands. "No. Worse. Much worse. She lost it. That's how she put it—that she lost our baby."

I shut my eyes—in part because the pain in my back and sides was growing worse, but also because I could see how much pain Paul was in and I did not want to take that on, too.

"A miscarriage?"

He didn't answer at first, so I looked at him

"You think she had an abortion?"

"I don't know." He took his hands away from his eyes, pain and disappointment distorting his face. "Here I went into the Navy thinking I'd have a paycheck and benefits so we could get married."

I said the first thing that popped into my weary brain. "Maybe it's for the best."

Paul lunged toward me, his eyes going fierce with anger. "How in God's name can you say that?" He clenched his fists. "And now she says she's going to marry her old boyfriend just because he's got a good job. Here I was trying to do right by her, and she betrays me."

Someone walked up behind Paul. When I looked over Paul's shoulder, I saw Ubel's face.

"Where's your sentry?" Ubel demanded.

His voice startled Paul, who spun around and then jumped to stand at attention beside me. He swiped tears away from his cheeks.

"Sir?" Paul said, "should I yell 'attention on deck'?"

"Call me Chief, not sir. That's reserved for those uppity officers who don't know their ass from a hole in the ground." Ubel grinned. "Well, son, normally in the daytime, you would do just that when an officer walks in. But at night, we like to let the boys sleep."

"Yes, Chief."

"Now, why don't you two explain to me what you've been doin' in the can together this late at night."

"Sir," Paul answered, "this recruit's sick."

Ubel stepped closer, a weird grin on his face. His breath reeked of booze. "Oh? Not feeling well? Needed this momma's boy to come hold your hand?"

I stared into his eyes. "Guess the food tonight didn't agree with me."

Ubel inched closer, smelling of Aqua Velva and stale cigarettes. He rested his left hand on my shoulder.

"Why, the food here is excellent, boy. Don't you think it's excellent?" he said, turning to Paul.

"Yes, Chief," Paul answered, staring straight ahead.

"What's your name, recruit?"

"Randall, Chief."

"Randall? Not just plain ol' Randy?"

He patted my cheek but then put his hand back on my shoulder. "I like Randy better, recruit. It ain't so... what's the word I'm looking for?"

"Unusual?" Paul offered.

Ubel grinned at me. "Pretentious. That's the word I was looking for. Don't you think Randall is a

252

pretentious name?"

I wanted his hand off my shoulder. "Yes, Chief." My heart pounded. Ubel's grin made me sick.

"Maybe you don't like to be called Randy 'cause you know what that word means. Is that it, recruit?"

I could feel my body tensing up..

Ubel pushed his head closer and squinted. "Say, I remember you. You were staring at me today during the ceremony, weren't you?"

My heart was beating so hard he must have heard it. "I don't think so."

"Sure you were. I never forget a face." He winked. "Were you admiring my beautiful eyes, recruit?"

"No, Chief."

"No? What... you don't like my eyes?"

I didn't know how to answer, so I just peered into his dark irises. If there was a soul in there, I couldn't find it.

"Why are you shaking? Are you cold, boy?"

"Yes, Chief," I lied.

Ubel rubbed both of my shoulders. "Well, you'll have to get warmed up. We can't have a strong, young recruit die of pneumonia here in the Florida heat, now, can we? Just wouldn't do, would it?"

I tried to step out from under Ubel's hands.

"Permission to return to my bunk."

"You don't like my hands on your shoulder, boy?"

It was like dealing with someone who was insane. There was no right thing to say. Only wrong answers.

Ubel reached over to Paul's shoulder. "You don't mind a little fatherly affection, now, do you boy?"

"No, Chief," Paul said. He seemed to be trembling, too.

"Good, boy. Is it cold in here?" Ubel asked, rolling his eyes around. "Why is everybody shivering? Oh, I see," he said, reaching down to Paul's boxer shorts. "No wonder I'm not cold, and you two boys are. You're practically naked!"

It was that moment, as I watched Paul Dowdy shudder under Ubel's hand, that I decided I would have to kill Ubel.

My heart pounded so hard, I was sure I'd black out.

Then Ubel's face, and seemingly, his entire character, changed. He stood straighter. The awful grin left his lips. He glanced from Paul to me, breathed in deeply and exhaled slowly—spewing the stench of alcohol and cigarettes.

"Well, now," he said, "you boys best git on into bed. You got one damn hard day ahead, and you'll need all the rest you can git. And, I got my own company to take care of tomorrow. You know that I'm commanding company 113, and they're in competition with you'll for the next nine weeks. I'm gonna work their butts into the ground to get those honor flags away from Chief Reed. So you spread the word among the other men that there's some stiff competition."

"Yes, Chief," Paul said. "Is that all?"

Ubel turned to Paul. "Yeah, boy. That's all for tonight. But I'll be seein' you again, you can bet on it."

Then Ubel turned and walked away, and it was as if it hadn't really happened.

I finally exhaled. "Jesus Christ! I thought we were going to have to kill that guy."

"You shouldn't use the Lord's name in vain," Paul said. He followed me as we walked back into the dark barracks. "You shouldn't swear like you do."

"Goddamnit!" someone yelled from a nearby bunk. "Shut the hell up so we can sleep."

I laughed, despite my pain. Exactly why, I wasn't sure. Everything that had just happened seemed surreal. It was hard to tell where the real world ended and the nightmares began.

Chapter 26

Dazed, I drifted back to my bunk. The encounter with Ubel had drained me. I was asleep instantly, and as instantly it seemed, a loud voice crackled over the P.A. system: "Reveille, reveille. All hands heave to and fall out."

I sleep-walked through the morning. The scrambled eggs tasted better—not as rubbery—and I drank as much cold water as I could. The coffee was nothing but mud, so I skipped it for the first time in years, as Ferguson had suggested. I also skipped the toast and decided not to sprinkle salt on my eggs. Ferguson sat down beside me with food heaped on his tray—eggs, hash browns, grits, and four pieces of toast.

"Feelin' any better?"

"A little."

"You doin' what I told you? No coffee or bread?"

I nodded.

"Cool. I bet by this time tomorrow, you'll be feelin' a lot better."

I watched him shovel a forkful of hash browns into his mouth. "How can you eat so much and stay so fit?"

"Got my daddy's metabolism, my momma says. Nervous energy, I call it."

I picked at my eggs.

"Hey, I heard they put salt-peter in these scrambled eggs so we don't get horny. Do you think there's any truth to that?"

"Who knows?"

"Well, if they are, it ain't working. I haven't gone this long without getting' some ass in years."

That made me think about Marion and Maggie, but when I saw Ferguson shake ketchup onto his eggs, I couldn't help but think of Sherry.

"What?" Ferguson said. "You don't like ketchup on eggs? You got one disgusted look on your face."

"It looks pretty disgusting."

He took his fork and mixed the ketchup into the eggs so they turned into a mass of orange goop. "How's that look?"

"A work of art."

He smiled. "Damn straight!" He shoved a forkful into his smiling face, then shook his head from side to side, as if it was the most delicious food he'd ever eaten. "Mmmm, mmm, that's so good!"

After breakfast, back in the barracks, Chief Reed appointed a recruit I'd never noticed before, Recruit Chief Petty Officer. The RCPO would act as a drill sergeant, calling orders for the company to march by, Reed explained. He lectured us on what we could expect for the next nine weeks and answered questions afterwards. Ferguson raised his hand at the end of the session.

"Are they puttin' salt-peter in the eggs?"

Everyone laughed, but Ferguson remained stoic.

"That's top-secret, recruit," Reed answered.

There was another round of laughter. A little while later, we filed out to the grinder's asphalt to be marched to lunch by our new RCPO.

The RCPO made many mistakes, and the mistakes seemed to irritate Chief Reed, but we eventually ended up at the mess hall, where we waited behind other companies for lunch.

Hagen sat down across from me, obviously disgusted about something.

"What's the matter, Hagen?"

He coughed out, "That c-clown Reed appointed RCPO is wh-what's the matter. He's such a d-dumb asshole!"

"Give him time."

"I should have got-got that position. I d-deserve that position."

"There are some other positions left. Maybe he'll pick you for one of those."

Hagen didn't answer, just finished eating the soggy meal. I ate a small portion of food—it was "shit on a shingle," which was some sort of gravy over toast with cubes of ham in it..

Before dinner, Hagen was appointed squad leader along with five other recruits. Each of them only had twelve men under them, but the new prestige seemed to suit Hagen well. At dinner, I patted him on the shoulder and congratulated him.

"I should have at least b-been a p-platoon leader," Hagen complained.

"You take all this pretty seriously, don't you?"

"I w-want to m-make the Navy my-my life."

After dinner, before taps, Reed rescheduled the sentry duty shifts. The eight hours between ten p.m. and six a.m. were assigned to four recruits. Their two hour duties would be to stroll among the bunks while everyone slept to make sure no one escaped. Reed established the order of the duty alphabetically, so I, Randall Wake, did not have to worry about guard duty for some time. After taps, I lay on my bunk. The pain in my back and sides was still there, but less severe.

Eventually, though, I had to pee. While the sentry was at the far end of the barracks, I slipped off my bunk and scurried into the head. After I relieved myself, I turned around and found Paul Dowdy standing a few feet behind me.

"Well, you can relax, Samaritan. For some reason I'm getting better. Must have been one of those hundred and sixty-eight hour bugs that's going around."

"You should say a thank you prayer. The Lord answered my prayers."

"Look, Paul. God has nothing to do with it. You can stop your holy visitations. You're going to get us both in trouble if you keep meeting me in here. We almost got accused of jerkin' each other off, and that's not the kind of reputation I want."

Paul didn't budge. I washed my hands and then went around him to get back to my bunk.

* * *

The next day was uneventful, except that Chief Reed appointed me the laundry P.O. for the company.

259

I'd voluntarily taken out the laundry bin a couple of times before, but this made it official. The duties were easy. Collect dirty laundry in two cloth bins at night after passing out clean laundry to the recruits. On a form, report any missing or damaged clothing, and tuck it into a special pocket of one of the bins. Then I would wheel the bins through the same hall that the officers used, to a spot outside the battalion building.

I was surprised and even a little amused by the appointment, and Reed seemed to notice. He said it was based on my college background.

"It's not as trivial as it might seem, recruit. You've got to be observant and even a little diplomatic when you're collecting clothes from the men. Lost clothes and towels account for a lot of lost dollars here, so take it seriously, Seaman Wake."

"Yes, Chief," I said. But I almost couldn't contain my laugher at being called "Seaman" Wake. Four years of college under my belt, and I was going to be pushing around the Navy's dirty laundry.

And actually, that night I enjoyed going around to the bunks, chatting with the other guys as they tossed their dirty clothes into the bin. They'd stop playing checkers or cards, nod and grin, and occasionally one would say, "Hey, aren't you one of the guys from California?"

"That's right."

"What the hell brought you all the way here?"

I'd shrug or say something meaningless, and they'd say, "You know, there's a base in San Diego. Why didn't you go there?"

"Well, I just wound up here," I'd answer.

As I pushed the laundry bins through the hallway

that joined the two wings of the building, I realized that I was still under the impression that being on the Navy base was like staying at a hotel—as if I could check out any time I wanted. I opened the back door and pushed the bins to a spot where they'd be picked up, and as I left them, I stared up at the muggy Florida night sky. The air was so thick with steamy humidity that I could barely see the stars. This sky was nothing like the beautiful clear moon-lit sky of St. Thomas. It felt claustrophobic, like there was a nearly invisible dome over the base. And it hit me. *I'm trapped for four fucking years!*

"What the fuck did you do?" I asked myself.

On the way back into the barracks, I started to panic, thinking about the turn my life had taken. As I rounded a corner in the hall that put the door to my barracks in view, I saw Ubel walking toward me. We'd received instruction earlier that day on how to salute, so I put my right hand up to my forehead.

"What are you doing, recruit?" Ubel spat out.

"Sir?"

"First of all, what are you doin' saluting indoors? And second, what are you doin in this hallway?"

Ubel walked up as if he would walk right over me, but stopped just in time, his nose almost touching my chin.

Lowering my hand, I said, "Guess I haven't practiced enough."

"Obviously," Ubel said, grabbing my hand. "You've got to hold your fingers tight together like this." He crushed my fingers together, making them form a flat plane. "Then hold this part of your arm horizontal to your shoulder," he continued, feeling

261

my bicep, "and bring your forearm up at a thirty-degree angle to the rim of your cap."

I stood rigidly posed as he'd instructed. Then his eyes softened, and he smiled. I thought he wanted to kiss me.

Fortunately, Chief Reed stuck his head into the hallway.

"What have you got there, Chief?"

Ubel's expression hardened again before he turned around. "A lost recruit, I believe."

"That's my laundry P.O., Frank. What's he saluting you for?"

"I was just showing him how."

"Let him go. He's a good recruit. He's had some college."

Ubel looked impressed. "College boy, huh?"

"Yes, Chief," I replied.

I'd been preparing to use my raised arm to hit Ubel in the throat. All the hatred returned. The image of Jimmy Collins dangling from a noose popped into my head.

"I said you can go, recruit," Ubel said.

"Yes, Chief." I walked calmly away, nodding at Chief Reed when I walked by, then scurried into the Head, and threw up.

After Taps, I must have slept for an hour or so before the pain in my back woke me up. I rolled onto my side, but that didn't help. Finally, I climbed off the bunk and walked into the bathroom, clutching my sides like a winded runner.

A bank of twenty urinals hung against the wall on the left, opposite the twenty sinks on the right. Another twenty toilet stalls continued on the left wall to the end of the room, and to the right were the showers. I stopped at the first urinal inside the door to relieve myself, and as I was doing so, I heard what sounded like someone whimpering, from deep in the back of the bathroom.

Before washing my hands, after I'd finished peeing, I walked quietly past the stalls. All the doors had been removed, so it was easy to check each one. Then I heard the sound again—something between an infant's whimper and a moan of pleasure—coming from the showers.

When I peeked around the corner, I saw Ubel standing in front of Hagen, his back against the wall. Ubel's hands were resting on Hagen's shoulders, and Hagen seemed to be staring over the officer's head.

Ubel leaned closer and whispered into Hagen's ear. "You want to do well, don't you, son?"

"Y-yes, s-s-sir."

Hagen's voice was low and shaky—I could tell he was afraid to do anything.

"You want someone like me to help you get ahead in this man's Navy, don't you?"

"S-sir, yes, sir."

Ubel's hands gripped Hagen's face. "We can help each other, son. What do you think?"

"W-what d-do you w-want from m-me?"

Ubel leaned forward again to whisper in Hagen's ear, and his eyes darted in my direction.

I pulled my head away. My heart raced and my vision blurred as I tried to think what to do.

My first instinct was to run into the shower and hit Ubel as hard as I could—to beat him to death. But then I realized I'd go to prison, probably for the rest of my life, for killing an officer. Boot camp was bad enough. How terrible would prison be?

Pain gripped my back and sides so intensely just then, I thought I might pass out. I looked in the mirror over the sink. Dark bags hung under my sunken eyes.

"Are you okay?"

Paul's voice made me jump. He walked toward me with his usual saintly sympathetic expression. I turned on the faucet and splashed cold water on my face, hoping the sound would stop Ubel.

"No," I said, keeping my voice low. "The pain's back, worse than ever."

From around the corner, I heard Ubel hiss, "Shhh."

Paul put his hand on my shoulder. "Did you say a prayer?"

I laughed. "Are you serious?"

He nodded.

"You're telling me God made the pain come back because I forgot to thank him. That seems pretty petty of the Almighty, don't you think?"

"Maybe he's trying to teach you a lesson in humility."

He said it so earnestly that I couldn't bring myself to laugh again. "Maybe I just need a doctor."

I brushed by him and left, knowing that Ubel had probably heard our conversation. I wondered if he suspected that I'd seen him, or if I'd kept my voice innocent enough that he'd assume I hadn't. I also wondered if Paul would make the same discovery I had, and that made me wonder how he'd handle it. Either way, I was sure Hagen was safe.

Back on my bunk, I lay on my side in the darkness, facing the entrance to the bathroom. Paul walked out a few minutes later and returned to his bunk. I kept my eyes on the doorway to see if Hagen would come out, too, but he didn't. At least not before I finally fell asleep.

Chapter 27

"Reveille, reveille. All hands heave to and fall out. Reveille, reveille."

The crackling voice made me jump off my bunk. We stumbled around each other, half awake. I made my bed as I'd been taught and took my things from the locker to the crowded bathroom. I was just starting to shave when Hagen walked behind me carrying his kit.

"Morning," I said.

He didn't even glance at me. My heart sank. I wanted to ask him what happened after Paul and I left, but that would mean telling him what I'd seen. It made me sick thinking about it.

At first, Hagen avoided me in the mess hall, but I managed to sit across from him, a few recruits away. He looked troubled.

"Everything okay?" I asked. "You get some bad news or something?"

He stared at me as if he didn't recognize me at first. "Nah. Just d-didn't sleep very w-well."

The guy next to him snorted. "Who the hell can sleep on those damn cots, anyway? Fucking uncomfortable."

"Damn straight," the recruit next to me said.

Hagen shoveled more food into his mouth before grabbing his tray and standing.

"Wait up," I called. But he left before I could get around the end of the table to join him.

Back in the barracks, he went inside the smoking room and lit a cigarette before I could grab him. I looked through the glass and watched him stare at the wall, and I just knew something more had happened with Ubel.

I needed to know what, and I wanted Hagen to know that I'd help him. I waited outside the smoking lounge, thinking I'd talk to him when he finished his cigarette. But then he lit another. I was just about to go inside the smoke-filled room when Chief Reed stepped out of his office. The RCPO yelled, "Attention on deck!" and we froze into position. Reed commanded us to grab the drill rifles and form up on the Grinder.

The sun beat down as we formed rows, spacing ourselves one arm's length away from each other. We held the rifles against our shoulders as if they were babies that needed to be burped. We had to maneuver the rifles into six different positions every time Reed called a command.

"Keep them babies up," Reed yelled. "Them babies getting heavy?"

We stood in rows, rigid except for our arms that volleyed the rifles to and fro.

"Hup, hup, hup," Reed signaled, as we twisted our arms and hands in the pattern of the drill. He strolled among us, watching. He stepped in front of me, so I tried to maneuver the rifle perfectly, but the pain in my back was catching at my muscles and I was wincing.

The Florida sun beat down like a sunlamp. My vision blurred, and the pain got so bad, I knew I was about to faint.

I looked at Reed. "Chief. Permission to pass-out."

His expression didn't change. "Permission denied, recruit." Then he stepped closer. "Is that my laundry P.O.?"

"Yes, Chief."

"What in hell's wrong?"

"Too hot, Chief."

He scanned the others. "Anyone else feel that way?"

Everyone stood at attention, the rifles resting against our shoulders, afraid to answer.

"Well?"

"Yes, Chief," some recruits finally admitted.

Reed looked disappointed and walked to the front of our ranks. He had the RCPO march us back inside the cool barracks where we locked up the drill rifles. We killed an hour doing nothing and then marched to lunch early, only to wait half an hour longer outside.

I made sure to find Hagen as we grabbed our trays.

"Hey, man, I want to talk to you."

"Yeah? W-what about?" He loaded silverware and a napkin onto his tray before grabbing a plate. I did the same.

I leaned in close and whispered, "I saw you last night."

He shot me a curious look. "S-saw me?"

268

"Yeah. I saw Ubel hassling you in the shower," I whispered.

He blushed and turned away. "Guy's a pr-prick."

"Hey, man, no argument from me. Did he try anything?"

"W-what d-do you mean?"

Someone behind the glass barrier loaded bits of hamburger meat smothered in dark brown gravy on our plates.

"Look, I can back you up, if you want to file a complaint or something. You know, if he made you... do something you didn't want to do."

He stared at me. "W-what the hell d-do you m-mean?"

I leaned in. "Did he do anything bad, like grab your crotch?"

Hagen's face crumbled. "It sh-sure seemed like he wanted to. Made me sick."

Someone else behind the sneeze barrier put bowls of fruit salad on our trays.

Hagen grabbed a carton of milk. I took a glass of ice water and we sat at one of the tables.

"He-he's not the k-kind of officer the N-Navy wants."

Keeping my voice just above a whisper, I said, "Look, Hagen, I heard that Ubel raped a recruit."

Hagen's surprise seemed genuine.

"You-you mean a female recruit?"

"No. A guy."

He shook his head. "F-fucking prick."

I nodded. "He's got to be stopped."

"H-how? W-what can we d-do?"

"Report it to Chief Reed. You could tell him

269

about last night. I can back you."

"B-but he d-didn't really do anything. P-put his h-hands on my sh-shoulders. Be-besides, he was d-drunk. I c-could smell the boo-booze on his b-breath."

Hagen took a bite of the meat and gravy, and I sat there thinking.

"We've got to do something," I said. "That guy needs to be stopped."

"I-I don't w-want to rat him out yet. We-we've got to have more p-proof."

"He's got to be caught in the act. By an officer."

Chewing his food, Hagen shrugged.

"What if you and I hang out in the Head tonight and wait for him to show up? I'll pretend to leave and you stay around, you know, like you were hoping to see him again."

Hagen shook his head. "No-no way."

"But I'll be around the corner, watching. When he starts to get too friendly, I'll find Chief Reed."

"F-fuck that. You-you stay behind with Ubel, and I'll g-get Reed."

"I don't know if that would work."

"W-why not?"

"He likes you better than me."

Hagen scowled. "F-fuck you."

"I'm not saying anything about you, man. It's just, you're smaller than I am. Less of a threat."

Hagen was about the same height and build as Jimmy Collins. He ate the rest of his food and guzzled his milk before turning to me. "You-you do w-what y-you want. I'm just going to avoid him." He grabbed his tray and left.

I examined the food on my plate, ate a few bites,

and then looked at the table knife on my tray. The distinguishing feature of a table knife is its rounded end. The origin of this, I learned from my father, is attributed by tradition to Cardinal Richelieu around 1637, reputedly to cure dinner guests of picking their teeth with their knife-points. Later, King Louis XIV of France banned pointed knives at his table to reduce violence. Dad had been a great conveyer of such trivia.

I ran my finger along the serrated edge. With enough force, I could probably drag that across Ubel's throat and open his windpipe. I slipped the knife into my pocket and then took the tray to the return window.

After lunch, Ferguson and I jogged back to Battalion Four together. Once everyone returned from the mess hall, Reed had us grab our drill rifles again and form up on the Grinder. We learned to march two-by-two in unison. It amused me to watch how seriously Reed inspected our feet and legs as we marched. He walked alongside us, bent over, as if one wrong move would bring the end of the world.

After almost an hour of that, we stood side by side in rows, rehearsing the drills with the rifle, tossing it from hand to hand, flipping it over, changing it from one shoulder to the other. If nothing else, it was a good workout for my arms. Once in awhile, a pain would catch in my back and I flinched, but fortunately Reed wasn't checking me when it happened.

We were spinning our rifles for about the millionth time when I heard Hagen grunt and looked over just in time to feel the butt of his rifle hit me on the forehead. I fell backward—more out of surprise than pain—and watched my own rifle slip from my fingers and flop on the asphalt like a stiff, dead eel.

"Oww," I said, grabbing my forehead.

Everyone around us stopped, and soon Reed screamed, "What the hell's goin' on?"

"Man down," someone yelled.

"S-sorry," Hagen said. "M-my g-gun slipped."

Reed yelled, "Attention," and everyone froze with their rifles leaning against their shoulders. Except Hagen. He looked down at me—a combination of sympathy and fear pulling at his face—unsure whether to help me stand or grab his rifle. He chose the rifle and then stood at attention as Reed hurried over.

"What happened?"

"My g-gun slipped, sir!"

Reed looked down at me. I was still on my butt, feeling the lump that was quickly rising on my forehead.

Reed reached for my hand. "Stand up, Seaman!"

I took his hand and let him pull me to my feet. I was dizzy—whether from the blow to my head or just the heat, I couldn't tell.

"Don't leave that rifle on the ground!"

"No, Chief!" I reached down and picked up the Remington, then leaned it on my shoulder and stood at attention.

"Let me see."

I took my hand away and saw the look of anger on Reed's face change to concern.

"Damn, son, that looks like it's gonna hurt."

"Already does, Chief."

272

"You look mighty pale, Recruit. You sick?"

"Feeling a little wobbly, yes, Chief."

He leaned in and examined my eyes. I could smell English Leather on his sweaty face. "Your pupils are still the same size, so no sign of concussion yet."

"Thank you, Chief." It was all I could think to say.

"Still, you'd better put a cold cloth on that."

"Yes, sir," I said, still standing at attention.

"You have my permission to go back to the barracks and put a wet paper towel on your forehead. You may lay down on your bunk until we get back. I will re-assess the situation then and determine if you need medical attention. Is that clear, recruit?"

"Yes, Chief," I said. But I didn't move.

"Well, then, go. You are dismissed!"

"Should I march or just walk, Chief?"

He smiled. "At ease, seaman. You may walk."

He stepped to the side, out of my way.

I lowered the rifle and stepped out of formation, then turned to walk back to the barracks.

"Now then, Mister Hagen," Reed said. "Let's see if we can improve your grip."

* * *

It was a luxury to be alone inside the air-conditioned barracks. Something about the small kindness Chief Reed had shown me made me feel better. I went to the bathroom and examined the lump. It was a raised little half egg, streaked blue and red and purple. I turned on the faucet and soaked a paper towel in cold water, then applied in to the lump, watching myself in the mirror. The steady hum of the air-conditioner merged with the ringing in my head.

The cold towel felt good. I closed my eyes and leaned against the sink, imagining how much better an ice pack would feel. Or a cold bottle of beer.

A hand gripped my shoulder. The face behind mine in the mirror belonged to Ubel.

"What in hell is going on here, recruit?"

Frozen with fear, I couldn't speak. I pulled the towel away from my head hoping the lump would speak for me.

"Turn around." He tugged at my shoulder.

My heart beat so fast, I thought I would pass out. But I turned.

Ubel stood much too close. His eye lids drooped—he already smelled of booze. A grin tugged his lips apart.

"You faint out there in the heat? Fall on your noggin'?"

Behind the booze on his breath was the smell of cigarette smoke.

No, Chief. One of the other recruits lost his grip on his rifle. It hit my head."

He touched the lump with his index finger. "That hurt?"

My tunnel vision was so bad, I couldn't see anything except Ubel's mouth.

"A little, Chief."

His finger brushed my eyebrow and then slid down my cheek. He didn't speak, but his hand went behind my head and pulled me closer. I pulled away, but he jerked my head down and planted his mouth on mine.

274

I squirmed away and swiped the back of my hand across my mouth. "What the fuck?"

Ubel's face hardened. "Do not use that kind of language with me, recruit. I am your superior officer."

That's when I remembered the butter knife in my pocket. My heart racing, I grabbed the knife, yanked it out of my pocket and held it up to Ubel's face.

He grinned. "Shit. You think you can hurt me with that? Pathetic."

To prove him wrong, I dragged the serrated blade across the palm of my other hand, slicing open a shallow wound. Then I lunged at him, trying to cut his throat, but he jumped back, avoiding the knife. He hit my wrist with his arm so hard, I dropped the knife. It clattered and clanged on the tile floor.

Ubel bent down and grabbed the knife, then turned to face me.

"Do you realize what this means, boy? You attacked an officer!"

I was trapped. Ubel stood between me and the door. If I tried to run around him, he'd be able to grab me.

"You're going to the brig, son. You realize that?" He waved the knife back and forth in front of my eyes. "You could get twenty years for what you just did."

My back tensed, my sides burned with pain and my heart raced.

"You got one chance here now, boy. One chance and one alone,"

My heart beat so hard, my head throbbed.

"Know what that is?"

I felt dizzy and knew I was going to black out. I reached for the sink to steady myself. My legs went weak, and I dropped to my knees.

Ubel smiled. "That's it. That's it." He stepped closer, reaching for his zipper. "You be nice to me, and I'll be nice to you. Understand?"

I looked up, feeling the bile rise in my throat.

"You make me feel good," he whispered, "and I'll make sure you don't go to jail."

"Is this how it went with Jimmy Collins?" I asked.

He stopped. "Who?"

My skin tingled and my jaws stung. "Jimmy Collins. Kid you raped. Remember him?"

"Jimmy Collins. Jimmy Collins. Come to think of it, yeah. Troubled kid."

"Troubled kid," I repeated. I didn't care anymore. I knew I'd black out soon and Ubel would do whatever he wanted. I was too weak to stop him. "You were his worst trouble, so go fuck yourself."

"No," he hissed, "that's your job."

Chapter 28

It may be true, after all, that your life flashes before your eyes right before you die. Images of childhood, fishing with my father, then him lying in his casket, the view from the Galleon House, Sherry and Maggie's laughing faces, Marion in the Miami moonlight—all flashed through my mind.

Ubel set the knife on the edge of the sink and stepped closer. He took my head in his hands and turned my face up. His eyes drowsy, his smile softened.

"Be nice and gentle with me. Understand?"

Gripping my head more firmly, he forced me to nod.

Too weak to fight back, I just floated between consciousness and unconsciousness.

"Keep those teeth in check, son. Just pretend you're sucking on a popsicle. A delicious popsicle."

He took one hand from my head and fumbled inside his zipper.

I looked down. My hand was bleeding, my head was throbbing, and I was about to gag.

A sudden burst of hatred gave me the strength to yank my head out of his grip. I fell on my side, then struggled to stand.

Then a loud crack echoed off the bathroom walls. Ubel's hand went limp. He fell to the floor, landing beside me with a thud.

Paul Dowdy stood over him, the Remington drill rifle in his hands.

"I saw the knife," he said, "and your bloody hand." His high-pitched voice was filled with panic. He dropped the rifle and reached down, helping me to my feet. "I didn't know what he was going to do next, but you needed help."

Ubel's limp body was like a rag doll on the floor.

Still dizzy, but standing, I swayed back and forth, looking at him. "Is he dead?"

"Sweet Jesus," Paul said, "I hope not."

We both stared at Ubel.

"Oh my God, I'll be court-martialed for this!"

Paul's pale face had gone even whiter.

"Why aren't you outside?"

"Chief Reed sent me to check on you."

Ubel groaned. He reached back and felt the lump at the base of his skull. Then he rolled onto his back and stared up as if unable to recognize us.

"What the hell happened?"

I glanced at Paul and he glanced at me, and for a second, I think we both hoped Ubel wouldn't remember anything.

"Which one of you sorry sons-a-bitches hit me?"

Paul started to speak, but I interrupted. "I did, you sick sack of shit."

Ubel sat up. "Well, your life is over, recruit. You hear me? It's over!"

I picked up the rifle and raised it over my head with the butt facing Ubel.

"Yeah, I hear you."

Even as Paul screamed, "Nooo," I smashed the rifle butt into Ubel's face. Blood splattered as bits of yellow teeth flew from his gaping hole of a mouth.

I took aim again, but Paul grabbed my arm.

Ubel clutched his mouth, eyes wide with fear.

I jerked the weapon away and smashed the butt into Ubel's forehead.

He collapsed, out cold.

"Oh my God, Randall, what have you done?"

"I did what had to be done. What he deserved."

"We're both going to the brig for the rest of our days. Holy Mary, Mother of God. My life is ruined."

Paul's eyes filled with tears. I hated to think of him in jail. He'd never survive it.

Then it became clear what I'd have to do.

"No, Paul, not you. Put it on me. You can tell them I hit Ubel. Me alone. You can be a witness."

"But that would be a lie."

"So what?"

"I can't let you take the blame for what I did. I can't bear false witness."

"It won't be that bad for me, Paul. Look, you can tell them what you saw. The knife in Ubel's hand and the cut on me. Say I acted in self defense."

"I've got to tell the truth. I hit him first."

"Paul, you're too good for your own good."

Ubel moaned. We looked down. His hands twitched. I absurdly thought of the scene in the old 1930s movie when Victor Frankenstein yells, "It's alive!"

"At least he's not dead, Paul."

"Thank the Lord Almighty!"

"I know things about him, Paul. He seduces young men. Forces them to do things. Bad things. Unholy things. Against their will."

Paul looked at me. "Are you speaking the truth?"

"He's why I joined the Navy. To expose him."

"So help you God?"

"So help me God."

Paul studied my eyes, searching my soul, I think.

"I met one of Ubel's victims when I was in the Caribbean. A kid named Jimmy Collins. Ubel raped him."

He winced, as if he actually felt Jimmy's suffering.

"That kid killed two innocent people I knew and seriously injured two others. Then he took his own life."

He shook his head, squeezing his eyes closed. "That's too horrible to imagine."

"But it's true. This man's responsible for a lot of pain and suffering. And who knows how many others he's harassed over the years?"

Paul opened his eyes and looked at me. He looked at the rifle on the floor, my bloody hand print on the grip, and he looked at the table knife on the sink—dry blood on the blade.

"I'm going to pray for wisdom, Randall."

He gripped my shoulders and exhaustion overtook me.

"You do that, Paul. Pray for both of us."

Then my world went black.

*   *   *

I awoke in a white room as small as the hotel room on St. Thomas had been. A needle with a tube attached to it stuck out of my right arm.

"What's going on?"

"You're in the hospital."

I looked at a slender man dressed in white. His pock-marked face seemed indifferent.

"Who are you?"

"An orderly."

My left hand was bandaged. I lifted my left arm but found my wrist handcuffed to the railing of the bed.

"Why am I handcuffed?"

"You assaulted an officer."

The memories flooded back as I tried to sit up.

"Ubel?"

The young orderly shrugged. He didn't look much older than me.

"But he attacked me."

"Someone will be here to take your statement."

"Let me tell Chief Reed what happened. He'll understand."

"You're out of commission for a while."

No one visited me that evening to "take y statcment," and the orderlies who took my pulse and brought my meals answered no questions. The worst indignation was being forced to us a bed pan because they would not unlock the handcuffs.

When I awoke in the morning, an orderly removed the needle from my wrist, the sun shone high and bright in the Florida sky outside the window, and a different orderly brought in a tray with scrambled eggs, toast, a small fruit cup, and a small glass of tomato juice.

"How are you feeling today?" he asked while taking my pulse.

He looked a little older than the previous orderly and had a kinder face.

"Confused." I jangled the handcuffs. "Am I under arrest?"

"Someone will explain it to you later."

He wrote some numbers on my chart, patted my foot, and left.

I picked at the rubbery eggs and ate the fruit.

Half an hour later, a doctor came in. Good looking, in his mid-thirties, with well-groomed dark hair—he reminded me of Jay, the dentist. I smelled Old Spice when he leaned close and looked into my eyes with a light.

"You've had a kidney infection," he said. "We've got you on antibiotics, so you should be feeling better. I don't think it's done any permanent damage, but we'll need to monitor you for a day or two."

"Would the infection cause all this pain in my back?"

His thick black eyebrows arched. "You have pain in your back, too? Not just your sides?"

"Yeah."

"Great pain?"

"Yes."

His head cocked to one side. "The infection could be the cause—kidneys rest closest to the back. Where's the pain exactly?"

I sat upright, running my finger up and down my

lower spine.

"We'll take a look."

I was X-rayed later, and the doctor returned before dinner.

"You often experience pain where you've showed me?"

I nodded. "Yeah, lately. I can't get comfortable, it hurts so bad."

"Okay. Let me get someone."

He stepped out and a few minutes later, an orderly came in with a wheelchair. He unlocked the handcuffs and told me to stand up.

I climbed out of bed, wincing with the pain in my lower back. But the pain in my sides was not as bad.

"Put this robe on, recruit," he said, handing me a thin, pale-blue robe. "Now sit down."

When I sat down, he handcuffed my left wrist to the arm of the wheelchair and rolled me out into the hall.

The doctor led us to a room where we viewed X-rays. He pointed to the image of my spine.

"See this," he said, "here and here?"

I looked more closely. The images of my vertebrae looked like a series of white butterflies stack one upon the other.

"The stems of two of your lower vertebrae did not fuse."

Just above my pelvis, a couple of the vertebrae did look a little different—as if the wings weren't attached to the body of the butterfly.

"This is a congenital occurrence. Mild spina-bifida. Spina-bifida occulta, to be precise. Because of the swelling from your kidneys, pressure pushed

283

against these malformations. This is what causes your pain."

"Is it serious?"

"Can be. The most extreme form causes paralysis and mental retardation."

"Is there a chance I could be paralyzed?"

"That's a possibility. If you were injured there sometime down the road. Those vertebrae are weak links in the chain, you might say."

The news slowly sunk in. I shuddered at the idea of sitting in a wheelchair my whole life. "How do we fix it?"

"We need to go in and fuse those vertebrae—try to get the wings attached."

"You want to operate on my spine?"

"It's not a question of whether or not I want to operate. It's what we need to do to repair the spine."

The idea of someone cutting open my back and messing around with my spine scared the hell out of me. I wished my father were still alive so I could get his opinion.

"Look," I said, "my father was a doctor. He told me always get a second opinion."

The doctor lowered his clipboard and scowled. "Are you refusing treatment?"

"No, not necessarily."

"If you want to stay in the Navy, then you're going to have to get this done. It'll take a few days to schedule the surgery, and it will be a week or two of recovery, so obviously you'll need to start boot camp over again once you're released. Unless, of course, you get court-martialed and go to prison."

I closed my eyes and imagined what the next few

weeks—and then the next few months after that—would be like.

"Can I be discharged because of it?"

"Is that what you want?"

"I don't want someone cutting open my back and messing with my spinal cord."

The doctor rested a hand on my shoulder. "Look, kid, assuming you don't go to the brig for striking an office, which is damn unlikely, you've got a congenital malformation that needs fixing. It's gonna plague you your whole life. Take care of it while you're still enlisted."

"You think I'll go to the brig?"

"Probably, but I'm not involved with that. The legal guys will deal with it, and they take forever. So my advice is, get this done sooner rather than later. You're innocent until proven guilty, so we can keep you here and get you all fixed up while the legal guys are doing the investigation."

I searched his eyes. He seemed honest and capable, but I didn't completely trust him. Maybe having been close to the philandering dentist had shaken my confidence in the medical profession.

"I've got to think about it," I said.

He shrugged. "Suit yourself, but…."

"What?"

"You get a medical discharge, that will be on your permanent record. Every time you apply for a job, it will come up."

"So?"

"Who's going to hire you if you have such a weak back that you had to be discharged from the Navy?"

I tried to imagine a scenario where a future

employer would look at my military records and refuse to hire me.

"I guess if it becomes an issue later in life, I'll get the operation then."

"That's an option," he said, nodding, "but it will cost a fortune. Even if you have good medical insurance, this is a pre-existing condition, so you'll still have to pay thousands of dollars. If we do the operation here, Uncle Sam picks up the bill."

The more the good doctor tried to convince me, the more skeptical I became.

"I'll think about it."

He scowled. "It's probably a moot point anyway."

"Why?"

"Because you'll probably be found guilty and get sent to Leavenworth, and the Navy won't want to spend money for back surgery. Not for a convict."

He spun on his heels and left, shaking his head. The orderly wheeled me back to my room and handcuffed me to the bed again.

I sat there, wondering how it would go. I'd seen trials in movies and on TV shows, of course, but I wondered what a military trial would be like. How different would it be from the courtroom scenes in *Law and Order*? Who would be called to testify? Paul Dowdy would certainly be a good witness for me, but would Hagen tell what had happened to him?

I made a mental note to contact the public defender on St. Thomas who'd been Jimmy's lawyer. He seemed like a decent guy. Maybe his testimony could help me somehow. Mike and Whitey, too. They could describe what we all saw the night Sherry was killed and Jimmy was arrested. But would their testimony even be admissible in a military trial?

My head was swimming with questions, and it was as frustrating as hell not knowing what would come next or how I would handle it. When I saw an orderly walk by, I called to him.

"Hey, man, I'm in a lot of pain here. Can I get some pain meds?"

He paused outside my door without answering and disappeared.

"Hey," I yelled, "I'm in a lot of pain!"

I just wanted to be knocked out so I could sleep. There was no other way to pass the interminable amount of time between now and the hell that awaited me.

Eventually, the young orderly came back with two white pills in his hand.

"This is the strongest medicine I'm allowed to give you," he said, proffering his hand.

"What is it?"

"Bayer aspirin."

Chapter 29

Chief Reed came to see me the next morning after breakfast. I was still handcuffed to the bed, and when I saw him walk into my room, I threw a corner of the blanket over my arm.

"There's my laundry P. O. How you feeling, Wake?"

"Embarrassed, Chief."

He nodded. "You've gotten yourself into a hellavu mess. No doubt about that."

"Can you tell me what's going on? The orderlies and doctors aren't saying anything."

He dragged a chair over and sat down.

"When you busted open Chief Ubel's head, you opened a big-ass can of worms, recruit. You and Dowdy both."

An image of worms squirming out of Ubel's skull jumped into my mind.

"Sir?"

"Turns out, Chief Ubel has been under investigation for a few weeks now. Something about a kid killing himself down in the Caribbean. Someone from the D.A.'s office on one of the islands sent a report to the base commander."

My heart started to race. I wondered if I should

admit to knowing Jimmy Collins.

"Don't know the whole story yet," Reed continued, "but I guess this kid killed a couple down there and then took his own life. He claimed Chief Ubel had molested him while he was here for boot camp."

"Like he tried to do with me?"

Chief Reed's face sagged. "Looks that way. About your situation, son, I'm not privy to the JAG's investigation, but I can tell you what I told them. And what I heard Paul Dowdy tell them."

I sat up. "I'd like to know, Chief."

"I told them you were an outstanding recruit, and I didn't think you'd attack an officer without a reason. Your friends came to me and told me what Chief Ubel had done to them. Ferguson told about an incident in the stencil room, and Hagen went into great detail about a very inappropriate encounter in the bathroom one night."

I nodded. "I witnessed that," I admitted, "but I was too afraid to say anything."

Reed cocked an eyebrow. "You could've come to me. In fact, you both should have reported it to me."

"But…"

"What, son? Tell me."

"You and Chief Ubel seemed to be friends."

He chuckled. "We were friendly because we worked in the same building, but he's never been my friend. I actually have never much cared for the man."

Reed seemed to be telling the truth.

"How's Chief Ubel doing? I'm not going to be charged for attempted murder, am I?"

Reed shrugged. "You two did a number on him,

that's for sure. Broken jaw, concussion. Claims he can't remember much."

"Ubel was trying to get me to… do something I didn't want to do." Admitting even that much made me blush. "He threatened me, Chief. I felt trapped."

"And that's what you'll need to tell the investigators. Of course, they've already heard from Paul Dowdy."

"Sir?"

"Dowdy told them that Ubel was trying to force you to, you know, go down on him. Says he saw Ubel put the bloody knife on the sink and then pressured you to get on your knees."

"Yes, Chief. That's true," I admitted.

"Dowdy says he snapped when he saw the gash on your hand, and he hit the Chief first."

"No, Chief. I hit Ubel. Paul tried to stop me."

Reed's doubt was obvious. "Son, Dowdy told us exactly what happened. Given the circumstances and what we've learned about Chief Ubel, I think you and Paul won't do much time."

I blinked. "But we will do time? Is that what you're saying?"

"Son, you struck an officer. Even if you felt justified, you committed a crime."

"But, Chief—"

"You should have reported the incidents and let the chain of command operate."

I felt sick to my stomach as much for Paul as for myself. "Yes, Chief."

There was nothing more to say. Chief Reed looked at me with sympathy in his eyes and I sensed his disappointment. I could see the kindness and empathy in his face that I'd often seen in my father's. *He's a good man*, I thought.

"I'm sorry for letting you down. I hope my actions didn't... besmirch your career."

Reed grinned. "Besmirch? A little bit of a black eye, I guess. Gonna have to do a better job of lettin' you boys know how the chain of command works. How to report something... out of line." He stood up and patted my foot. "Stay strong, recruit."

"Yes, Chief."

I watched as he turned and walked out of the room. I wondered if I'd ever see him again. Maybe at my trial.

That afternoon, I was half asleep when two officers in dress whites walked into the room and stood on either side of the bed. They could have been brothers. Tall and fit, with square jaws and piercing dark eyes. The one on my right had a slight cleft in his chin that made me think of a young Kirk Douglass.

"Wake up, recruit. You've got some questions to answer."

I sat up and pulled the covers over my bare chest, feeling very exposed.

"Who are you guys?"

The one on my left answered first. "We're with the NIS. You know what that is, or are you too green?"

I looked at the other officer.

"Naval Investigation Service, recruit," he stated. "We're here to investigate the Article 90 charges that will probably be filed against you."

"Article 90?"

"Any person who strikes a superior officer or lifts any weapon or offers violence against an officer can be charged with an Article 90 violation."

My heart raced and my vision blurred. "Even if it was in self defense?"

The two men exchanged glances.

"You care to elaborate?"

I held up my bandaged hand. "Chief Ubel attacked me first. He tried to force me to give him... oral sex."

The officer on my right—Kirk Douglass—fished a small recorder out of his black leather briefcase. "Are you ready to make a statement on the record?"

My mind raced. This was all suddenly very real and very serious. "I guess so."

"Good. State your name and rank for the record."

"Randall Wake. Rank? I guess I'm an E-3. I'm just a recruit."

"Tell us what happened on the day you and Seaman Paul Dowdy struck Chief Ubel."

"But it started before then. At least, for me it started weeks ago."

I told them everything. My first encounter with Jimmy Collins at the Galleon House, the next few encounters, breaking his nose at the bar, then seeing him in the bedroom where he'd killed Sherry and Stewart. I told them what Jimmy had revealed about Ubel while he was in the DA's office in The Fort on St. Thomas, and then I told them what I'd seen the night Ubel had Hagen pinned in the shower.

"Tell us about the day you and Recruit Dowdy struck Chief Ubel."

I told them about how ill I'd been, and then how

Scott Evans

Hagen had accidentally hit me on the head with his drill rifle. "Chief Reed sent me into the barracks to put a cold compress on the lump. Next thing I knew, Ubel had snuck up behind me and was acting, I don't know, belligerent."

"Belligerent?"

"Yeah, like he was pushed out of shape that I wasn't on The Grinder with the rest of my company. I told him Chief Reed had ordered me into the barracks, but I guess he didn't believe me. When he got closer, I could tell he'd been drinking, like before."

"What do you mean, like before?"

"Every other time he got close to me, I could smell the booze on his breath."

"Go on. What happened that day in the bathroom?"

"Like I said, he got up in my face and started to threaten me. Said I'd go to jail if I didn't do what he wanted."

"Where'd the knife come from?"

"It just sort of appeared," I lied. "Suddenly it was in Ubel's hand and my hand was bleeding. It's still kind of a blur to me."

"To be clear, you're accusing Chief Ubel of slicing your left hand open with a table knife?"

I didn't want to answer, so I stared at the officer as coldly as I could. "Let the evidence speak for itself. My blood is on that knife blade, my left hand is sliced open, and I'll bet you'll find Ubel's fingerprints on the handle."

Again, the two officers glanced at each other.

"So what happened next, after Ubel threatened

you?"

"I heard a cracking noise, like someone had dropped a coconut on the floor, and then Ubel collapsed, and I saw Paul Dowdy standing behind him with his drill rifle."

"So you're saying on the record that Paul Dowdy struck Ubel in the back of the head with the butt of his rifle."

"Well, I didn't actually see him do it. I just saw Ubel collapse after I heard that cracking noise."

"What happened next?"

"Paul was terrified. He knew right away he'd done something awful. He dropped the rifle and started to cry. And pray. He's very religious."

"And then what?"

"Ubel rolled over. He started threatening both of us, telling us our lives were ruined. Unless we did what he wanted."

"And by that, what did you think he meant?"

"I knew exactly what he wanted. He was going to force us to have sex with him anytime he wanted it. That's when I snapped. I thought about Jimmy Collins and picked up Paul's rifle and hit Ubel. I would have hit him until his head was caved in if Paul hadn't stopped me."

"What happened next?"

"I have no idea. I blacked out after that and woke up in here with my arm handcuffed to the bed."

The officer with the recorder looked at the counter on it. "You want to add anything else before we go?"

"Yes, sir."

"Go ahead, but be quick. This is about to run out."

"I'm sorry for what happened. I should have gone

to my CO and reported what I'd seen that night when Ubel was abusing Hagen. I should have followed the chain of command. But I've been pretty sick. Haven't been sleeping, and I've been feeling confused. And scared. I was afraid of Chief Ubel, which is why I probably over reacted."

"Anything else?"

"Yes. Paul Dowdy shouldn't be charged with anything. He was just trying to be helpful and check on me. He's like that. A Good Samaritan. He doesn't deserve to go to jail or the brig, whatever you call it."

"Is that it?"

I nodded, and he turned off the recorder and slipped it into his case.

"Can I ask you something?"

The officer nodded. "You can ask, but we might not answer."

"If I'm found guilty, what will happen to me?"

"You're probably going to be court-martialed and dishonorably discharged, which means you'll forfeit all pay."

I stupidly said, "That's okay. I don't need the money."

The other officer added, "And you can be confined for up to ten years."

"Confined? You mean jailed?"

"Affirmative, recruit. It's serious."

My heart did a flip inside my chest.

"How likely is that?"

The one on my left smiled. "Have you heard about the Tailhook Scandal?"

I had no idea what he was talking about, so I shook my head.

"Last year there was a big sex scandal. A lot of careers were ruined."

"What's that mean for me? For my case?"

"It means you're one lucky son of a bitch."

"Why's that?"

"The last thing the Navy wants is another sex scandal all over the news."

"Meaning what, exactly?"

"Yet to be determined, but our superior officers might want this whole matter to go away quietly."

They left me to my own fears. I tried to imagine what would come next. More investigations, a court-room trial, years in a prison somewhere. Ten years possibly. Could I finish college after serving time? Would I be admitted to medical school anywhere?

I wished my father were still alive. He'd know what to do, how to handle the legal issues. What would he do? He'd tell me to get a lawyer.

My dad was gone, but my brother was alive and well. I needed him.

I pressed the button for the orderly and waited. After pressing it repeatedly, he came into the room looking annoyed.

"What is it?"

"Can I make a phone call? I want to call my brother and let him know what's going on. He's my only living family member."

"I can't authorize it, but I'll ask the Doctor when he comes back for rounds after dinner."

"After dinner? But I can't wait."

"Sorry, recruit. You'll have to. You're a prisoner, remember, so you don't have a whole lot of clout."

He disappeared as I absorbed being called a

"prisoner."

I suddenly understood why Jimmy Collins had hanged himself. My own vain, idiotic choices had led me down a similar self-destructive path as he had traveled. I—and I alone—had destroyed my future. Whatever life for myself I'd imagined was now completely out of my control. I felt a strong, sudden desire to find Maggie or Marion and get married, have children, go to work, accomplish something—anything—with my life. Do something meaningful.

"What a waste," I said aloud. "What a fucking waste."

Then I burst into tears and cried harder than I'd cried since my mother's death.

Chapter 30

The doctor did check on me after dinner. He took my temperature, listened to my breathing, and felt the pulse in my wrist. I waited until he finished listening to my heart.

"No fever and your color's good. I'd say you're on the mend, recruit. Except for the spine. Does your back still hurt?"

"Not as much as it did."

"Well, then, I guess my theory was correct. The swollen kidneys were putting pressure on your spine, which was causing the pain. Curing the one alleviates the other."

"Can I make a phone call, Doctor? I need to tell my brother what's going on."

"Where's he live?"

"Plainfield, Indiana."

"Plainfield? Sounds about as boring as it gets."

"Yes, sir. But he's my only living relative."

"That would be a long-distance call, recruit. Don't think I can get authorization for that."

"I've got to be allowed a phone call, don't I?"

"If you were a civilian, yeah. But the Navy owns

you."

My mind raced—what the hell was I going to do?

"Can I at least write a letter?"

"Sure. I'll even get you some nice stationary with the base's letterhead."

"Will you make sure it gets mailed?"

He grinned. "Got any stamps?"

"Not on me, sir. They're back in my footlocker."

The doctor stared at me with bored eyes. "You write the letter, and I'll get it mailed for you."

"Thank you, sir."

He came back a few minutes later and handed me an envelope and three pages of stationary.

"Can I have a pen, sir?"

"May you have a pen?"

"Sir, may I please have a pen, sir?"

He felt the breast pocket of his white coat and pulled out a cheap ballpoint which he handed to me with a ceremonial gesture.

"Thank you, sir."

When he left, I pulled the rolling table over my lap and started to write my letter. I summarized everything, writing on the front and back of each sheet, finishing with a plea for him to get to Florida as soon as he could and get me out of this hellish situation. I signed it, "Love, your foolish brother, Randy."

Writing it all out made me feel a tremendous sense of relief. It would take maybe three or four days for the letter to get to Richard, and then maybe another day or two for him to get to Orlando. With a pleased sigh, I folded the letter and tucked it into the envelope which I licked and sealed and then addressed. I rested the envelope against the plastic water pitcher on the table and stared at it. It hadn't even left my hospital room, but it was already transporting me away from the Navy base.

*   *   *

Marion stood beside my bed dressed in a white lab coat like a doctor. "How are we feeling today?"

Had she joined the Navy just to be near me? "I'm much better now that you're here. Will you stay with me?"

She smiled. "If you want me."

Did she mean if I wanted her to stay or if I wanted to make love to her? "I want you," I told her. "I want you."

She lit a cigarette that suddenly appeared between her red lips and blew smoke into my face.

"You smoke?"

She didn't answer, but the stale, exhaled smoke made me choke.

*   *   *

I woke up coughing. Someone was standing beside the bed in the darkness. The door to the room was completely shut. Whoever was standing next to me took a long drag on the cigarette. By the orange glow, I could make out Ubel's swollen face. He blew another stream of smoke in my direction.

Choking, I sat up and reached for the little silver chain that would turn on the light, but my arm was still handcuffed to the bed.

I felt for the call button, but I couldn't find it.

Ubel took another long drag and exhaled as he spoke.

"You fucking kids." His whispered voice was strange as if he were forcing words through clenched teeth. "I show you a little attention," he hissed, "and you turn on me."

I rolled onto my side so I could reach the light with my other hand, but before I could grab the chain, Ubel took it.

"Looking for this?"

He tugged the chain and the fluorescent light blinked on, illuminating his bruised face. Ubel's jaws were wired shut and the bandage on his forehead barely hid the swollen gash. His eyes were black and blue... and filled with rage.

I sat up as straight as I could, expecting him to hit me . . . or worse.

"What do you want?"

He lifted his head to the ceiling and rocked it back and forth, hissing, "What do I want? What do I want?"

Then he lowered his gaze at me and held the tip of the cigarette close to my left eye. "I want to make your eyeballs sizzle and pop and cut your vocal chords out of your fucking windpipe and drive a stake through your beating young heart."

I smelled alcohol and searched for the call button but couldn't see it. Ubel followed my eyes as I looked over the edge of the bed. He saw the envelope on my table, grinned at me and picked it up.

"Addressed to Richard Wake, in stink-hole Indiana. A letter to your father?"

He held the envelope against his forehead the way Johnny Carson used to when he played Carnack. "Let's see. I bet it says, 'Dear old Dad, I find myself in a bit of pickle down here in Orlando. Mean old Mister Ubel wants to rip my heart out of my chest and piss all over it.' Is that about right, son?"

Hatred filled me. "Don't call me son, you sadistic son of a bitch." I grabbed for the letter, but Ubel jumped away, grinning in the greenish light. "I wish Jimmy Collins had bludgeoned you to death."

Ubel nodded and smiled, tucking the cigarette into his puckered lips. Then he took a lighter out of his robe pocket and lit the corner of the envelope. His grin widened as the envelope went up in flames.

"God damn you!" I screamed.

As he let the ashes fall to the floor, he said, "God damn me? I think he already has, son."

Ubel dropped the last corner of the envelope onto the foot of my bed, and it flared up as if someone had poured lighter fluid on the blankets.

He stared at me and grinned. "Amazing what a little rubbing alcohol can do. Burn in hell, motherfucker."

I kicked at the blanket which made it bunch at the foot of the bed. Suddenly, a tornado of flames swirled up to the ceiling.

I tried to stomp out the fire, but it spread even faster.

Ubel bowed before pulling the door closed as he left.

The flames marched toward me. I jerked to the right, but my left arm was still attached to the railing. I tried to roll over top of the bed rail, but couldn't quite make it.

"Help!" I screamed, jerking the railing back and forth. "Help me, please! My bed's on fire!"

I grabbed my pillow and swung it at the flames. The hot orange flames retreated momentarily, but then the pillow itself caught fire and I threw it to the door.

"Help! Help!"

I squirmed as close to the head of the bed as I could, my left arm stretched as far as it would go. The room filled with heat and smoke. I crouched against the headboard to escape the tower of flames inching toward me, and I started to cough, choking on the unbreathable air.

"Help!" I screamed, but the smoke gagged me. Flames singed the hair on my bare legs. I knew I had to make one last effort to leap over the railing, even if it meant breaking my arm. Otherwise, I was going to burn to death.

Then a miracle happened.

Water rained down from the ceiling. The flames sputtered and died as the cold water washed over me. An alarm began honking like a trucker's horn, and the door to the room swung open.

"What the hell?" the orderly yelled.

"Ubel," I told him. "He tried to kill me."

Water continued to rain down from the sprinklers as the orderly and I stared at each other. We were both drenched.

The orderly shook his head as if trying to clear his mind. "Chief Ubel tried to kill you? How?"

"Isn't it obvious? He set my bed on fire."

He wiped his face, like someone might while

taking a shower and blinked a few times. "You all right?"

I unfolded myself and stretched out on the soggy, blackened bed. "Right as rain."

The orderly shook his head. "What a fucking mess."

Chapter 31

There was a flurry of activity in the hallway outside my room for hours after that, but no one cared to tell me exactly what was going on. Around 3:00 a.m., two large MPs came in, unlocked the handcuffs, and led me to a different wing of the hospital, where I was given dry pajamas and a dry bed to sleep on in a ward with eleven other men. The MPs didn't handcuff me to the bed, but one of them laid a meaty hand on my shoulder.

"Do not leave this ward, understand?"

I nodded.

"You leave this ward, and you could be shot on sight."

He didn't seem to be joking, and I didn't feel like arguing.

I changed and slid into the clean bed, wondering what had happened to Ubel.

In the morning, I ate breakfast in bed. The other guys seemed happy to scarf down the rubbery scrambled eggs though a couple doused theirs with tabasco sauce. Some of the men were very sick—there was a serious bout of mononucleosis going around—but most were recovering from some illness, like I was, and felt fine.

The best part was the television mounted on the wall at the foot of my bed. I was halfway through a rerun of *St Elsewhere* when the doctor came in carrying a chart.

"I had to have a new chart typed up for you, Mister Wake. It seems your old one perished in a fire last night."

"I almost perished, too, you know."

"That's what I heard. Thank God for sprinklers."

He set the chart on the foot of my bed and looked into my eyes and ears with his little light. Then he listened to my breathing and thumped my chest.

"Inhale," he commanded. "Exhale. Again."

I did. Nothing hurt.

"Lungs sound clear. Good news. I heard you'd inhaled a lot of smoke."

"Yeah. Luckily, I've had a chance to do a lot of breathing since then."

"Don't be a smartass with me, recruit." He put the cold stethoscope on my chest and listened to my heart. Straightening up afterward, he said, "I'm releasing you today, Mr. Wake."

"Releasing me? What's that mean?"

"You no longer need medical care, so I'm releasing you."

I sighed. "Does that mean I go back to Chief Reed's company?"

He raised his eyebrows. "Do you want to go back?"

"Hell, no... sir."

"Because if you want to return to finish your training, then we'll have to schedule that back surgery

306

I told you about. Otherwise, I'm transferring you to the holding company where you'll wait for your discharge papers."

I shook my head. "So I'm going to be discharged?"

He nodded.

"What about the charges? The Article 90 charges or the Catch 22 charges or whatever they were?"

He shrugged, and I detected a faint smile. "Like I told you before, that's for the legal guys. All I know is, I got orders to release you to the holding company if you were healthy enough to be discharged."

I looked around the ward. The other guys were propped up in their beds watching TV as if everything in the world was completely normal.

"I don't get it. What happened to Ubel?"

"That gentleman will be going away for a long time, I understand. And you're getting an honorable medical discharge, which means full pay until discharge. Not a bad deal, Mister Wake."

"So all I have to do is be quiet, right?"

"Be quiet about what?"

"About Chief Ubel and what he does to the recruits."

He turned away and picked up his clipboard before answering.

"It seems to me you'd want to be quiet about that."

"No! I want that asshole to pay for what he's done!"

"That means a trial. What good can come from you going on trial for assaulting an officer? The Navy would be forced to re-open the case against you, and you would go to Leavenworth, for a few years at least. This way, you get what you want and Ubel gets what he deserves."

"What do you mean, he gets what he deserves?. The public needs to know the damage he's done. People have died because of him, damn it!"

"Trust me, son, people know about his crimes."

"What people?"

"His superior officers."

I snorted. "Won't they just whitewash it? I mean, you don't know the horror he's caused. He raped a recruit name Jimmy Collins, and that twisted motherfucker murdered two of my friends."

"I'm sure all of Ubel's crimes will be investigated. I know for a fact that he's now in custody and will be court martialed. Believe me, once they find out what kind of man Ubel is, his new pals at Leavenworth will make his life a living hell."

I could imagine it—Ubel pressed against the wall of a shower the way he'd cornered Hagen. "Is that justice?"

"Justice?" The doctor's penetrating eyes held my gaze. "Of a sort, yes. Listen to me, son. You've done enough. You played a big role in bringing Ubel's crimes to everyone's attention, and now he's going to pay dearly. In fact, after the Tailhook fiasco, the entire Navy is going through some major soul-searching."

I shook my head and started to say something, but I couldn't think straight. The doctor stepped closer and patted my shoulder. I could not help but remember my dad.

"You can let yourself off the hook now, son."

Scott Evans

I didn't mind him calling me "son." It wasn't twisted and disgusting, the way Ubel had said it.

"Do you have children, sir?"

He smiled. "Yes. Two boys."

"How old are they?"

"One's ten and the other's eight. Why do you ask?"

"If Ubel had molested one of them, what would you want done to him?"

He pulled his hand away. A scowl tugged at his mouth. "I'd want to kill him with my own two hands, of course. But we have laws and a system of justice. We've got to trust it."

"I don't know if I can, sir. When I think about what I've seen, it's just too much."

He nodded. "Get some rest, son. Everything will seem clearer after you've had a little more time to sort it out."

"What about Paul Dowdy? Is he going to be charged?"

"As I understand it, Mister Dowdy has already gone back to Company 112 with Chief Reed, and he's decided to become a chaplain."

"A chaplain?" I laughed. "Guess he found his true calling."

"Yes, Mister Wake, it looks like he has."

We exchanged grins.

"How about you?" he asked.

"How about me what?"

The doctor smiled. It was a good smile, like my father's.

"Have you found your calling yet, Mister Wake?"

I shut my eyes and thought about that. A memory

309

of my father, dressed in his white lab coat, a stethoscope around his neck, bloomed in my mind. I'd dropped by his office to say farewell before driving back to the City after Thanksgiving. He was smiling at me as I left and threw his hand up to wave. He was the picture of contentment.

"Yes, Doctor. I think I have."

Epilogue

———————◦———————

Three years later, I was grabbing a ham sandwich between classes at the medical school in Sacramento when an article in the *Sacramento Bee* caught my eye. The Orlando Naval Training Center was going to be closed—one of many military bases closing after the fall of the Berlin Wall to cash in on what President Clinton called the Peace Dividend.

"Good riddance," I muttered. But then I realized that, if it hadn't been for my experiences there, I probably wouldn't be where I was, devoting myself to the healing profession. I wondered if the sex scandal involving Ubel had played a role in the decision to close the base.

Charley came by just then and tapped me on the shoulder.

"We're going to be late for class," she said.

Her real name is Charlene, but she prefers to be called Charley, and I respect that. She's bright—smarter than I am—and tall and slender and pretty. She still possesses a rare quality—a fragile innocence—that I hope to protect. And she reminds me of an elegant young woman I once knew on a half-forgotten island, remembered through a haze of rum and the music of steel drums.

NOTES:

The *Tailbook Scandal* refers to incidents in which over 100 Navy and Marine Corps aviation officers were accused of sexually assaulting approximately 83 women and seven men at the Hilton Hotel in Las Vegas, during the 35th Annual Tailhook Association Symposium in early September of 1991.

From an article in the *New York Times*, by JAMES DAO
Published: June 23, 2013
Sexual assault has emerged as one of the defining issues for the military this year. Reports of assaults are up, as are questions about whether commanders have taken the problem seriously. Bills to toughen penalties and prosecution have been introduced in Congress.

But in a debate that has focused largely on women, this fact is often overlooked: the majority of service members who are sexually assaulted each year are men.

In its latest report on sexual assault, the Pentagon estimated that 26,000 service members experienced unwanted sexual contact in 2012, up from 19,000 in 2010. Of those cases, the Pentagon says, 53 percent involved attacks on men, mostly by other men.

From "Male Rape Survivors Tackle Military Assault
in Tough-Guy Culture
By Bill Briggs, NBC News contributor, May 2013

Amid the legislation and indignation sparked by
the military's sexual abuse crisis, male rape survivors
are stepping forward to remind officials that men are
targeted more often than women inside a tough-guy
culture that, they say, routinely deems male victims as
"liars and trouble makers."

The Pentagon estimates that last year 13,900 of
the 1.2 million men on active duty endured sexual
assault while 12,100 of the 203,000 women in
uniform experienced the same crime — or 38 men per
day versus 33 women per day. Yet the Defense
Department also acknowledges "male survivors
report at much lower rates than female survivors."

About the Author:

Get in touch with Scott and find out what he's working on next via his website:

www.scottevansauthor.com

About the Publisher:

You can find us on Facebook or via our website.

88601410R00180

Made in the USA
San Bernardino, CA
21 September 2018